a girl like that

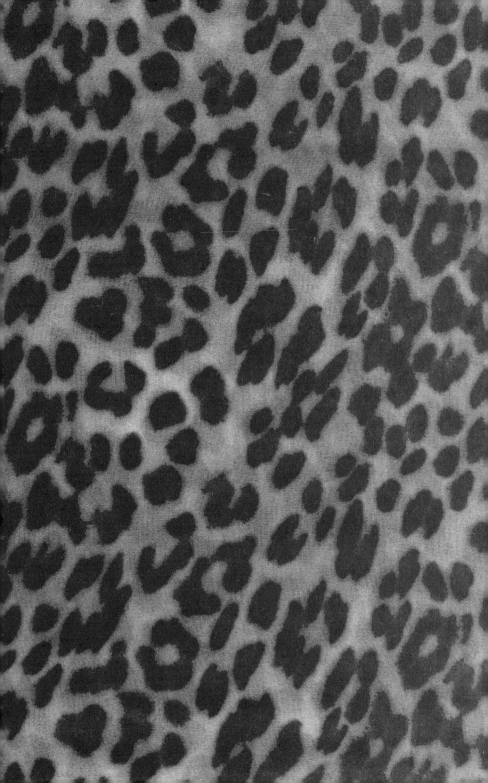

a girl like that

tanaz bhathena

Farrar Straus Giroux · New York

Farrar Straus Giroux Books for Young Readers
An imprint of Macmillan Children's Publishing Group, LLC
175 Fifth Avenue, New York, NY 10010

Printed in the United States of America
Designed by Elizabeth H. Clark
First edition, 2018
3 5 7 9 10 8 6 4 2

fiercereads.com

Library of Congress Cataloging-in-Publication Data

Names: Bhathena, Tanaz, author.
Title: A girl like that / Tanaz Bhathena.
Description: First Edition. | New York : Farrar Straus Giroux, 2018. | Summary: In Jeddah,
  Saudi Arabia, sixteen-year-old half-Hindu/half-Parsi Zarin Wadia is the class troublemaker and top subject for the school rumor blogs, regularly leaving class to smoke
  cigarettes in cars with boys, but she also desperately wants to grow up and move out of
  her aunt and uncle's house, perhaps realizing too late that Porus, another non-Muslim
  Indian who risks deportation but remains devoted to Zarin, could help her escape.
Identifiers: LCCN 2017011020 (print) | LCCN 2017033224 (ebook) |
  ISBN 9780374305451 (ebook) | ISBN 9780374305444 (hardcover)
Subjects: LCSH: East Indians—Saudi Arabia—Juvenile fiction. | CYAC: East Indians—
  Saudi Arabia—Fiction. | Dating (Social customs)—Fiction. | Rape—Fiction. |
  Bullying—Fiction. | Religion—Fiction. | High schools—Fiction. | Schools—Fiction. |
  Jiddah (Saudi Arabia)—Fiction. | Saudi Arabia—Fiction.
Classification: LCC PZ7.1.B5324 (ebook) | LCC PZ7.1.B5324 Gi 2018 (print) |
  DDC [Fic]—dc23
LC record available at https://lccn.loc.gov/2017011020

Our books may be purchased in bulk for promotional, educational, or business use.
Please contact your local bookseller or the Macmillan Corporate and
Premium Sales Department at (800) 221-7945 ext. 5442 or by e-mail at
MacmillanSpecialMarkets@macmillan.com.

To my parents and my late grandparents,
with gratitude and love

a girl like that

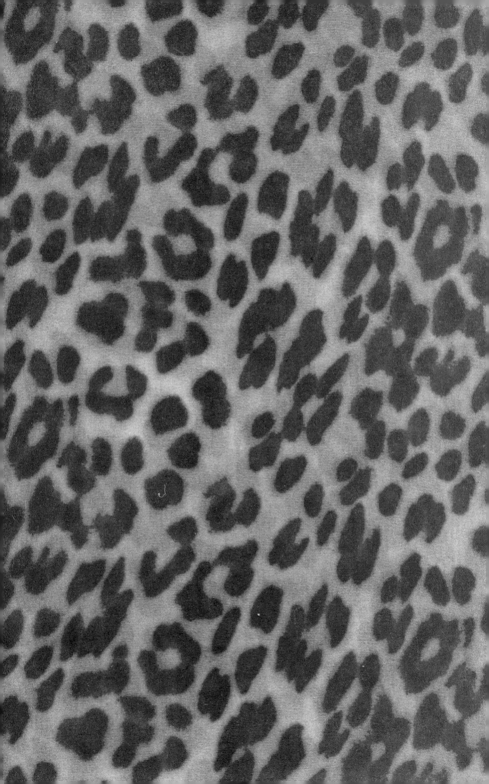

PROLOGUE

Zarin

THE WAILS MASI LET OUT WERE SO HEART-wrenching, you would think I was her only daughter lying dead before her instead of the parasite from her sister's womb, as she had once called me. She should have been a professional funeral crier. Porus's mother knelt in a pool of his dark blood and joined Masi in a cacophonic duet. Masa was more somber. He dabbed his eyes with the sleeve of his shirt, took deep breaths, and tried to compose himself. The officer in charge of the accident scene told Masa that our corpses would be kept in a local morgue till arrangements for the funerals were made.

His loud voice floated upward to where Porus and I now hovered, a few meters above the wreckage on the Al-Harameen

Expressway in Jeddah—completely dead, yet not entirely gone.

We stared at the scene below: Porus's smoking Nissan crumpled like a Pepsi can, the green-and-white squad cars, a flashing Red Crescent ambulance, the Saudi police in their long-sleeved khaki uniforms with black berets, our mourning families. The police had blocked off several kilometers of the highway shoulder and most of the right lane with bright orange construction cones. The area around the car was marked with yellow tape.

It had taken them an hour to remove our bodies from the Nissan, and even that had been fairly messy. There was blood everywhere. Blood that smelled like metal and gushed from our bodies like springs. Blood that had splattered across the windshield, and pooled on the floor of the car. A tire that had somehow come loose during the accident lay a few feet away, coated with the same dark, gleaming liquid.

"Aunt," I heard Masi tell the police officer in English when he asked her how she was related to me. "Mother's sister."

Masi gare de phansi, I used to taunt her in Gujarati when alive. My aunt who would strangle me with a noose. Strangulation and suffocation were common ways of getting rid of unwanted children in India, the country where I was born. Quick and easy fixes for daughters who were supposed to be sons, for orphans like me who were foisted upon reluctant relatives. Once, on a vacation in Mumbai, I heard the Dog Lady tell Masi that there were rare occasions when very rich families paid their maids to do the job. Strong, limber women from slums like Char Chaali who used pillows or sometimes their own hands to snuff out the life of a newborn.

Masi's hands were shaking now. A side effect of the pills my uncle made her take for her "sleeping problem," as he liked to call it. With Masi, everything was a side effect. Tears, mood swings, the beatings she gave me over the years, the raging fits she sometimes threw when I did something that reminded her of my dead mother, or worse, my dead father.

A few feet away, Masa stood talking to another police officer—a short and potbellied man who was gesturing wildly in the air. We were not Saudis or Muslims, so I knew that neither Porus nor I would be buried here. Expatriates who died in the Kingdom were shipped back to their home countries for funeral rites. There were procedures to be followed, paperwork to be taken care of at the morgue and the Indian Consulate. Rites before the last rites.

But it was obvious to me, even from up here, that the potbellied officer wasn't talking about paperwork. He pointed toward our bodies, shouting in a mix of English and Arabic. If I moved a little closer, like Porus had, I could probably hear everything he was saying. But I didn't need to. From the context of the scenario it wasn't that difficult to guess the reason for the police officer's displeasure. Few infractions riled up the authorities in Saudi Arabia more than a girl voluntarily seeking out the company of a boy, especially one who wasn't her brother or husband.

"I will miss my mother," Porus told me softly.

I did not reply. I didn't think I would miss anyone, really. Perhaps I would miss Masa for the times he had been remotely sane: the few instances when he spoke his mind in spite of Masi's constant henpecking. But I tried to forget Masi as a matter of convenience. I wasn't exactly Mother Teresa during the short span of my earthly existence, so there was no guarantee that I would spend my afterlife on a stretch of white heavenly sand. Why rack up more unpleasant memories if I ended up going to hell?

A police officer removed my school ID card from my ripped handbag. I saw him glance at my name and copy it down in his notebook: *Zarin Wadia. Female. Age 16. Student. Car accident.* If my English teacher, Khan Madam, was there, she would have added more: *Bright student. Debating aficionado. Troublemaker. Disturbed.*

The officer lifted an edge of the white shroud and compared my face to the photo on my ID. It was one of those few pictures where a photographer had managed to capture me smiling, a curl of black hair peeking out from behind my scarf, the hair partly veiling my left eye. Masa said the photo made me

8

look like my mother during her teens. This was not a surprise. For as long as I could remember, people had told me I was my mother's mirror image. A replica of dark curls, fair skin, and brown eyes, right down to the beauty mark on my upper lip.

I did not remember my mother that much. Sometimes I could recall the soft hum of a lullaby, the cool press of a glass bangle on my cheek, the smoky fragrance of sandalwood and *loban* from a fire temple. Memories that were few and far between, never more than flashes of sensation. I could often recall with more clarity the first day I grew aware of my mother's absence. A hollow, nearly tangible silence in a warm room. Dust motes dancing in a stream of light from the window. November 28, 2002. The autumn of my fourth birthday. It was the week after my mother died—of cancer, they said, even though I knew it wasn't.

It was also the day a neighbor escorted me from my mother's quiet two-room flat in downtown Mumbai to the north of the city, to the one-room flat owned by my maternal aunt and uncle in Cama Parsi Colony. Masa liked the idea of having me around, since Masi couldn't have kids. She, on the other hand, was furious.

"Watch the chalk!" she snapped the moment we entered the flat. "*Khodai*, look at what this girl has done."

I looked down at where she was pointing—at the chalk designs she'd made on the tiles by the flat's threshold. White fish with delicate scales and red eyes surrounding a banner that now said *G . . . ck—Good Luck*, as I discovered later on. *Good Luck* with my shoe printed in its center, powdery pink creases blurring out most of the *Good* and the *Luck*.

"All these years I've lived my life in shame because of my sister," she told Masa that night when she thought I was asleep. "At least marrying you took me away from that and shut up those horrible gossips at the Parsi Panchayat."

I didn't have much status in the world—bastard orphans usually did not—and everyone in Cama colony was quick to remind me about that, even after Masa adopted me and gave me a surname to fill in the blank left by my father.

"You don't know how lucky you are, child," said Masi's neighbor, also known to the colony kids as the Dog Lady, a woman who always smelled of 4711 Original Eau de Cologne and Pomeranian sweat. "So many children in your state usually end up on the streets! Or worse."

A month after I moved into Masa and Masi's flat, my father's lawyer managed to track me down. It was through the lawyer that Masi found out about my father's will and bank account.

"How much is in the account?" The lawyer had repeated Masi's question. "Around fifteen lakh rupees, madam. The girl's guardians are in charge of this account till she turns twenty-one."

"Thank goodness she's here with us," Masi told Masa when

the lawyer left. "Who knows what would have happened to that money if she'd fallen into the wrong hands?"

Two years later, Masa accepted a new job—assistant plant manager for a meatpacking factory in Jeddah, Saudi Arabia. He said we needed a fresh start.

And, for a time, we had it. In Jeddah, with its shimmery coastline, giant roundabouts, and brightly lit malls. Where the air was hot and dense and somehow always smelled of the sea.

During our first week here, Masa had taken us to Balad, the city's historic center, on a friend's recommendation. "It will be like traveling back in time," the friend had said. And it was. If the glittering lights and skyscrapers of the Red Sea coast were the city's ornaments, then Balad was Jeddah's ancient, beating heart, its narrow streets linked to the main shopping square like arteries. The smell of roasted coffee and salt lingered in the air like perfume: at the souk, where men chewed *miswak* and hawked everything from ropes of gold jewelry to leather sandals; between alleys of abandoned old Hijazi homes, where veiled women with hennaed fingernails peddled potato chips, candy, and toys. We returned home at night, carrying bits of the old city back with us in plastic bags filled with roasted almonds and Turkish delight, in the green-glass bottle of jasmine attar Masa had bought for Masi from a local perfumery. The next day, however, Masi had complained about the smell of the perfume giving her a headache and tossed the bottle into the trash. It was the sort of happy day that had never happened again.

Now, my life having ended, I watched the police officer continue to interrogate Masa, while Masi watched him from a few feet away, her face pinched with worry. The look on her face reminded me of that Syrian boy from the Red Sea Mall. The one with the curly black hair, the hooked nose, and the scar over his left eyebrow. He was the first guy I'd ever gone out with after he'd thrown me his number, scribbled on a crumpled bit of notebook paper, from behind one of those fake, overly tall palm trees inside the mall. He was also the first guy I'd skipped school for, even though I never really had a crush on him. We'd spent most of the date driving in his car, nervously looking around for the religious police. There had hardly been any conversation; his English was bad, my Arabic even worse. We'd kept smiling at each other, until even smiling became awkward. I still remembered the end of the date: the way he whipped his head around to make sure the coast was clear, the slight furrow in his forehead, the quick, nervous kiss on my cheek. I was fourteen at the time.

Next to me, Porus let out a sigh. He was getting depressed and heavy. I could feel myself being pulled down with him. I had a very bad feeling that if we floated back down, we would be shackled to the scene of the accident forever.

"Let it go, Porus," I said. "We can't return. We must move on."

I took hold of his hand.

When I was nine, a high priest at the fire temple next to Cama colony in Mumbai made us write a description of what we thought happened after we died. Even though I knew that the exercise was pointless (no one in our summer theology class at the fire temple ever had the right answers to the priest's questions), I found myself writing out two pages. It was a fun change from the endless finger snapping to ward off satanic spirits and the droning monotone of prayer that formed the background noise of most of my vacations to India.

I wrote of souls the way I imagined them, featherlight and invisible, floating upward through a layer of clouds that looked like flat white cotton, but felt cool, misty, and very wet. By the time the souls would get through the cloud covering, their earthly clothes would be soaked with moisture. Then they would pass through a sunny, heated zone that smelled like toast, and then another cold, wet layer. Hot and cold, cold and hot, until the air thinned and the sky darkened from light blue to navy to black.

I wrote of outer space. Stars everywhere in diamond pinpricks. Bright white fire crackling in the tails of the comets. Meteors falling in showers of red, orange, and blue. Colorful planets revolving around fiery suns. The souls would continue ascending through this vast, glittering space for a very long time until they reached utter darkness and their heads brushed against something that felt like a ceiling: a delicate, thinly veined membrane that tore easily with a poke of a finger. Beyond that membrane lay heaven or hell, depending on how the souls had behaved on earth.

The priest gathered our papers and skimmed through the descriptions. "Some of you have good imaginations," he said. "But this isn't what really happens."

Zoroastrian death, he explained, was followed by a journey that began three days later, at the foot of a silvery bridge arching up into a brightness that blinded the eyes. The bridge, called the Chinvat, had to be crossed by every soul three days after death.

As I grew older, I liked to think of the bridge as the Walk of Fame or of Shame. Your fate lay in the Hallowed Brightness Up Above or the Dark Abyss Down Below. If you had sinned too much, the bridge would become blade thin and you'd fall into the Abyss, but without the eternal damnation that plagued so many monotheistic religions. For Zoroastrians, there was only a temporary hell, somewhat like the Jewish and Roman Catholic concepts of purgatory.

I thought the concept of the Chinvat itself was unique to Zoroastrians until I turned twelve, when Mishal Al-Abdulaziz, the meanest girl in Qala Academy, informed me about a similar bridge in Islam called As-Sirat, or the Bridge of Hell.

There were times over the years when I found the whole process of arguing with Mishal over this subject futile. After all, Mishal's true knowledge of what happened after death extended to corpses in boxes and rectangular graves. Similarly, mine was limited to shrouded bodies being carried up a set of stairs by pallbearers—bodies that would end up as entrées in a meal for the vultures circling the Towers of Silence on Malabar Hill in Mumbai.

Emergency lights flashed below: a new van had arrived at the scene of our accident. Two men in white uniforms emerged with a stretcher, probably to carry our bodies to a morgue. Porus didn't seem to notice. He continued staring at his mother—the only one who, apart from my uncle, seemed to be shedding real tears.

Porus

THE SKY IN JEDDAH WAS BLUEBRIGHT. LIKE the sari Mamma wore to my *navjote* eleven years ago, blue and yellow like my father's matching tie. Down below, dust gathered: the dust of traffic, the dust of people, our bodies turning to dust like the Christians, burning to ash like the Hindus, while the policemen in their dusty uniforms hovered over our bodies like vultures from a Zoroastrian Tower of Silence.

It would have been normal for Zarin to make some smart-ass comment by now—something about the way her *masi* was blowing her nose, or maybe about how uncomfortable she seemed to be making the policemen with her constant crying. But nothing was normal today. I could feel Zarin floating next to me in total silence. Her hair, which used to curl like smoke, was all smoke now. Smoke and fire.

"Girlfriend?" The police officer pointed at our bodies as he shouted at Zarin's uncle. Zarin's undamaged cell phone glinted silver in his hand. "Boyfriend?"

I wondered now if he had called our families to the scene of the accident specifically to ask this question instead of telling them to come directly to the morgue. My boss, Hamza, once told me that the police sometimes made examples of people for breaking the laws against dating. *Khilwa*, Hamza had called the offense, followed by a diatribe about how nothing good ever came out of a boy and a girl going out alone without supervision. But what could they do to us now that we were dead?

I watched Zarin's *masa* open his *iqama* to the photo page. "Please sir," he pleaded. "Please look at her. She was a child . . . a young girl . . ."

It was painful to hear him. Even though we weren't related, Zarin's *masa* had still treated me like a son when I first met him. "Call me Rusi Uncle, my boy. Or just Rusi, if you feel like it," he'd said with a twinkle in his eyes. "I'm not so old yet."

Not as old as today, when it looked like the years had crept up on him in a matter of hours. If he could hear me, I would have told him that pleading with this particular officer wouldn't work. I could tell from the sneer on the officer's fat face, from the way he held his clipboard—almost lazily, as if nothing anyone said mattered anymore now that he'd come to his own conclusion about the situation. Though most police interrogations were fairly reasonable ("One hour max, *ya habibi*, and then they let you go," my boss had told me), there were times when they could make your life miserable.

"Girlfriend?" The officer was bellowing now, and pointing at the area where a tow truck flashed orange, hooking itself to the smoking heap of metal and plastic that used to be my old car. "Boyfriend?"

"Sister!" Rusi Uncle shouted back. "Brother!"

Behind the policeman, a black GMC stood ready, the round gold seal of the Saudi religious police painted on its doors. Two men waited nearby, their beards long, their short white *thobe*s exposing bony ankles, their noses wrinkled against the combined smells of sweat, exhaust fumes, metal, and blood.

The job of the religious police, who were locally referred to as *muttawe'en* or the Hai'a, was to enforce Sharia law— from raiding shops for selling contraband like pork and alcohol to asking women to cover their heads in public places—though they needed to be with the city police to make any actual arrests. The mark of a *muttawa* was usually the absence of an *egal*, the round black cord that most Saudi men wore on their heads, over a red-and-white-checkered *shemagh*.

"When you see one, run in the opposite direction," Zarin had said. "Unless, of course, you want to get stuck in a prison cell for being seen with me."

She'd succeeded in scaring me with this comment a couple of times, until I realized that the men she was pointing to at the mall weren't religious policemen, but civilians out and about with their families.

"You should have seen your face!" she had said, laughing. "Porus, even if he *was* a real *muttawa*, he wouldn't start chasing us the second he saw us together!"

The religious policemen at the scene of our accident were, however, the real deal. I could see it by the careful way they were scrutinizing our families, the casual authority with which one of them finally walked up to the policeman interrogating Rusi Uncle and murmured in his ear.

Somewhere in the distance, beyond the GMC, within the flat expanse of dusty palm trees, streetlights, glass skyscrapers, and apartment buildings, lay Aziziyah, and Zarin's school, Qala Academy, where the whole nightmare had begun.

A sheen of moisture coated the police officer's face. He tapped a pencil against his clipboard and then, with a sigh, scribbled something down.

"Why different surname?" He pointed behind Rusi Uncle, where Khorshed Aunty and my mother were crying, their arms wrapped around each other. "You have two wife?"

Rusi Uncle went red and started swearing in a way I had never seen before, calling the policeman all sorts of names in Hindi. Names that could have him arrested and tossed into a deportation center if the policeman understood him. Khorshed Aunty screamed his name.

The police officer's hands balled into fists. The sun shifted slightly and for a moment I thought, *This is it: Rusi Uncle is done for.* Then, finally: "*Khallas!*" The officer clipped his pencil back onto the board. "Go!" he spat out. "GO!"

I let out a breath I had not known I was holding and watched Zarin's aunt and uncle help my mother back into their car. I watched as my mother continued to stare at me, or what remained of me: the bigger of two human-shaped stains on the tarmac.

I am so sorry, Mamma, I wanted to tell her. I did not want to leave you alone. Not like this. I did not even know how this accident had happened in the first place.

"Let it go, Porus," Zarin said, as if sensing my thoughts. "We can't return. We must move on."

She took my hand, her fingers sliding into the gaps between mine, something she had never done voluntarily when we were both alive.

Something inside me unclenched. I watched the *muttawa* follow the policeman who had been interrogating Zarin's uncle, both of them speaking in rapid-fire Arabic.

"What do you think they're saying?" I asked Zarin, who knew some of the language.

She let out an irritated sigh. "I'm not listening, Porus. They're talking too fast for me in any case, and I don't want to know what they're saying. I don't want to go back there."

"I'm sorry," I said. She had reasons enough—reasons aplenty, really—for not wanting to return. I hesitated for a second and then squeezed her hand gently; it was surprisingly soft and smooth—or did it feel that way because I was dead?

"You have tough hands." She sounded surprised.

So it *was* soft.

"Yeah. But I thought you already knew that. From my job and all."

"I thought you worked behind the counter."

"There are many things behind the counter. Like a loading dock and delivery trucks."

Now I knew she was smiling even though I could not look into her face. Not directly. There was something bright around her that prevented me from seeing her clearly. But we could feel each other's reactions. We could touch. It was strange.

We were holding hands now the way my father and I had on my sixth birthday. Palm to palm, fingers laced together like two people afraid of tipping over and falling into the Arabian Sea—me more so than Pappa, whose hand I had clung to as he guided me into a fisherman's boat near the ferry wharf in

21

Mumbai. "Careful, now," he had said as the boat rocked under my feet. "Careful when you step inside."

I gripped his hand even tighter and tried to steady myself, hoping I wouldn't tumble overboard in my excitement. "It will be special," Pappa had promised the day before. "A glimpse of heaven, right in the middle of the sea."

Overhead the sky was thick with clouds. Rain, the fisherman predicted before murmuring a prayer to the goddess and pushing off.

In the daytime, we saw clouds floating over the growing slum onshore, over women washing clothes and utensils in the stagnant pools while children bathed nearby, their dark skins covered with a fine watery film. The fishermen, by then, were already at sea, their painted boats and trawlers bobbing somewhere in the middle of an undulating blue. When the fishing season was hard, they picked up passengers like Pappa and me for a bit of extra money, taking us into the middle of the sea whenever we wanted, sometimes into waters that were so black we could barely see anything except for the faint gold glimmer of the city lights on the water close to the shore.

"Mad," Mamma had called them and Pappa. "Utterly mad."

I recalled her words in the darkness, amid the sounds of Pappa's breaths and the crush of the fisherman's paddle against the water. Moments later, however, the paddling stopped.

"Now we wait," Pappa said. The fisherman lit a match and brought it close to his face, lighting a *beedi* that he first offered to Pappa, who refused.

It had been another half hour before the first rays cast orange into the sky and then yellow before the sun finally rose, as round as a peach and glowing. The dark water turned pale and translucent, tiny sea creatures shimmering gold underneath. "This is what I have dreamed of, my son, what I've always wanted to show to your mother," Pappa had told me. "This is what heaven will look like after we die."

A year later, when we went out to sea again, the boat began to sink midway, forcing us to swim back ashore, a skill Pappa had had since he was a boy, but I'd never learned. Water, I discovered then, could go into your mouth and your ears. Could burn your throat like fire when it finally came out of you. Pappa had had to pull me back to shore with him. After CPR, our first stop was at the hospital to make sure I was okay. It was the closest I'd ever come to seeing heaven firsthand. My mother had been furious.

"Stop!" Zarin commanded. "You're doing it again!"

"Doing what?"

"Weighing us down."

And now I could see that we were closer to the ground, closer to the voices that were louder than before, to the crush of the Jeddah traffic below, vehicles snaking around my old car and the police, their hoods gleaming in the afternoon sun. If I wanted, I could get close enough to touch the shapes of the people standing below, the faint trail of moisture on my mother's cheeks.

Zarin squeezed my hand hard and we floated up once more. "Do you want us to be stuck there forever?"

"As long as I'm with you, it doesn't matter," I said, and could instantly feel her roll her eyes.

"You scared me," she said.

Not as much as she'd scared me when she went out with those assholes over the past year.

"Did you swear in your head?" she asked me suddenly.

"How did you know?"

"I don't know. I could . . . I don't know, feel your hostility, I guess. I never heard you swear before . . . or technically even now."

Of course she hadn't. After Pappa's death I had become quite adept at hiding my anger from the people I loved. Though I had the feeling that Zarin did see, or maybe hear, me bash in that one guy until he saw the sun and the moon and a few stars. I wasn't too sure. Our one and only conversation about it had not gone too well.

Here and now, however, the boys in her past no longer seemed to matter.

"A gentleman doesn't swear in front of a lady," I recited in perfect English, some line I'd heard somewhere, now popping out of me as if it had been waiting for this very moment.

She laughed and I felt myself growing lighter.

English was not my first language. I rarely spoke in English with Zarin, normally preferring to use Gujarati, the language of instruction of my old school in Mumbai—a language I was certain to have better command of when talking to Zarin, who with a single look could still sometimes leave me fumbling for words.

Below us, my mother was now praying. I could tell from the way her lips were moving. When someone died, a simple Ashem Vohu would suffice, she had told me once, though I never understood why even that was needed. "Who understands prayers anyway?" Zarin had always said, and I had agreed with her. Especially when they were spoken in a language that few priests back in India could translate.

It was Zarin who had told me the story of the three wise men from the Bible—how they were actually Zoroastrian priests, who the Christians called the magi.

"No one at school would believe me if I told them this," she'd said with a laugh. "Except maybe Mishal. But she'd pretend ignorance to spite me."

"How do you know this?" I'd asked her, awed.

"How do you not?" she'd teased back. "I'm not even technically Zoroastrian and I still do!"

Having a Hindu father meant that Zarin was permanently barred by the fire temples in India from being inducted into the Zoroastrian faith. Though Zarin liked to pretend indifference about this fact, I knew it bothered her. Between the two of us, it was always Zarin who knew more about Zoroastrianism, who had spent hours reading up on it during trips back to Mumbai. I, on the other hand, was no longer sure if I believed in God, especially after my father died.

"My mother wanted me to become a priest, you know," I said now. "She came from a priestly family."

"A priest?" Zarin sounded interested. "Well, why didn't you?"

"Pappa was from a nonpriestly family. So I couldn't." I still remembered the look on my mother's face, the disappointment she couldn't quite hide.

Zarin squeezed my hand again, but this time in reassurance.

There were things I still wanted to tell Zarin: things we'd never had the chance to talk about, things I had told her before but she'd ignored. But we were now fading—or was the light growing brighter?—and I could no longer remember what they were.

"I'm going to hell, aren't I?" Zarin asked me suddenly.

And then I remembered everything again, bit by bit, my memory jogged not by Zarin's voice, but by the fear I heard

behind it—an emotion she'd expressed in front of me once before, on that nightmare day when everything went wrong.

Memories, Pappa had said, can be like splinters, digging
into you when you least expect them to, holding tight and sharp
the way wood did when it slid under a fingernail.

I felt Zarin's fingers tighten around my hand.

"I'm not letting you go," I said.

Mishal

THE DAY AFTER SHE DIED, I CALLED THE number again.

"Hello?" The woman at the other end had a voice hoarse from crying.

I did not speak. Did not breathe. It was something I'd learned to do during those blank calls, in the early practice sessions years ago—before Caller ID became nearly as commonplace as a Happy Meal—when I would prank Father's second wife, Jawahir, who by her very existence had turned my mother into a basket case.

The number I'd dialed now did not appear to have Caller ID. Or if it did, Zarin Wadia had never confronted me about it—never bothered asking about the blank calls I had made to her in the past. A silence that in itself seemed uncharacteristic of her. Zarin had been a loner, but she had never exactly been quiet about the things that pissed her off. I knew that firsthand.

". . . trailer . . . accident . . . highway . . ." My left ear tuned into the words floating faintly up the stairs to my room; Abdullah was watching the news again on Channel 2.

My right ear, however, was still focused on the woman over the phone, whose breaths were growing quicker now, impatient. I could almost feel them on my skin.

"Who is this?" Her voice was louder. "What do you want?"

Deviant, they called her at school, I wanted to say. A girl who stood out the day she first came to the academy. A square peg in a round hole.

I wanted to tell the woman about that time in Class II. The time we found out about Zarin lying about having parents. How her face had turned red like a poppy when I confronted her. *Shame, shame*, my friends and I had chanted whenever she'd stepped out on the playground after that. *Shame, shame, poppy shame.*

I wanted to tell the woman about that time in Class IX, when I first smelled the cigarettes on her. When she stuck her tongue out and blew a raspberry, spraying my face with her spit. "I'll report you for this," I told her. And I had. Though by then, she hadn't seemed to care.

My fingers brushed the name and number scribbled on the photocopied page of the class phone list. Careless strokes, uneven in weight, some characters darker than others. She put a dash through her sevens and through the *Z* in her name. The same number, year after year, ever since she first showed up in Class II with her short hair and weird brown leggings, no new cell number added, even though I knew that she'd started carrying around an ancient flip phone sometime last year.

I wrapped the phone cord tight around my fingers.

It was nothing, I wanted to tell the woman. Just a bunch of girls saying crappy things, sharing crappy pictures on Facebook and Twitter. Stuff like this happened all the time at school. Zarin knew that. She had to have known that! She used to laugh at the rumors before. *Pea brained*, she used to call anyone who believed them. How could we have known that she would try to run away?

I opened my mouth to speak.

"Mishal?" Abdullah called up to me. "Where are you?"

I hung up instantly, heart pounding. I cursed my brother for his voice—that loud Sports Captain voice he used to bark marching orders to the Qala Academy boys during Sports Day presentations—a voice that must surely have penetrated the woman's ear on the other end of the phone as it had mine.

"Come down here!" he shouted. "They're showing the news about your friend."

The same news they'd announced this morning at a special assembly held on the school grounds. The headmistress made a speech, the teachers dabbed at their eyes with the edges of their saris or *dupatta*s, prayers were recited, and everyone observed the obligatory Two Minutes of Silence for the Dead. Seconds after the assembly was complete, however, everyone around me burst into whispers about the details.

Inna lillahi wa inna ilaihi raji'un! Ya Allah, what a tragedy!

Tragedy, my foot. It was probably her fault, with all those cigarettes she smoked. One of them probably set the car on fire!

How can you say such things about someone who died?

What? What are you guys talking about? The headmistress said it was a crash in the assembly. Like the wheel came off the car she was in or some—

Forget about that—was she with that deli boy again?

On my Tumblr account, random anonymous tippers were going wild with even more theories, forcing me to post the following message when I got back home from school:

You have been asking a lot of questions about a certain Class XI student (you all know who she *was*). I understand that you have your own theories and honestly I appreciate the asks and tips you guys send me. But I am NO LONGER going to post anything else about this person on Tumblr as I don't think it's fair to her or her family.

31

POSTED 2 HOURS AGO BY **BLUENIQAB**, 45 NOTES
*#seriously #anonymous #ily #but let's not speak ill of
the dead okay #blue's announcements #QA gossip*

On Zarin's Facebook page (one she rarely used, from the
looks of her twelve-person friend list) there was a lone status up-
date dating back to October 13, 2010: *so this is facebook? looks
boring.* She hadn't even bothered putting up a profile picture. Her
timeline, set to Public, had a slew of messages: some from our
classmates, but most from strangers, their sentiments ranging
from *Ding dong, the witch is dead* to *May your soul rest in peace.*
My own message, one I'd typed out and erased several times
before hitting Enter, had been a short *R.I.P.* and nothing else.

I sat on my bed and opened my Physics textbook. *My* friend,
Abdullah called her, as if I was the only one who'd known her,
as if she was a complete stranger to him.

"Mishal?"

"I'm studying!" I shouted back. "I have a test tomorrow!"

He fell silent. The days when he and I would run into each
other's rooms without knocking and drag the other out to watch
something we'd seen on TV were long gone. In those days,
Father lived with us on the weekends, playing games with
Abdullah and me, sometimes even coaxing Mother to join us.

Of the two of us, Abdullah resembled Mother the most,
with his wide mouth, his fair skin tanned by the Jeddah sun,

and the black hair that curled around his head. Mother's hair, on the other hand, was long; in her days as a student of classical music in India, she had often left it loose. "It was the first thing people noticed about me," she said. "My hair, which hung to my hips."

Hair that she had, after marrying my Saudi father, to tie up in braids and cover with scarves, never to be seen again by other men. "I didn't mind," she said when I asked her about it. "Your father married me against the wishes of his family, you know. They didn't want him marrying a woman who wasn't Saudi, even if she was a Muslim. I was very lucky."

In the room next to mine, I heard the faint hum of Mother's old CD player: a classical song I recognized from my childhood. When she was younger, my mother had played the *sarangi*, a stringed boxlike instrument that she'd brought with her from Lucknow to Jeddah after marriage. An instrument that she did not relinquish even after marrying my father, much to the general disapproval of his family. "I've already given up far too much," she said.

She turned to her instrument more and more after Father married Jawahir, often growing frustrated by the lack of interest Abdullah and I showed in her music, not understanding that it was an alien language we both resented, a language that, to us, had had some mysterious hand in separating our parents into two houses. "Feel it, Mishal!" she would cry out in those days, often taking my hand and placing it over my heart. "Here, Mishal. Feel the music *here*."

She noticed neither my grades nor Abdullah's prolonged absences from home, a fact that Abdullah took full advantage of once Father bought him his first car, a GMC that he drove around in with his friends, sometimes not returning for two or three days.

At school, girls were often surprised to find out that Abdullah was my brother, which to me wasn't that surprising. While my brother had inherited my mother's looks, I had inherited my father's, my skin as dark as his even though I did my best to keep out of the sun, my eyes large and protruding in a face that was much too long and thin.

"Your brother is *so* hot!" my classmates would gush whenever they got the chance. They hoped I would play matchmaker to their Bollywood dreams and give them a happy ending with a guy they'd stalked on Facebook and at the annual school fair that brought the boys and girls of Qala Academy out of their segregated buildings and into the enormous boys'-section parking lot.

Unlike the academy's girls' section in Aziziyah, where the courtyard was enclosed by four white buildings, leaving the school buses to line up outside the gates, the boys' section's parking lot remained open to the public and functioned as a soccer field during the school year. On fair days, it was the only plot of land the school administration considered large (and therefore safe) enough to accommodate hormonal males and females at the same time without pissing off the parents or the religious police.

"He snorts Pepsi through his nose," I would tell some of these giggly girls, most times getting the grossed-out reaction I'd been hoping for—a *yuck!* or an *eww!* followed by an end to an irritating conversation. My brother chose his own girls, as far as I knew from snooping through his texts or from eavesdropping on the conversations he had with the friends he sometimes invited over to our house. He had a preference, I wanted to tell them, for blondes with big boobs.

The girls, of course, did not know this. They did not know of the magazine I'd come across in Abdullah's room when I was thirteen, or what he'd told me when he saw me flipping through it, part fascinated, part horrified.

Instead, they called me names behind my back. Some even called me jealous, thinking that my feelings for Abdullah were more than sisterly: "She probably wants to keep him to herself."

But no one had the courage to say those words to my face. Not only were they intimidated by my sharp tongue, they wanted my friendship for the information I provided to them—the gossip, the scandals, the stories I knew about everyone in school.

Except for Zarin, of course. The only girl Abdullah had ever asked me about, probably because she'd completely ignored him at the school fair when she was fifteen. The girl everyone in school would now discuss for ages for being found with a boy—evidence, they would call it, for the rumors that had been circulating around her. Zarin, a girl as scandalous in death as she had been in life, the memory of her etched into my skin like the bite she'd marked me with when we were both seven, in the courtyard behind the school bookstore.

My hand automatically went to my arm and rubbed at it even though the marks had long since faded.

The fight had begun with an innocent question spurred by that morning's Social Studies lesson: "What are you? Hindu, Muslim, Christian, or Jew?"

I had posed the question to the girls during break—or at least to the ones who weren't chasing one another, skipping rope, or playing hopscotch in a chalk-drawn grid on the tarmac.

Muslim, Muslim, Hindu, Muslim.

Christian, Muslim, Christian, Muslim.

"Zoroastrian," Zarin said.

"There's no such thing."

"There is." Lines appeared on the skin over her brows, reminding me of the pictures I'd seen of the Hindu men the teacher had shown us in class—three pale skin-colored streaks on a forehead that was now pink with anger.

"Come on," I said, irritated by the sound of a word I'd never heard before, a word that to me sounded like something Zarin had made up out of the sheer boredom of having no friends in class. "You don't have to lie to us. What are you? Hindu, Muslim, Christian, or Jew?"

"I'm not lying." Her dusty black Mary Janes scraped the ground as she got to her feet. Her knees, darker than the rest of her legs, were bruised, red blots and scratches slowly turning purple from the fights she sometimes got into with the girls in the classroom beside ours.

I felt myself growing stiff, even though outwardly my voice showed no change. "Well, you told us you had parents too. But you don't. You live with your aunt and uncle."

"I'm not *lying*," she said, snarling the last word.

"You are too," I insisted loudly, in an effort to be heard over the general din on the playground. "You don't have parents and you don't have a religion either."

In fact, my voice was so loud that many of the girls playing nearby had fallen silent and stopped their game-play to watch Zarin's reaction.

And what a reaction she gave them.

Before I realized what was happening, she caught hold of my arm and sank her teeth into it. We rolled in the courtyard, bit, pulled, scratched, and screamed, until a teacher yanked us apart and called us a pair of hooligans.

Of course, Zarin wasn't lying about her religion, and my mother told me as much when I came home that afternoon.

"You learn this now, Mishal," Mother scolded, "while there is still time. Tomorrow you will go and say sorry to that girl."

Yet, though I filed away this fact on Zoroastrianism for future reference, I had no intention of apologizing to Zarin. She did not apologize to me either. Instead, we always tried to top each other in the classes we liked best, though I'd never beaten Zarin in English and she'd never beaten me in Arabic. When not competing in the classroom, we competed outside of it, usually on the school bus we both took home, our battles limited to taunts and name-calling.

I stared at the page in my textbook: *Consider the motion of a car along a straight line . . .*

From the mosque outside my window, the *muezzin* sang a call for the *isha* prayer.

Downstairs, Abdullah switched the channel to *The X Factor Arabia*. On another night, I might have shouted at him for turning up the volume so loud. I might even have unrolled my mat and prayed. But I couldn't study anyway. And I was not sure if any of my prayers would be accepted after the things I'd done. I tossed my book aside.

In the room next to mine, Mother had begun another song. Quiet plucks of the strings that were slow at first and then quick. Staccato notes, I think she called them. Rapid little jabs to the heart.

BEGINNINGS

Zarin

THERE WAS SOMETHING ABOUT THE BOY'S
back that caught my eye, that made me pause on the way to the
used-books stall and watch him string lights over a painted
wooden stand at the annual school fair the summer I turned
fourteen. Hours later, when the air cooled and the sky darkened, the lights would flash red, blue, green, and yellow and
hordes of students would squeeze into the parking lot at Qala
Academy's boys' section in Sharafiyah to stuff their faces
with popcorn and cotton candy, buy bangles and DVDs, and
throw darts at colored balloons to win cheap two-riyal toys
made of old sofa foam and lint-covered velvet.

Maybe it was the translucent white polyester of his shirt that
revealed the absence of the white undershirt worn by most

schoolboys. Or the breeze that pressed said shirt to the long, smooth indent of his spine: a tunnel that trailed from nape to waist, flanked with thick muscle on both sides. Or maybe it was simply the novelty of being able to leisurely stare at a boy, without Masi constantly hovering around me like an overprotective bulldog.

"She's growing up fast," I had often heard her complain to Masa. "Too fast."

Too fast based on the looks she said I got from boys and even from some men at the deli, the supermarket, and the mall. From the way I walked, my "hips swaying like a loose woman's," if the boy that followed me home from the DVD store when I was eleven was any indication—even though at the time I had not known what it meant to be a loose woman.

Too fast, like my mother. A woman who, even as a teenager, wore no *sudreh* under her clothes and tied no *kusti* around her waist.

"How could she?" Masi's voice would boom through the house, as loud as a priest's at prayer time. "With those small-small shirts that she wore? 'It wouldn't be *fashionable*,' she would always say."

According to Masi, the story of my birth could have been made into a tragic film for Indian parallel cinema. My mother had worked as a bar girl in Mumbai, a woman who danced to remixed versions of popular Hindi songs in a shower of

Gandhi-faced rupee notes, accompanied by drunken compliments and whistles. After my great-grandfather's death, it was the only way she could make money to support herself and her younger sister, my *masi*—not that Masi was ever grateful. My father worked as a hit man for a Mumbai don. He and my mother fell in love, did not marry, but had me. Then my father abandoned my mother, went off to Dubai, and got blown up by a pair of guns. The End.

There had been several articles in the newspapers about my father's death. "Fugitive Mumbai Gangster Shot Dead in Dubai." "Massacre in Deira." "Suraj Shinde's Final Salaam." On a trip back to Mumbai, I looked up these headlines one afternoon in the archives of a public library and even managed to find a small color photo of him—a broad-shouldered man with a square jaw, warm brown skin, and a frown exactly like mine.

My mother's death, on the other hand, was not documented anywhere, except perhaps in a Mumbai morgue. I would hear Masi talking to the Dog Lady about it at times over the phone—how some of my mother's bar patrons had shown up at the funeral—until the talk inevitably turned to me and the way I behaved after my mother died. "Never even cried, that girl," Masi would always say. "You'd think she had no feelings whatsoever. She makes me so angry sometimes. Keeps egging me on until I hit her."

My uncle had never approved of her hitting me. I had heard

them fighting about it once a couple of years ago, when she'd left a bruise on my cheek for failing a Math test. But apart from that, he rarely, if ever, intervened about any other form of punishment Masi doled out. My disobedience was something he didn't approve of either; he often told me that Masi and I would get along better if I listened to her more, if I tried harder at school, if I didn't make her so angry by being argumentative.

In any case, Masa could never stay mad at her for long. The night they had argued, Masi woke us up with her screams. "I won't let you!" Masi's body jerked upward as she struggled against my uncle's grip on her wrists. Her teeth gnashed. White drool gathered at the corners of her lips. "She isn't—she isn't going with you!"

I'd watched Masa gently coax her out of the episode, the way he had several times before in Mumbai. "It's okay, Khorshi. It's okay. Did you forget your medicine again?" It took him two hours to make her take the pills and then soothe her back to sleep, crooning an old Hindi love song. A lullaby for a grown woman. Neither of them seemed to notice that I was there, watching from behind the partly open bedroom door.

I, on the other hand, never screamed when I had a nightmare. Neither Masa nor Masi knew about the cold sweats I woke up to late at night when I first came to live with them in Mumbai, or the ones I sometimes woke up to even now in Jeddah. Most nights I dreamed of my mother, saw candles glowing, tasted chocolate flakes on my lips. "Smile!" she would say, and a flash would go off repeatedly, until I woke up with a start. Other nights, I would have different dreams. Scarier ones of a man tossing me up high into the air. A loud cracking sound. A woman's scream. But then, just as quickly, the mornings would come and Masi's voice would rise, sonorous in prayer. I would turn once more into the Zarin they knew—a girl who no longer cried or jumped back in surprise when her aunt gave her a beating.

One day she made me so angry that I stuffed my underwear in a clothes drawer, allowing the navy-blue cloth of my academy *kameez* to touch my skin without hindrance, resisting the itch of the rough cotton. It had been worth it to hear Masi screech when she saw the outline of my nipples through the cloth—even more satisfying than the way her face purpled each time I winked at a boy at the mall or exchanged smiles with one at the supermarket.

It no longer mattered what Rusi Masa said in her defense— "She means well!" or "It's for your own good!" By then, I was fourteen and I already knew the truth: that Masi's protectionism stemmed not out of a genuine concern for my well-being, but from a paranoia of having males around me, especially those who reminded her of my "good-for-nothing gangster father."

It was basic psychology, Mishal Al-Abdulaziz told us at school. Girls were often attracted to boys who reminded them of their fathers, and boys, in turn, to girls who reminded them of their mothers.

But that day, at the academy fair, I was not looking for a fight with my aunt. I glanced around quickly, scanning the faces of the growing crowd of fairgoers for the glint of her big gold-rimmed spectacles or my uncle's bald head. I couldn't see either, which meant they were still talking to that man from Masa's office on the other side of the fairgrounds. It had been the man who'd suggested the used-books stall when Masa told him that I liked to read.

"Let her go," Masa had told Masi. "Maybe she can find those Harry Potter books the kids are always talking about."

Masi had frowned for a moment, but to my surprise, she did let me go, probably unwilling to create a scene in front of Masa's colleague. "No wandering around," she had told me in her curt voice. "We will join you very shortly."

The faint call for the *maghrib* prayer floated through the air from a nearby mosque. It would soon be followed by the rustle of prayer mats being rolled out in front of the stalls on the tarmac, the snap of shoelaces and the scrape of Velcro as men slipped off their shoes, splashed their faces, hands, and feet with water from a bottle, and stepped onto colorful rectangles with paisley designs, their heads covered with kerchiefs or netted skullcaps.

The sound of *salah* was one I always associated with Saudi

Arabia, a time when work came to a pause and shops rolled down their shutters for several minutes, five times every day. In Mumbai, life went on as usual, the blare of traffic horns competing with mosques, temples, and churches alike. In Jeddah, however, a sort of stillness fell over everything. Here, prayer's melody was distinct, audible over every other sound. As a six-year-old, I'd often fallen asleep listening to a *salah* after a nightmare. Even as I grew older, the sound had never failed to ease my restlessness. Until now.

The boy stretched back his arms and then leaped off the chair, his sneakers throwing up dust as they hit the ground. Unlike the men near the stalls, he didn't kneel or turn in the direction of Makkah, but spun around to face me.

Black hair. Tanned skin. Narrow jaw. But it was his eyes that caught and held my attention, the irises hazel, almost pale gold in the fading afternoon light. They traveled over me: from the top of my scarf to the tips of my sneakers peeking from underneath the black *abaya*. I was aware of the shapelessness of the garment, the worn laces of my shoes, the boyish crop Masi had been forcing on me ever since I was four years old. For a moment I wished my *abaya* was fancier: a pastel shade of white, sky blue, or yellow instead of the usual black, or embroidered and sequined like the ones Mishal and her friends wore. I wished I could, like some other girls at the fair, feel bold enough to leave my *abaya* open at the front and show off glimpses of a

47

colorful new outfit. But even underneath the *abaya*, my clothes weren't much better—an old T-shirt and the cheap jeans that Masi bought by the dozen from Manara Market.

"It's not like anyone's going to see what you're wearing," she had always said and I had never found a reason to question this rationale. Until tonight.

The boy tilted his head slightly and then flashed me a smile—white teeth, a dimple deep in his left cheek.

My face warmed. It was ridiculous, really. I had never blushed in front of a boy before—not even in Masi's presence. *Smile back*, my mind told me. *Smile back*.

However, by the time I felt the corners of my mouth turn up, the boy was distracted by other matters, more specifically by the head girl, who jogged by us with a money box clutched in her hands, her big breasts bouncing like a pair of water balloons.

"Nadia!" the boy called after her. "Hey, Nadia, do you need some help?"

"Farhaaaan." I'd never heard the head girl sound so breathless. She held the box out to him. "Oh Farhan, you're a lifesaver. May Allah forgive me for missing my prayers today, but I've been so busy! Could you please get this to the headmistress for me?"

"Of course, Nadia." This time his smile was for her, only turned up in brightness. The dizzy, megawatt grin of a guy who'd finally been noticed by a girl he'd been eyeing for ages.

Instead of walking away, they continued to talk, the head girl giggling at something the boy said, seemingly oblivious to the glares they drew from the praying men. By the time they walked off, the *salah* had ended and voices around me rose again, indicating that the stalls had reopened for business.

"There you are." Masi's voice floated to my ears a moment later, as pleasant as the snap of a rubber band on skin. "We've been looking everywhere for you."

I turned away from the boy and the head girl, my face burning. My aunt and uncle approached: Masa, smiling, with plastic packets of blue and pink cotton candy in his hands, and Masi, frowning, her magnified bifocal eyes focused somewhere over my head.

"Who's that boy?" she asked.

"No one."

"You were staring at him. Clearly he isn't no one."

"So is it now a crime to look at people?"

"Stop it," Masa interrupted. He gave me one of the packs of cotton candy. "Stop it, both of you."

I tore out a chunk of the spun pink sugar with my fingers and stuffed it into my mouth, barely listening to Masi's lecture about bad manners. To my relief, we did not see either the boy or Nadia again for the rest of the evening—not that we stayed there very long.

Hours later, I pulled out the school yearbook in my bedroom, turning page after page until I came across one with his photo. Farhan Rizvi. Captain, Qala Academy soccer team. Second-place winner at the regional school debate held last year in Dubai.

His smile didn't seem that special now. It was too toothy, I told myself, too white. Like he was modeling for a toothpaste commercial. His nose looked like it had been modeled by a plastic surgeon, it was so perfectly shaped and centered. Fake, I decided. Completely fake.

I stared at the photo for a few more moments, remembering the way his gaze had traveled over my body, almost as if he was mapping it, the slight narrowing of the eyes, as if something was missing, as if there was something about me that fell short of his expectations.

"It will be difficult," I'd heard Masi telling Masa once, in reference to me. "So difficult to find her a good boy once they find out about her family."

"That happened a long time ago. It won't matter."

"Not everyone is like you, Rusi." It was the first time I'd heard her sound sad, resigned. "Most boys listen to their parents. And they are not going to ignore her past."

The taint of bad blood, the Dog Lady called it. It didn't matter how good your reputation was or how pretty you looked. Though I had never thought about marriage before, I could imagine what the Dog Lady and Masi would say when the time came.

"She will be lucky if she can even *find* someone," the Dog Lady would say in her patronizing tone. "As is, it is so troublesome, you know, Khorshed dear, when it comes to finding someone for a child from a mixed marriage, and in her case . . . well, you know how people talk."

Of course Masi knew. I knew as well.

Illegitimate. Half-Hindu. Gangster's daughter. I'd heard the words before.

I looked at Farhan Rizvi's photo again. Blood rose to my cheeks and I was suddenly angry with him for reminding me of these things. For ogling me first and then chasing after the head girl. For flashing me his perfect smile: a crumb of affection for a lovesick little girl. Pain flickered deep inside my chest. I snapped the yearbook shut and tossed it aside.

The first time I smoked a cigarette, it felt like I'd swallowed a piece of burning coal. Asfiya, the girl who'd offered it to me on the academy roof, did not seem surprised by my coughing fit.

"It happens," she said in a gravelly voice. "You'll get used to it, though."

It was the longest thing she had said to me since I'd started coming up here, halfway through Class IX. Neither of us had

51

planned that first meeting. In those days, I would skip Phys Ed and sneak off to a quiet stairwell on the second floor, where I read a novel I had borrowed from the school library. One day, however, instead of going to the stairwell again, I'd climbed up to the top floor of the academy, a roof terrace that acted as storage for broken desks and blackboards, and a water tank with white paint chipping off its sides. Atop the water tank sat Asfiya—a senior I knew only by her first name mostly because everyone kept saying she was a bad student and a smoker. A smoker! You'd think she was Satan incarnate, the way the girls in my class spoke about her.

She had been blowing smoke rings into the air, one short puff after another, squiggly white circles that rose toward the blue sky before dissipating into nothing. I had expected her to stop when she saw me, maybe even yell, but she hadn't done either of those things. We had stared at each other for a long moment until I pointed to the base of the water tank and asked: "Can I sit here?"

Asfiya had shrugged and simply said, "Whatever."

As the weeks went on, it became a sort of ritual—me sitting at the base of the water tank and reading, her sitting on top and smoking, both of us with a bird's-eye view of three of the four whitewashed buildings that made up the enclosed Qala Academy girls'-section complex, and parts of the neighborhood that lay beyond—shadowy apartment buildings with their clotheslines and dusty satellite dishes, the crescent tip of a mosque glinting in the sunlight. On windy days, I didn't read and Asfiya didn't smoke. We simply sat together, enjoying the respite from the moist Jeddah heat, and watched the grounds below, where girls played volleyball, basketball, and cricket, their voices high and thin from down there, the sort of voices I imagined dolls would have if they ever came to life.

"Is it interesting?" Asfiya asked me a few days after she gave me my first cigarette. "That book you're reading?"

I looked up. "It's pretty good. Animals making up their own rules. Running a farm. The pigs are kind of creepy though."

"Hmm, I guess. Not much of an animal person myself."

I stared out into the distance, my vision blurring slightly in the heat. "I had a kitten once," I said. "I found him here in the academy four years ago, in the second-floor corridor. His mom had died."

The dead cat was a pile of ribs draped with dirty white-gray fur, its back pressed against the freshly painted wall. "Call the maid," the headmistress had said. As if the body was a stubborn piece of chewed gum to be scraped off the speckled marble tiles. It was then that I'd seen something move out of the corner of my eye. The kitten stared up at me with wide lamp-yellow eyes and shrank behind its mother's body. I slowly reached out to touch it. Tiny claws dug into my hands. The kitten wailed and tried to get free. My head had spun from the combined smells of fresh paint and dead cat. "It's okay," I had told the kitten. "My mother is dead too."

"Did it have a name?" Asfiya said, interrupting my reverie.

"Fali."

Masa was the one who had helped me come up with the name. Masi had hated Fali from the very beginning—she called him an Unwanted Expense. "Does money grow on trees?" she had snarled at me, her nostrils flaring. "Who is going to pay for the animal's food?" When I pointed out that she could take the money from the bank account my father left me, she slapped me for "being impertinent."

"Calm down, *jaanu*." Masa always called Masi his *jaanu*, or his life, during her temper tantrums. "What is the harm in a few tins of cat food? We can easily afford it with my new raise."

Since Masi did not really have a good excuse in the face of Masa's reasonable explanation, she switched tracks from cat food costs to household cleanliness. She started off small at first—with complaints about Fali shedding on the sofa and coughing up fur balls. Typical Masi mumbles and grumbles that I'd trained myself to ignore over the years. Then, one afternoon, when I was doing my Science homework, she snapped.

"Bringing in allergies and feces in our house!" she shouted

at Fali, as if he could understand what she was saying. "Who is going to clean this?" She caught Fali by his scruff, threw him out of the apartment, and slammed the door shut.

Then she locked me in my room, kicking and screaming, until Masa came home from work. "Have you seen the way this girl answers back to me?" she demanded. "And the way she fights and pulls at my arms? Acts like a bloody woman wrestler!"

I flew out as soon as Masa unlocked the door. We found Fali lying in a pile of garbage outside the building. Stiff. Bloody.

She didn't mean it, Masi kept telling Masa. Pleading with him as if Fali had belonged to him and not me. She didn't mean for the cat to die. She was sorry. So sorry.

I had never believed her.

"I hate you," I'd said. "You're nothing but a mean old witch."

Neither Masa's pleas nor his threats made me take back my words.

Asfiya remained silent for a long time after I told her the story. Then, with a sigh, she nudged me with a cigarette. "Come on. Let's see if you can smoke without coughing today."

When she graduated the following year, I found a half-used pack tucked into a crevice behind the ladder, likely forgotten—a surprise because Asfiya usually hoarded her cigarettes with great care. It was not until I was smoking my second cigarette that afternoon that it struck me that she may not have forgotten them. That she may have intentionally left them there for me.

Over the years, I learned to deal with my nightmares by focusing on my surroundings. The good things in my life, as I began to think of them. The bedside lamp Masa had gotten me from the souk in Balad, its shade made of green-glass leaves glowing like a fairy bush in the dark. The crunch of the Lion bars that I kept hidden in my drawers, followed by the sweetness of chocolate and caramel melting on my tongue. The call for prayer from the mosque across our apartment: loud, nasal, soothing.

Some nights I allowed myself to remember Porus Dumasia—the closest I'd come to having a friend in the two years I'd stayed at Cama colony.

I first saw Porus a couple of months after my mother's death. By then I had discovered that evenings were the only time I would get some semblance of peace from Masi's constant scrutiny, when the Dog Lady would come over for tea, to gossip with Masi about everyone else in the colony.

Masa often escaped as well, usually on the pretext of

talking to his brother, Merzi Kaka, who lived in the building across from ours, where I watched them growing red and smiley each evening as they downed peg after peg of whiskey on the balcony. One of Merzi Kaka's sons would sit cross-legged on the floor behind them, wearing headphones, his eyes focused on the flat gray remote control–like object he held in his hands. Merzi Kaka kept saying the kid needed to get out more and play something other than video games, but right now even Merzi Kaka didn't seem to care where he was. Not like Masi, whose eyes seemed to follow me wherever I went.

That evening, I glanced back to make sure that Masi and the Dog Lady were still talking and then stepped out onto the common balcony shared by the second-floor residents. Cama colony was a cluster of six buildings facing one another with a large, unpaved courtyard in the middle. Outside the colony, autos, buses, and cars blared horns. Inside, music from radios and CD players clashed: the high voice of Freddie Mercury combating with a popular Hindi song from an Aamir Khan movie about cricket. Here and there, smells emerged. Mothers frying fish and stewing dal in their kitchens, peering out windows from time to time to watch their children playing below.

On my balcony, however, there was no one. When I sat down, I spread out my skirt like a cloud, feeling the tiles, cool against my bare skin. I then moved forward inch by inch, using my hands and shoulders. I got closer and closer, until I could wrap my arms and legs around the wooden banister and watch the children playing below—girls of my age skipping rope, the older ones racing bikes; boys from the colony's junior cricket club racing up and down a long, well-worn strip of dirt. One of them, a boy in a pale blue Tendulkar jersey, squinted when he looked up at me, his eyebrows knitting together. I squinted back. He gave me a wide, gap-toothed smile that nearly split his face in two. Though he looked like he was a couple of years older than me—maybe six or seven—he didn't look as old as the other boys, who were nine or ten years old. It was probably why they bossed him around, making him field the whole time, chase the worn ball around the colony on his stubby legs. After someone hit a ball that zoomed right out of the gate ("SIX! SIX!" the other boys chanted), he plopped onto the dusty ground, panting, and looked toward my balcony again. Pleased to see that I was still there, he gave me that goofy grin again and waved. This time, I smiled and waved back. The older boys were laughing. "Looks like Porus has found himself a girlfriend," one of them said, making the boy in the blue jersey blush.

I did not hear the voices behind me cease conversation; in fact I noticed nothing until a pair of skeletal, long-fingered hands curled around my arms, yanking me upright.

"What are you doing?" Masi shook me by the shoulders.

58

"Spreading your legs and sitting like a boy! Do you have no sense?"

"I-I'm s-sorry . . ." I pressed my knees together. I did not know what exactly I'd done wrong, but I knew that I didn't want her to see me shaking. She marched me back into the flat and slammed the door shut.

Even the Dog Lady looked startled. She cleared her throat. "Khorshed, she is a child."

"I don't care." Streaks of red colored Masi's cheekbones. "She may be young, but not everyone around her is. I saw those boys. The way some of them were gawking. In this day and age, you can never be too sure."

She walked to the cupboard where my clothes were kept, next to a framed photo of my mother on the wall, now garlanded with sandalwood flowers to signify her death. Masi pulled out a neatly folded pajama set and handed it to me, two hours before bedtime. "Here. Put these on."

A week later, she called the *kabaadi* to the colony and sold my frocks to him at a bargain price.

"They were getting old," she lied when Masa asked her why. "She'll grow out of them anyway."

"But what about her hair?" Masa looked perplexed and, for some reason, a little angry. "She had such pretty hair, Khorshi. Did you have to cut it off?"

"Do you want her to have lice, then?"

Crawling gray things that would eat away at my head, Masi had explained moments before she had made me lower my head into the bathroom sink, dousing my curly, shoulder-length hair with a shock of cold water before slowly, methodically snipping it off with a pair of scissors.

Masa frowned. "She looks like a boy now."

"It doesn't matter." Masi let out a strange, bitter-sounding laugh and then pressed down the iron on the secondhand pair of corduroy pants she'd bought for me at the thrift store across the street. Steam rose from the cloth, partly shielding her face. "She's my sister's daughter. She won't look like a boy forever."

It didn't take long for the kids at the colony to notice the change in my appearance or remark on it—especially Merzi Kaka's sons, who instantly began calling me by a boy's name.

"Is that Zarin?" my oldest cousin asked, pretending to be astonished. "Why, she looks exactly like Snot-Nose, doesn't she? That little brat from school? All she needs is phlegm running down her mouth and an open fly."

A few days after this, I often had boys from the colony, mostly my cousin and his friends, shouting at me from different directions and then bursting into laughter when I threw a rock at them in frustration.

The teasing grew worse when a new milkman started

delivering bottles to the colony. "Ey boy, need any milk today?" he would call out whenever he saw me. Or, "Is Mummy-Pappa at home, boy?" I never knew if he was doing it on purpose or was simply myopic. None of the other deliverymen called me a boy; but then again, they had probably seen me when I still wore dresses and had longer hair.

I saw the boy from the cricket pitch from time to time, usually going out with his parents during the evenings or cycling with the other boys in the compound. He was one of the few kids at Cama colony who didn't call me names. There were times when he would glance up at the balcony where he'd seen me before, almost as if he could sense my presence there, as I peered at him through a gap between Masi's curtains. I always ducked when this happened, remaining hidden until I was certain he was gone.

My heart leaped to my throat when I saw him one evening on the second-floor balcony of our building—*my* balcony, as I'd begun to think of it. He was wearing the blue jersey again and his lips were curved up slightly. Had he noticed me spying on him? Was he going to complain to Masi? I hoped he wouldn't. It had taken me two months to work up the courage to come out here again during the evenings. Two months of being holed up inside, on my cot, staring out the window while Masi and the Dog Lady jawed about boring things like *rava* recipes and vacuum cleaners or the people they worked with at Zoroastrian community organizations like the Parsi Panchayat.

"Hi," he said after staring at me for a few moments. "How are you?" His voice was raspy and a little shy.

I glanced back quickly and edged along the balcony, closer to the boy, out of Masi's line of vision.

"You shouldn't be here," I told him sternly, careful to keep my voice quiet. "My *masi* doesn't want me talking to boys. And if you're here to make fun of me, I will kick you."

I didn't like the way he frowned. It made his lips turn down and the space between his eyebrows wrinkle. I much preferred his goofy, gap-toothed smile. But obviously I couldn't say that to him.

"*Ey su che?* I won't make fun of you. I want to be friends with you." Unlike my cousins, who flaunted their convent education by speaking in English whenever they could, this boy spoke in the smooth, flowing Gujarati common to the kids who went to the vernacular school run by the Parsi Charitable Trust in Mumbai.

"I can't be friends with you. I don't even know you." I felt bad the moment I said the words, mostly because the boy looked hurt. But I didn't take them back. Masa had promised to get me a book next year for my fifth birthday. One of those big Disney picture books with perfect sketches of ragged street urchins, bookish French girls, and dancing lions on the African savanna. I was desperately looking forward to those pretty pictures that would take me away, far away, from the life I lived here, if only for a few hours. If I made Masi angry by talking to this boy, I wouldn't even get that.

After a moment, the boy nodded, a strange, determined look on his face. "My name is Porus. What's yours?"

"Zarin," I said, too puzzled to think hard about this line of questioning.

"Okay, so now you know me." He grinned when I scowled. "And your name is as pretty as you are."

"Don't lie to me. I know I look like a boy. Everyone says so."

"Those people are lying, then," Porus told me seriously. "You're too pretty to be a boy." Then, to my astonishment, he leaned forward and sniffed my shoulder. I pushed him away.

"What are you doing?"

"See? I was right. You don't even smell like a boy," he said. "You smell like Pond's Magic Powder and flowers. Boys don't smell like that."

"Zarin," Masi called from inside the flat. "Zarin, where are you?"

"I have to go." I turned around, grateful that I had an excuse to avoid him—this strange boy who went around smelling people to prove a point. Except for the few times I had told my cousins and their friends to shut up when they called me Snot-Nose, I'd never even talked to a boy before. He was probably making fun of me. However, unlike my cousins, whose words sometimes made me stew for hours on end, Porus's words made me feel strangely good about myself. I replayed them in my head that night, over and over again, long after Masa and Masi fell asleep.

In the weeks to come, I saw Porus more often, though never again on my balcony. Maybe I'd scared him off. Or maybe he somehow sensed that I would get in trouble with Masi for encouraging his friendship. In the mornings, when Masi was busy praying, I sometimes sneaked out onto the balcony to watch the comings and goings of the other residents. This was where I usually saw Porus, clinging to his father's hand as they walked to the bus stop across the road. Porus's gaze would somehow always gravitate toward me and he would grin and wave each time. Sometimes Porus's father would wave as well, and I would be treated to older and younger versions of the same smile.

Slowly, after a week or two of this, I began to wave back. It was the polite thing to do, I reasoned. And though I didn't like to admit it, I almost always felt calmer on the days I saw Porus and his father walking to the bus stop. Some mornings I even walked around with a smile on my face—a fact that did not escape my uncle's notice.

"Someone looks happy today," Masa said. "Did something special happen?"

I shrugged, saying nothing. I kept it hidden away—this strange "waving friendship" of ours—along with the memories of my last birthday cake, my hopes for a Disney picture book, and the toothy smiles from a boy who thought I was pretty.

By the time I was sixteen, I'd learned a couple of things.

I learned that Thursdays were the best days for sneaking out of school with a guy—by catching the sweet spot between the last two periods (Home Science and Phys Ed) and slipping out the unmanned side gate at the south end of Qala Academy and into a waiting car. I would have an hour and a half to eat a shawarma and smoke a cigarette or two, maybe talk if the boy was chatty, before he dropped me off a block away from our apartment building moments before the school bus drove by.

I'd also learned that, when faced with the threat of being locked up forever in my room or in an unwanted marriage, I could school my features into a mask and lie to my aunt with conviction.

"Where were you?" Masi had shouted one Thursday when I had come home later than expected. "I was about to call your *masa*."

"We had debate practice at the last minute and I missed the bus. My friend Noor's father dropped me off." I didn't even know anyone by the name of Noor, but luckily Masi didn't ask any more questions.

After that, however, I didn't take any chances. Dates were cut shorter, despite the boy's complaints, and I came home quicker. Normally debate practices took place on Mondays and ran for about two hours after school. If Masi made inquiries with my teacher or the headmistress, I would be in deep trouble. I might have learned ways to pull one over on my aunt and uncle, but I couldn't use that excuse again.

For the other girls, Thursdays held a different sort of allure. They marked the end of the school week in Saudi Arabia, a time when most academy students threw aside their books for two days of respite from the rigorous Class XI coursework.

"Any year without board exams is a good one," our class monitor, Alisha Babu, declared to everyone on the day school reopened after two months of summer vacation. "Too bad our teachers are such poor sports about it!"

Our teachers, who piled us up with essays and problem sets the day we returned, who scolded us for not completing our holiday homework on time, who reminded us of our dismal scores from the first term test in May. They started handing out punishments by the dozen, usually in the form of more problem sets or lines to write out.

Even Khan Madam, our mild-mannered English teacher, grew irritable. "Don't forget—you will still have the boards next year," she said one day when she caught Mishal Al-Abdulaziz yawning in English class. "So *failing* English this year will not help you much, my dear Mishal."

It was really quite an unfair statement, a surprising and rare display of temper that had most girls diagnosing Khan Madam with early-onset menopause. I couldn't really blame them. As much as I disliked Mishal, she was by no means a poor student. Thanks to our perpetual rivalry since Class II, she was only five marks away from the highest English score in our class—mine.

Unlike other subjects, English was easy for me—so much easier than Hindi, which needed a lot more than a rudimentary knowledge of Bollywood songs. My edge over Mishal in the subject often lay in debates; arguing with my aunt over the years had given me enough practice with snappy comebacks.

English, Masa told me once, had been Masi's favorite subject too. "She used to read lots of books!" he had said cheerfully. "Like you, Zarin."

My interest in reading had been a surprise to Masi as well, not that we had many books in our apartment except for a few old Famous Fives and a tattered copy of *Jane Eyre*. Trips to Jarir Bookstore, the only place you could get any interesting novels, were extremely rare. Jarir was expensive—even Masa said so—and who was going to spend forty-two riyals ("Six hundred and seven rupees?!" Masi exclaimed) on a book about a group of teenagers trying to kill each other on reality TV?

"Sorry, dear," Khan Madam had said when I asked if the school library kept these books, "but these aren't usually on our prescribed teaching lists." Her eyes twinkled like dark gems and for a moment I did not see the pouches underneath. "Why don't you borrow them from one of the girls?"

It was a nice idea, except that most girls would not lend me a broken pencil. My reputation as a smoker and my general unfriendliness often preceded everything I'd ever done in school, good or bad. At one point, some girl had been blunt enough to tell me straight up, "My mother wouldn't like it if I was friends with someone like you."

"I want to borrow your book. It doesn't make us friends."

Alisha Babu, who eventually lent me her own copy of *The Hunger Games*, told me that most of my classmates found me intimidating. "If you were a little friendlier, people would begin to like you more. You'd see that the rest of us aren't so bad."

But I knew better. I could see the sly curiosity beneath their offers of friendship. I'd seen women like the Dog Lady in action at the colony, women who were experts at such backbiting friendliness. First they would ask questions about your life. *Really? Tell me more!* Then they would tell everyone else. *Do you know what* she *did? I would never have imagined it!* They would first giggle about you and then criticize you and later converge on you as a pack. *You know there are things about yourself that you should change. We're telling you this because we care.*

The Dog Lady was part of the reason Masi was so neurotic. My aunt depended on her for advice even here in Jeddah, sometimes making long-distance calls to Mumbai for up to thirty minutes. "What do you think, Persis?" I had heard her often ask. "Do you think I did the right thing?"

I wondered if Masi knew how ridiculous she sounded when she spoke like that, how weak. You couldn't win anyone's approval by trying to fit in or even by doing what they expected you to do, I wanted to tell her. I had learned as much when I was seven.

It was easier, much easier to say nothing. To skip Phys Ed and go up to the water tank to smoke in silence, to think instead of talk. Talking, I'd learned from observing these girls and the Dog Lady, only led to revelation of secrets. Secrets that could open up again like a barely healed wound under a bandage and bleed through the white surface.

Class XI wasn't Class II. We were sixteen now and other things were going on apart from rivalries over being a teacher's pet or student of the year. Boys had entered the picture. Not only celebrities, but real ones, mostly captains and vice-captains from the boys' section in Sharafiyah. Many of the girls didn't get to see them up close, let alone go out on dates with them (unless you counted texting each other from different stores at the same mall), which made those who did automatically become objects of envy and derision.

"Slut," Mishal had called a girl for going out with Farhan Rizvi in Class X. "Wore a scarf around her neck like a muffler to hide the marks he'd made on her skin."

"That's gross," her friend Layla Sharif had replied before bursting into giggles. "But I don't blame her. He's so hot."

That Farhan Rizvi had been appointed head boy this year added to his hotness. The title allowed most girls to overlook the many rumors that had been floating around about him ever since he had broken up with the head girl: that he was drifting down highways in his black BMW, partying with Saudi boys from a local college, changing girlfriends like pairs of socks.

"That face." Another girl sighed. "Oh my God, I swear it has grown better looking every year."

A face that I still could not look at without remembering that day at the fair, without feeling the old sting of rejection.

However, not everyone in our classroom was susceptible to Farhan Rizvi's charms. Mishal Al-Abdulaziz hated him, often bringing us rumors of his wild escapades, some of the stories so far-fetched that I wondered if she spent her free time making them up.

"You should have *seen* the way he and his friends were behaving at the fair this year," Mishal said the week we returned to school after the holidays. "Getting together in groups of six or seven and cornering three or four girls in a stall to dry hump them. I swear! I'm not lying! It was disgusting, really, the way they were going about it—and those girls were giggling, encouraging their cheap behavior!"

I rolled my eyes, wondering if Mishal even knew what dry humping meant. The fair was certainly one of the few times the boys and girls from the academy could see one another without the interference of the religious police, but it was still a public place, with stall owners, teachers, and parents milling about. Poking a girl on Facebook or throwing her your number in the mall was one thing, but the idea of a boy—or a group of boys—attempting something like that in such a chaperone-heavy location was so ludicrous that even Mishal's friends had burst out laughing.

Mishal may have talked about penises and vaginas with the detached inflections of a college biology teacher, but everyone knew she would jump a mile if a boy so much as winked at her. She would probably have blown a fuse if she'd found out about me dating her brother, Abdullah, a boy whose advances I had initially ignored, mostly because I knew who he was related to.

Tall, handsome Abdullah, with his broad shoulders and curly black hair. Abdullah, who glared at boys for eyeing his sister, but had no problem eyeing girls himself, which was quite evident when I finally met him face-to-face this past summer at the school fair.

"Hey." He'd paused by the used-books stall I was standing

next to and leaned an elbow across the counter. "You in Class XI?"

In response, I had pulled out a magazine on display and studied the cover—an old copy of *Vogue* featuring an American pop singer, her bare legs colored over with Magic Marker. Neat black lines followed the curves of her calves and thighs, giving the appearance of leggings.

"Hellooo." Abdullah snapped a finger next to my ear.

"Not interested," I said out loud. Good-looking though he might have been, I knew who Abdullah was. I had seen enough of his pictures in the school yearbook, read enough newsletter bulletins about his trophies and track team records. In any case, his last name, on a badge clipped to the lapel of his navy-blue school blazer along with the title Sports Captain was a dead giveaway. There was only one Al-Abdulaziz in the boys' school who had been appointed to that position that year, and he was the brother of a girl who hated my guts.

"You're being rude, you know," he said, following me when I left the stall. "I wanted your opinion on the Independence Day exhibition stalls. I'm writing an article for the newsletter and I wanted an eleventh-grade girl's opinion."

"Oh really?" I raised my eyebrows. "Why don't you ask your sister, then?"

"Well, because she's my sister, duh," he said with a grin. "What's the point of writing an article if you can't interview pretty girls?"

I couldn't help smirking. "You'd be guilty of *khilwa*, you know."

His eyes widened in mock horror. "Uh-oh, don't tell me that I found another religious policewoman at QA. I thought Mishal was the only one!"

The joke made me laugh out loud. It stuck with me through the rest of our conversation, as he showed me the Independence Day exhibits and asked questions, taking notes whenever I said something. The Dog Lady always said that if you could make a girl laugh, you could make her yours. Maybe there was some truth to that statement, because at the end of the interview, when Abdullah finally asked for my number, I scribbled it down on his interview sheet along with my name.

"You're fairly brave," I told Abdullah a week later as I slid into the front passenger seat of his big maroon GMC. "Most guys would be worried about getting in trouble with the cops. Or the Hai'a."

Unlike the other boys I'd dated, Abdullah never seemed threatened by the religious police, which might have partly been the effect of having a Saudi father with connections in the government. Jeddah, Abdullah told me, was considered Saudi Arabia's liberal city even though its name translated to *grandmother* in English. A city seemingly devoid of sentinels from the Commission for the Promotion of Virtue and the Prevention of Vice: an old lady with mischief up her black sleeves. Here, it seemed perfectly natural for elaborately designed mosques to coexist with giant sculptures of bicycles and geometry sets. Jeddah offered those few courting opportunities that couples were denied in most other parts of the Kingdom, even though few such relationships lasted long. I'd learned from experience that a love story that began with a phone number tossed on a piece of paper at a crowded mall could end abruptly, within days, leaving behind radio silence.

Abdullah laughed at me now. "You're talking about trouble? You'll be in more trouble than me if we're caught. At least I'm a Muslim. You're not that; heck, you're not even a Christian. You could die in an accident tomorrow, but you'd still get jack from the government. Let me think—what *is* the going rate for Parsi chicks found dead in ditches?"

"Three thousand three hundred thirty-three riyals," I replied. "Not even half your father's salary, *ya walad*."

He laughed even harder at that. "Your Arabic accent is so *Indian*."

The comment brought out a question I'd been thinking of ever since Abdullah and I had started going out. "How come you and Mishal didn't go to a Saudi school?"

Segregation in Saudi Arabia wasn't limited to gender alone.

Apart from rare gatherings to celebrate Eid at offices, there seemed to be a natural divide between the Saudis and the expatriates, each community keeping to itself in matters of education and socializing. The Saudis had their own school system with an all-Arabic curriculum and a focus on Islamic studies. There were also private schools that Abdullah had told me about where wealthy Arabs sent their kids for an English education, whose graduates had the chance to apply to universities in America and Europe. It seemed more likely to me that both Abdullah and Mishal would have gone to one of these schools instead of Qala Academy, which wasn't that fancy, and where the curriculum mainly focused on South Asians planning to return to their home countries.

He gave me a tight-lipped smile. "My mother wanted it. Father agreed. Besides, I'm half-Indian too, remember?"

There was a brief, awkward silence before he pulled out a pack of cigarettes and a lighter. "Want one?" He offered them casually, in a way that told me he didn't really expect me to take him up on his offer.

"Sure." I flicked one from the pack and lit up.

He smiled. It was a nice smile, accentuating a cleft in his chin that I had not noticed before. "You're different," he said. "Different from any other girl I know."

"You're different too," I admitted. "I'm surprised you're even related to Mishal."

Which made him laugh again.

A year ago, Mishal had tried to get me in trouble by reporting to our sadistic Physics teacher that I carried cigarettes in my backpack. It had been a close call. It was sheer luck that I'd run through my last pack that morning and thrown it away before I entered the classroom; luck that my breath smelled of mint and not tobacco when the teacher made me open my mouth and sniffed like a rabid bloodhound. After that, I never carried cigarettes on my person, usually stashing them in little nooks and crannies at school—in that space behind the ladder at the water tank on the terrace.

By the time I was sixteen, however, it was boys like Abdullah who would help me skip school, who offered me their own cigarettes and smoked with me in their cars, parked in a deserted lot by the Corniche on Thursday afternoons.

Only Abdullah became a lot more than a guy I simply went out with for cigarettes or food—and that became evident when he kissed me on our third date—a light, pleasing dance of lips and tongues that made me forget for a few moments that we were in a public place.

"What's the matter?" he asked when I pushed him away. "I thought you liked me."

I laughed, gently tracing his frown away with a finger. "I *do* like you. But maybe we should not keep doing this *here*."

I gestured toward the railing in the distance, where a lone man stood, staring at the sunlight glittering on the waves.

Abdullah rolled his eyes. "He's so far, Zarin. He's not even turned this way."

"And when he does turn, we're going to be the ones in trouble. I'm not taking any chances."

"Come on." Abdullah was grinning. "You're telling me you've never done this before?"

"It may surprise you to know that I haven't," I said truthfully.

As reckless as I was under most circumstances, I did not want to kiss every guy I went out with on these dates. Half the guys I'd gone out with had been far too worried about the religious police showing up to catch us red-handed, while the other half had been far too intimidated by me and never attempted more than a timid kiss on the hand or the cheek.

Abdullah was an exception in many ways. For one: I genuinely enjoyed his company. He was intelligent. He made me laugh. And he smelled nice too. Which was why, when he leaned in to kiss me, I let him.

There were times when we talked when Abdullah would mention Farhan's name. "Rizvi and I did this," or "Rizvi and I did that," or "Rizvi's such a loser sometimes, I don't even know why I'm friends with him." I listened closely to these little stories—bits and pieces of information about a boy I had only,

77

as of yet, seen in pictures or from a distance during school functions. Those were the nights I would imagine Rizvi's lips on mine instead of Abdullah's—a wisp of curiosity that fluttered through my brain when I was falling asleep—a thought I managed to squash before it bloomed into heat. I instantly felt guilty afterward, sometimes even refusing to go out with Abdullah when he texted me a week later, making an excuse of a doctor's appointment or a test.

The beauty about Abdullah was that he never followed up on my lies or asked additional questions. *Cool. Next week then*, he always wrote back in reply. It was almost as if he expected me to have a part of myself that I kept private the way he kept parts of his own life a mystery, evading any questions that might have anything to do with his family or childhood.

"Some things are too messed up to explain," he said, and I agreed.

It made perfect sense for us to be together; to meet up each Thursday to talk, smoke, and sometimes kiss; to lose ourselves in random conversations about school or movies or music for an hour and forget who we really were.

Mishal

THE STARS WERE BRIGHT THE NIGHT LAYLA
called.

They pricked the sky like diamonds, like the gems studding
the expensive *abaya* Father's second wife wore to a cousin's
wedding last weekend, with a matching scarf and *niqab*.

"It cost me two thousand riyals," Jawahir had said when the
women at the party asked her about it. As if she was the one
who had earned the money for it, as if it wasn't Father's plati-
num credit card that she used every time she went to a mall—a
card that I knew he had never offered to Mother or to Abdullah and me, even for basic household expenses, let alone friv-
olous shopping sprees for designer clothes.

"Witch," Abdullah had called her when I told him.

"Money-hungry, gold-digging witch," I had corrected, making him laugh.

Cursing Jawahir together was the closest Abdullah and I ever came to expressing affection these days, our concentrated hate for her temporarily allowing us to forget the anger we collectively held against Father for ignoring our existence, against Mother for turning into a zombie, and mostly against each other for growing up and changing—in Abdullah's case, changing so much that there were days we couldn't even look at each other, let alone talk.

"Mishal?" Layla's voice crackled over the telephone line. She grumbled to herself and then I heard her moving to a room where the reception was clearer. "Mishal, you got my text, didn't you?" She emphasized the *got*, shouted it for good measure to show me how angry she was.

As for the text—of course I'd gotten it. She knew I'd gotten it. I knew she'd seen the little check mark under the image she'd sent me, right next to *Read 8:45 p.m.* Right after which I shut off my phone.

Minutes later, Layla had called me on my landline, demanding explanations in that nagging, mother-hen way of hers. In hindsight, I should have known she would do that. Things like shutting off phones and ignoring texts and e-mails did not affect Layla Sharif when she wanted to get hold of someone. It was probably why we were such good friends.

"Are you sure it was them?" I asked, even though the picture she'd texted was clear enough.

"Positive! I wouldn't lie to you about such a thing. They were in Abdullah's car. My brother saw the license plate number when he was driving past the Corniche this afternoon. And it was her. It had to be. Who else do we know who has a penchant for sneaking out with boys and smoking?"

I stared out my bedroom window. Across the compound where Abdullah parked his car, the neighborhood mosque glowed, its spires outlined with tubes of neon-green light. Speakers circled the main minaret on four sides, crackling slightly, the way they did moments before the *muezzin* sounded the call for prayer. To the left of our compound, in the garden where I'd once played as a child, everything was dark. In the daytime, you could see an old tire hanging from a neem tree, still held in place by the rope Father had bound to the branches eleven years before, when I was five years old and Abdullah, six. Orange-and-blue nylon, now faded and worn, forming what I used to think of as *rope henna*—strange, braided designs imprinted on my palms after a long day of swinging.

"Higher," I remembered calling out to Abdullah the day the swing was set up. "Higher, *ya akhi*." *Akhi*, a word that the dictionary defined as *my brother* but that, for me, also stood for *playmate* and *best friend*.

Abdullah would push the tire as hard as he could before

81

climbing onto it at the last moment and then using his feet as leverage so we could both swing together. I couldn't remember ever feeling so buoyant or laughing so hard, ever feeling so close to another person the way I had that night with my brother, my arms wrapped tight around his waist, my ear pressed to his heart, hearing it beat hard through his rib cage.

My brother had always held me during our parents' fights in those early years, whispering that it would be okay, that we would be okay, until the day he turned eight, when Father enrolled him in soccer lessons at a local club. Suddenly, seemingly overnight, Abdullah had a whole bunch of new friends. Friends he spent hours with outside the house, friends he sometimes brought over to play in his room, never allowing me to see them. He became irritable whenever I tried to join in. "No girls allowed," he'd say, refusing to unlock the door despite my repeated knocks and pleas. The days his friends did not come over, he took to tripping me in the corridors of our house, laughing at my confusion, sneering at the way I cried out in pain. "My friends are right," he had said. "Girls are silly crybabies."

Though Mother made him apologize for his behavior later, I knew that this was only the beginning—the first crack in a relationship that I had once thought unbreakable, a shade of gray in a photograph that, until then, had always appeared black and white.

"Mishal." Layla's voice penetrated my thoughts. "Mishal, are you okay?"

"Y-yes," I managed to say. "I'm fine, Layla. I have to go now, okay? Will talk to you tomorrow."

I put down the phone.

I encountered my brother's friends again when I was fourteen, when the Qur'an Studies teacher my father had appointed for me called in sick and I was forced to stay up in my room, counting the stars on my ceiling, while Abdullah watched television in the downstairs living room with a group of guys he'd invited from the academy.

They were older boys from classes X and XI—fifteen- and sixteen-year-olds who, for the most part, I'd always been hidden from, because Abdullah never wanted them to see me, even though he never told me why.

"They're good guys," he said, "but sometimes they can get a little rowdy. If at any point you get nervous, remember to lock your door."

The way Abdullah had begun to lock his door the previous year, after I found the porn magazine hidden under his mattress. The one he read between the pages of a comic book or a newspaper, thinking he could fool me the way he did our mother, not expecting me to sneak in when he was at school, to have a look at the kind of magazine that I had, till then, only heard about at school from the other girls, but never seen.

It had been a shock when I first saw her. The woman spread out across a large, glossy centerfold, her legs stretched in a split, in nearly perfect symmetry. I may have been a teenager, now officially surrounded by girls openly giggling about boys in the classroom during breaks or drooling over posters of bare-chested Bollywood heroes. But in matters of nudity, I was little better than an eight-year-old, my knowledge limited to what I saw of myself in the mirror and the Barbie dolls Mother bought for me as a child—plastic women with painted faces, nipple-free breasts, and hairless vaginas—women I strove to make modest by dressing them in maxi-length dresses I made myself out of old hankies and scarves, women whose shiny hair I braided like my own, a single plait that fell to their waists, and then covered with my handmade scarves.

"Miniature Mishals," Abdullah had called these dolls, sometimes ripping off the scarves I'd so painstakingly wrapped around their hair, or lifting up the skirts of the dresses so he could peek underneath. In those days, these were the only times that we fought—my screams would even bring Mother out of her musical reverie to scold the both of us. Abdullah would then run out of my room in disgust and Mother would hug me and say, "Stop being silly."

The woman I saw in Abdullah's magazine, however, had nipples the way I did, though hers were considerably larger and pierced through with silver rings. A thin strip of black hair ran down her crotch; the hair on her head was dyed blond. The shock I felt at seeing her nude wasn't as great as the shock of finding her in my brother's room.

I remembered the look he'd given me once when I bent over to pick up a pencil in the living room, the way his gaze had lingered on my legs and butt even after I'd straightened. It was only when his gaze reached my face that he started and stepped back. We both went red—I, for reasons I did not know back then—and then Abdullah had simply frowned at me, which made me feel as if I'd done something wrong.

I flipped through more pages, ignoring the text and focusing on the pictures—all of them women, all of them naked. I spent so long in Abdullah's room that I didn't hear him come back from school or enter until he was towering right over me, his shadow censoring my view of the page.

He seized me by the arm and threw me out the door. "If you tell Mother about this I will screw you so bad, you will not know what hit you."

"Like you screw those girls, you mean!" I shouted, even though I didn't know what *I* meant in throwing his threat back at him.

Then Abdullah leaned forward and grabbed hold of my

arms. His thumbs dug into the sides of my breasts; I could feel his nails through my clothes. His teeth were gritted, his mouth so close to my face that I could smell the potato chips on his breath.

"Stop it! You're hurting me!"

"Children?" A voice floated toward us from the other end of the hallway. "Children, what is it? Why are you fighting?"

I do not know what Abdullah would have done had Mother not suddenly emerged from her room. He released me as suddenly as he'd caught me. "I do not want you inside my room again. If you do that, I will show you what I can do."

Out of fear, then, rose an emotion that I would carry always in reaction to Abdullah's threat: an anger that made me shove him with both hands against the closed door. There was surprise on his face—he had, I realized, not expected me to hit back—then wariness, a look he would always give me when we were alone together after that, before he stalked off into his room.

In the weeks and months that followed, I began to look up terms in the dictionary—*intercourse, sex, masturbate*. From the girls at school, I learned the slang words—the forbidden four-letter ones they scribbled on the doors of toilet stalls—and looked those up as well, putting new meaning to the words my brother used on the phone with his friends.

By the time I was fourteen, I had a rough idea of what

happened between a man and woman when they had sex. We learned about reproduction in biology, saw crude drawings of the male and female organs in our textbook. At school a girl brought in *The Diary of a Young Girl* and showed us a chapter where Anne Frank described her own body in detail. I had learned enough to giggle at these descriptions, to hide my own prudishness in front of the other girls.

It was the year Father instructed the family driver to give Abdullah driving lessons in his car—a brand-new GMC that Abdullah was expected to chauffeur me and Mother around in once he got his driving permit. Father's visits to our home also decreased that year as he spent more and more time managing his new electronics store in Bahrain. Now, in Father's absence, Abdullah was officially the man of our house and our legal guardian—the one who would be allowed to sign papers permitting me or even Mother to travel anywhere outside the Kingdom, even though he was fifteen and Mother forty.

Forbidding me to see his friends was the first of Abdullah's many dictums, though that never really bothered me that much. I had heard plenty about these boys at school, and had no inclination to see them or to let them see me. What bothered me was Abdullah's refusal to allow me to accompany him and Father on our family's first ever pilgrimage, our first ever Hajj, to the holy city of Makkah the following month, even though Jawahir and her sons were allowed to go.

"You cannot!" Abdullah had insisted when I complained. "You're fourteen years old, Mishal. You have your whole life ahead of you. Besides, if we both go, who will take care of Mother?"

"We could take Mother with us! I promise I'll take care of her!"

"Mother is not capable of going at this time and you know it." Abdullah's eyes softened slightly when he saw the anger on my face. "Look, I'll tell Father to take you with him next year, okay?"

Rationally, I knew my brother was right. While the pilgrimage was one of the five pillars of Islam and obligatory for Muslims, it needed to be undertaken only once during a lifetime, health and finances permitting. Abdullah also had a point about Mother's depression, which often got worse after spending time with either Father or Jawahir, even with her medication. There was no way she would be able to manage the five days of the Hajj with both of them *and* their kids.

A part of me couldn't help wondering if these were the only reasons or if there was more behind Abdullah's refusal to take me along. By now, my brother and I had reached a truce of sorts, which we maintained by staying out of each other's way. He did not want me around him, which should have been more relief than it was offense, I had told myself.

The evening Abdullah's friends came over, I was still

thinking about the Hajj. About the luxury Makkah Clock Royal Tower hotel, where my father had booked a suite with a view of the Grand Mosque and the Kaaba. I thought about how once they got there, Jawahir would fawn over Abdullah as if he was her son. How they would pretend to be one big happy family—like my mother and I didn't exist.

I emptied my bag. Books fell out onto the bedspread, along with a few pencil shavings and a folded piece of paper. I unfolded it again and stared at it. The result of the Class IX aptitude test had come the week before, hours before Mother had one of her fights with Father over the phone and locked herself in her room.

The test suggested that I had a good grasp of body language and human interactions. Psychology or counseling was one of the recommended career paths—one that instantly made me the butt of an Abdullah joke. "*You?*" Abdullah had said with a laugh. "A psychologist? Those poor, poor patients!"

I leaned out my bedroom window now, the way I sometimes did when left alone, bending my waist as far as my upper body would go without losing my balance and somersaulting two stories down onto the paved driveway, where the cars were parked.

Normally I would have been watching the sky. I always loved watching the sunsets in Jeddah. Sometimes the sky turned orange or pink or violet and soaked everything—the iron gates and white outer walls of our villa, the potted palms at the entrance, the driveway—in a single pastel shade. It was like seeing the world through different-colored lenses, depending on the day.

Years before, when the weather wasn't too hot or humid, my parents, Abdullah, and I had spent hours in our small garden. While my parents talked over pitchers of nonalcoholic Saudi champagne made with oranges, apples, and mint or rose-flavored Rooh Afza, Abdullah and I often sneaked away to the back, where the gardener kept his ladder, and climbed up to peek at the world outside the villa's walls. We both stood there, precariously balanced, Abdullah always one rung below me, and pointed out familiar sights to each other. The tall minaret of the *masjid* we went to every Friday with Father and Mother. The brightly painted walls of Al-Fajr Elementary School. The Indian and Somali construction workers on the steps of the building next to it, their hard hats and blue coveralls coated with dust, cigarettes glowing between their fingertips. Back then, I did not know that once Father left, our visits to the *masjid* as a family would stop as well. I did not know that Al-Fajr Elementary would reject Abdullah's school application, sending my father into a rage.

"Qala Academy?" He had bristled at Mother's suggestion. "That school for Indians?"

Mother had said Father did not mean to be that insensitive.

"It's family pressure and disapproval. It can take a toll on him, you know," she had told us both.

Going down memory lane added to the storm broiling inside me. To distract myself, I examined the cars parked in the driveway. Abdullah's GMC was there, of course, along with a shiny black car I'd seen there once before. I squinted my eyes against the setting sun, trying to make out the logo on the car's hood.

The owner of the black car was a friend of Abdullah's, I knew. A boy slightly taller than my brother, with black hair and hazel eyes. A month earlier, he had been standing outside next to his car, smoking a cigarette. He had looked up. I'd sprung back like a jack-in-the-box, guilty by instinct, even though I was sure he hadn't seen me.

This evening when I looked out, no one was there. I was leaning out even farther, testing the limits of my balance, when a knock sounded on the door. My fingers tightened on the sill and as I fumbled back inside, I grazed my arm on a sharp metal edge. I winced—a cut had appeared on my skin, a thin line interspersed with dark, blooming beads of red.

"What?" I wanted to yell. It was probably Mother or Abdullah wanting something or another. But for some reason, my mind warned me to keep my mouth shut, and my mouth obeyed. I slipped out of the pink sequined slippers I usually wore indoors and quietly made my way to the door.

Another knock, this time louder. "Hell-lloo? Anyone home?"

A male voice, low and deep. One of my brother's friends. The voice made me uncomfortable. I moved closer and, without really thinking, clicked the lock in place. Beyond the door, a laugh and then more—there could have been three, maybe four of them there.

"Come on, little girl," the boy said again, and I suddenly knew it was him. The boy who owned the black car. "We're all friends here."

He hammered the door now; it shook within the frame. I caught hold of the badminton racket lying on the floor next to me and held it close. My left eye twitched. Blood pulsed at the bases of my ears.

"Rizvi!" a sharp voice said. My brother's.

I let out the breath I had been holding.

"I'm fooling around, *ya* Aboody." The boy used the nickname Father used for Abdullah, his voice clearer now, less deep. "We meant no harm."

"I *told* you not to come up here." Abdullah's voice tightened my insides more than Rizvi's had. "I told you that my mom is sick and that my sister is studying for exams."

"Come on, man, you're acting like—"

"GO!" Abdullah shouted.

There was a pause for a moment and then Rizvi laughed again. "Okay, man. Your house, your sister, your rules!"

I slid down to the floor and pressed my ear against the door, listening to the squeak of a sneaker on the tiled corridor outside and then footfalls on the carpeted stairs, retreating to the living room once more.

Another knock on the door, hesitant this time. "Mishal?" Abdullah said. "Mishal, are you okay? They were kidding—they didn't mean anything, okay? It was—I'm sorry, Mishal. I'll make sure it doesn't happen again."

It didn't.

Though a week later, Abdullah was gone from home again, returning at five in the morning, a couple of hours before I had to get ready for school.

"How can you stay friends with such guys?" I demanded, rising from the sofa the moment he entered. "You know what they're like, how they harassed me."

"What do you mean? You know I was at a friend's house after the Qur'an Club meeting. I spent the night there."

"What friend?" I demanded, but Abdullah didn't answer. "I'm not a fool, Abdullah. You were out with those guys again."

Abdullah stared at me for a moment and then sighed. "Look . . . Mishal, I'm really tired right now, okay? Can we talk about this later?"

"But I—"

"They're my friends, okay!" Abdullah snapped. "My real

friends. Besides, you should've listened when I told you to stay in your room."

"What do you mean? I *was* in my—"

"Rizvi saw you, he said. He *saw* you when you leaned out the window—in your nightgown, your hair uncovered. What do you *think* he was going to do?" Abdullah's eyes made a harsh, unforgiving perusal of my floor-length housecoat and lingered on the scarf draped over my breasts. "Have you learned nothing about men and the necessity of a proper *hijab*? Or did you want his attention?"

My face burned. "No!"

As sick as Abdullah's words made me, he wasn't saying anything that I hadn't heard before from teachers at school or from my Qur'an Studies tutor at home. They had told us about women who forgot their place, who sought out a man's attention by intentionally wearing *abaya*s that revealed the curves of their bodies, by accentuating their eyes with makeup even while wearing a *niqab*. I remembered the way I had leaned out my window. Had my posture revealed the shape of my body in a way that was alluring to the boy in the black car? Wanton, even? Had he seen in it a form of invitation?

Abdullah raised a finger and quietly wiped a tear from my cheek. I slapped it away, disgusted with him and myself.

"Please, Mishal." His voice was soft now, almost consoling. "Please try to understand. A woman's honor is like a tightly wrapped sweet. If you unwrap a sweet and leave it lying around, you expose it to everything out there. If, by accident, it falls into the dirt—tell me, Mishal, will anyone want to eat it?"

"Stop it," I whispered.

But he persisted: "Don't you remember what happened to Reem?"

Of course I did. Everyone knew what had happened to our cousin. Sweet, innocent Reem, with her big brown eyes and shy smile. Who seemed to have the perfect arranged marriage when she fell in love with the man she was engaged to—until she slept with her fiancé a week before the wedding ceremony. It wasn't her fault, the fiancé claimed when he broke off the wedding. But many who knew the truth had blamed Reem for it. He had been surprised, I'd overheard our aunts whispering over a family gathering. Suspicious that she had enjoyed the experience instead of suffering through it like a proper virgin.

"That was wrong, what happened with Reem," I said. "It shouldn't have happened that way!"

"It would not have happened if she had remembered her place like a proper Muslim girl," Abdullah said. "You're not a child anymore, Mishal. One day, it will be your turn to get married. I won't always be there to protect you."

If that's the case, you probably shouldn't *protect me,* I thought angrily. Unlike Reem or most of my other cousins, for me marriage had never been enticing. It was one of those "realities of life" I chose to ignore—mostly because I knew that my prospects were limited to creepy grooms nearly twice or thrice my age. Dark-skinned half-Saudi girls weren't prize commodities on the marriage market, Jawahir reminded me every time I saw her at a family gathering. "At least you still have your youth on your side," she always said. Even Mother seemed to agree, sometimes emerging from her little musical bubble to ask me if I had used the skin-whitening creams she'd ordered for me from India, creams that I'd dumped in the trash after they'd either made me break out or had no effect on my pigmentation.

"Why are you blaming me for this?" I asked Abdullah. "Isn't your friend—as a *boy*—responsible for lowering his gaze if he ever comes across a girl in an immodest state of dress? Have you both forgotten *that* part of the Qur'an?"

Abdullah's face turned pink, a sure sign he was losing his temper. "I don't have time for this nonsense," he said before leaving the room.

Though the black car continued appearing in our driveway now and then, its owner never ventured up to my room again. From time to time, I heard stories of it parked in other driveways, outside other apartment buildings, but mostly I saw it parked in the shade of the eucalyptus trees outside the Qala Academy's girls'-section compound.

I saw the boy who had spoken to me from behind my bedroom door—his navy-blue Academy blazer tossed over a shoulder, a hand tucked into the pocket of the jeans he would swap for the navy pants of the school uniform when classes began at the boys' section, miles away in the district of Sharafiyah.

There were moments when, on seeing the car, I would pull the top of my scarf forward so that nothing of my face showed when I passed it. But Farhan Rizvi never seemed to notice me. Often, he simply sat in his car, head leaned back, his shades reflecting the green of the leaves overhead, until a girl slyly detached herself from the crowds of *abaya*-clad girls pouring out of the school buses and, instead of following them into the gates, casually walked toward the eucalyptus trees, to the passenger seat of the black car.

After the incident at my house, I made it a point to keep track of the girls who went to sit in that car, though I did not always see them. My blog on Tumblr grew incredibly useful in this regard.

Created on a boring Friday afternoon after Jummah prayers, the blog was something I initially used as a space to anonymously rant about school stuff—mostly complaints about the Class IX finals at Qala Academy, which I likened to the head crushers used in the Spanish Inquisition, and passive-aggressive Internet memes complaining about English teachers who wanted to know the symbolism behind blue curtains in a book.

Later I began posting gossip as well. Not much. Just tidbits that I heard around school.

PRINCIPAL AND BIO TEACHER IN
CLINCH IN GIRLS' SECTION!

Okay. So maybe they were only hugging, but you know what hugging eventually leads to, right?

The reason behind the hug? The Bio teacher was crying because a few girls were making fun of her and Princi was being your typical knight in shining armor.

Note to teachers: Your students are not mean. Really we aren't. But if you try to walk like a runway model in a school corridor AND have a butt like a certain Kardashian, you are asking to be mocked.

POSTED 4 MINUTES AGO BY **BLUENIQAB**, 2 NOTES

#sorry not sorry #but shouldn't our teachers set better examples? #QA gossip

No one was more surprised than I was when my little blog began to get followers. My first inbox message had come from our very own head girl, Nadia Durrani, who demanded I delete the gossip I'd posted about her and some guy she'd hooked up with over the summer (the fourth one over the course of two months). She made a number of ridiculous and hilarious threats, claiming to have *wasta* with someone high up at the Ministry of Communications and Information Technology, who would, in her words: *Shut down ur stupid blog, track ur IP, and put u in jail.*

Why? I wrote back, making sure her question and my response were visible to every blog follower. *Did you hook up with him as well?*

I added a GIF file to the post—the image of a cartoon cat rolling on the floor laughing its furry behind off. Underneath I wrote: *I'm scared, Nadia. Really scared. Maybe you should tell your contact about that. Maybe he can do you a favor and ban Tumblr and every other blogging platform for you as well.*

The fight finally ended with Nadia deleting her Tumblr account and me gaining another fifty followers, many of whom wrote to congratulate me:

Way to go, blue! That's telling her!

rofl this made my day thanks

nadia is such a hypocrite. pretending to be a good and honorable head girl when she's screwed most of the senior boys in QA. good on you for calling her out, blueniqab.

And on and on.

It was easily the most fun I'd ever had online.

No one—not even Layla—knew who BlueNiqab was. Anonymity was key to running a blog that blabbed other people's secrets, and I trusted no one with mine. If a teacher found out I was behind the whole thing, I would be in big trouble.

I knew that things were going well for the blog when even the nerds of our class began talking about the gossip I'd posted there instead of the next Math test, and a steady stream of tips, asks, fan mail, and hate mail began trickling into my inbox.

By Class XI—the blog's third year running—most of the gossip usually came to me hours, sometimes even minutes, after the incident happened. Most of my tippers were girls, and it made sense that they would seek and disseminate information about boys like Farhan Rizvi.

Stories began circulating about girls going off with Rizvi to an abandoned warehouse near Madinah Road, stories that I often verified by snooping through the texts on my brother's cell phone.

On the rare occasion that my brother called his friends over to our house, I would sneak out of my room and hide behind the wall near the staircase to eavesdrop, often picking up things that most girls at school would, under normal circumstances, have learned about only weeks or months after the incident.

To my surprise, no one mentioned Zarin Wadia, who by then was acquiring quite a reputation. Insubordination in the classroom, smoking cigarettes, skipping classes for hours on end to see a boy, only to return in the afternoon in time to board the school bus back home. Our English teacher's little pet. A girl who seemed to have no concept of boundaries.

———————————

Which was why when in Class XI, instead of hearing more rumors about Rizvi as I expected, I was shocked to hear rumors about my brother.

Abdullah and Zarin. Zarin and Abdullah. Seen by Layla's brother at the Corniche in a maroon GMC two weeks ago, laughing and smoking.

"Hey, Mishal," Layla teased during break. "If you're not careful, you and Zarin may become relatives soon."

"Yeah." I slammed my lunch box on our shared desk. "Right."

"Whoa, relax." Layla raised her eyebrows. "You know I'm pulling your leg. In any case, I think they may have already broken up. She hasn't skipped a class since my brother last saw them."

"I . . ." I forced myself to lower my voice. "I can't *believe* Abdullah would go out with someone like that."

"I know, right?" Layla rolled her eyes. "But let's be reasonable. Abdullah doesn't go to school with her or know her as well as we do. Maybe he even *likes* her for some reason."

Of course he liked her. Zarin Wadia with her perfect body, with that fair skin prized by every matriarch I'd ever come across at Jawahir's parties. Though Abdullah hadn't told me that he was dating Zarin (he never told me anything about the girls he went out with), I had seen him smiling to himself when he thought no one was looking, the way his face lit up each time the phone rang on a Wednesday night, how it fell when he found out it wasn't her, but one of his friends.

"You didn't tell anyone else about this, did you?" I asked her sharply. Layla may have been my best friend, but she had the tendency to blab.

"Of course I didn't!" She sounded irritated, which was a good sign. An offended Layla was an honest Layla. If she was lying she would have tried soothing me with gentleness and clever words. "Do you think I'm going to send something like this to bloody BlueNiqab?"

I forced myself to remain impassive.

"He's your brother, Mishal," Layla told me. "You need to cut him some slack. Even good guys like Abdullah can make mistakes."

I let out a bitter laugh. "Yeah, like he would cut *me* slack if I went out with some guy and then said it was a mistake."

Layla's eyes widened. She turned around to make sure the other girls were still busy talking or eating their lunches.

"What are you talking about?" she whispered. "Do you want to go out with a guy?"

"Of course not," I said impatiently, "but—"

"Seriously, Mishal." Layla frowned. "I don't know why you're talking like this. You know—we both know—that these rules for segregation have been made to protect us."

"But don't the rules apply to boys as well?"

"Of course they do."

"Then why always blame the girl if things go wrong?" I demanded. "Why aren't boys held responsible?"

Layla sighed. "Mishal, you've seen my brother. You know how shy he is around girls. Neither he nor his friends date. My parents have always treated both of us equally in that way. But let's be realistic. This world does not always operate on theory. I mean, would you go out alone at night in a deserted area, anywhere?"

"No," I said reluctantly.

"Exactly! Why go looking for trouble where you know it exists? Especially when you're a girl?"

"But—"

"Girls like Zarin are different," Layla interrupted. "They don't care about the rules or the future. See how dangerous that is? First she tempted Abdullah with her wanton ways, and now she's confusing you with her deviance."

Images clashed in my head: Abdullah swinging me in the

garden next to our house as a child; the naked blondes in his magazine; my brother violently pinning me to the wall; boys hammering on my door, laughing; my brother shouting, driving them away.

I held my head between my hands. "I don't know, Layla."

"Please." Layla placed a gentle hand on my shoulder. "Don't let her turn you against your own brother."

That evening, I switched on my cell and dialed Zarin's number several times, my first three calls unsuccessful—hanging up on Zarin's aunt twice and her uncle once. Then, on the fourth try, Zarin herself picked up the phone.

The sharp "Hello" startled me and almost made me hang up. "Who is this?"

I said nothing and fell once more into the routine of being silent, letting my breaths pass through the phone to let her know there was someone at the other end.

After a moment of silence, she spoke again, her voice softer, more encouraging, almost as if she was expecting me to be a boy who had called, a boy far too nervous to speak. "Hello?" A hesitation. "Abdullah, is this you?"

Witch, I wanted to say. *Slut.* But my voice choked in my throat. I disconnected the line. In the days that followed, I kept a close eye on her. The times she went out during break, the times she skipped school. The times she talked to my brother over the landline—though those conversations were short and to the point. "Same time, same place," Abdullah would say. "Bring cigarettes," she would reply.

"What are you doing?" Layla whispered one day. "Always watching her like some obsessed boy. Are you trying to catch her smoking red-handed this time?"

I shook my head. I did not know what I was looking for, but I knew it would not be to report her for smoking again. I'd overheard enough conversations between Abdullah and his friends now to know that he and Zarin were still dating. "Hot *and* not a hypocrite," he'd described her over the phone. "She never freaks out if we joke about sex the way some other girls would."

Googling Zarin Wadia didn't bring up much information— at least not on the Zarin Wadia I wanted. She wasn't on Twitter or Tumblr or Snapchat or Instagram. Her Facebook was barely used. It made sense somehow that she wouldn't use social media. Like me, Zarin had her own need for secrecy.

I felt my nails dig into the soft flesh of my palm. "I want to know everything about her," I told Layla.

Farhan

AGE 12

They were going at it like dogs, Abba and the maid. My father, who my mother said I would look like when I got older—tall, dark, and handsome—banging the maid so hard that he banged the headboard against the wall and left a mark in the paint.

It was one of those evenings when neither Ammi nor my sister, Asma, were home. Asma had gone over to a friend's place. Ammi was at the beauty parlor—"Gone to shave the beard off her chin," Abba said contemptuously. Abba, who came home early that evening, then shut himself up in his room.

It could've almost been scripted. The noises in my parents' bedroom. Me, crawling off the sofa, where I'd been dozing in front of the TV, padding quiet and barefoot across the carpet, noiselessly opening the bedroom door. Abba, heavy and hairy, his body heaving up and down; the maid, small and smooth, her eyes closed and mouth open, scoring his back with her nails. I watched until they switched positions, putting her on top and my dad on the bottom. His eyes opened and then locked with mine.

I fled.

Ten minutes later, the maid went into the kitchen, fully dressed, to cook dinner before my mother and sister came home.

Abba emerged, wearing a pair of striped pajamas and a dark blue robe. "Farhan."

I looked up from the television, stood reluctantly, and walked over to where he was standing. Standing and swallowing, as if the words in his mouth were all wrong.

He smiled at me and put a hand on my shoulder. "There's no need to be afraid."

He took my limp hand in his and pressed a note into my palm. Fifty riyals. New and crisp like the press on his shirt. Fifty falafel sandwiches from the school canteen. Half a Nintendo Game Boy. A twelve-year-old's temporary silence.

"It will be our little secret," he said. I looked up and saw something different in his eyes—fear, where there previously had been none. I put the note in my pocket, feeling strange about this sudden shift in the tectonic plates, the sickness in my belly mingling with a sense of power.

"Yes, Abba."

AGE 15
DATE #9

"*This* is the special place you were talking about?" Nadia glared at the warehouse's faded, hand-painted sign (*Al Hanood* it read now, the *y* long gone), the rusty gates, the cigarette butts littering the unpaved lot. "Why couldn't we have parked at the Corniche?"

Ants were crawling up the broken wall, up my pants it felt like, when a red T-shirt flashed behind one of the concrete holes, lookout points for Abdullah and Bilal the Charsi, who I had told it would be done by today—scoring a home run with head girl Nadia Durrani, also called Double Dome Durrani because of her fantastic breasts.

"Yeah," Abdullah had said when I told him about my plan. "Right."

He'd given me the same reaction at the beginning of the year, when I'd scored Date #1 with Nadia, and then asked if

I was on drugs. Bilal, who had once been Nadia's neighbor and spent most of his free time stalking her when he wasn't selling cigarettes and twenty-riyal weed joints behind the municipal garbage bin outside the academy's boys' section, didn't believe me either.

"She likes Arabs, mostly. Syrians. Falasteenis. Black guys. White guys," Bilal said with a shrug. "Most of them end up at the parking lot of the old Hanoody warehouse on Madinah Road. No offense, Farhan, my man—you may be one of my best customers, but I've never seen Nadia go for an Indian or Pakistani yet. And especially not a horny fifteen-year-old schoolboy."

But not all horny fifteen-year-old Indians or Pakistanis had access to their father's black Beamer whenever they liked, and that's what Abdullah and Bilal had been pissed off by, even though they didn't admit it.

Nadia had liked the look of my car, especially the black tint on its windows. "This is nice." She had skimmed a finger lightly over the glass. "But are you even old enough to drive?"

"Officially, no. Unofficially, yes," I had replied, forcing a bravado I did not feel. "Dad works for the Interior Ministry. He's almost always traveling outside Jeddah on business. I've been chauffeuring my mom and sis around for about six months now."

Nadia had scanned me from head to toe, her gaze lingering

briefly on the bulge between the front pockets of my jeans. I felt myself go red and cursed myself for not keeping it under control. But, somehow, it worked.

"Okay," she'd said with a slight smile. "I'll see you this Wednesday, after school."

It had taken nine more Wednesdays over the course of five months to get to the warehouse stage. Five months of e-mails and secret telephone calls. Two hundred and fifty-four riyals and seventy-five halalas' worth of CDs and coffees at private five-star restaurants where we would not be seen by anyone from home or school, or by a *muttawa*. These dates usually ended at a deserted part of the Jeddah Corniche with a hurried lip-lock that Nadia refused to take further. "No, no, it's too risky," she would say, or "I see someone coming," or "What's the rush, big boy? We have plenty of time."

"She's sucking you dry," Bilal had told me. "And not in the way she should."

"You gotta take initiative, man," Abdullah had said. "From the looks of it, Nadia needs a guy with a bit of aggression."

My heartbeat accelerated now as Nadia's head turned toward the warehouse wall.

"I know this place is gross," I said quickly. "But this is way better than having that waiter at the Sofitel police our every move, isn't it?"

"Whatever." Nadia grimaced. She turned away from the

wall. "It's too late to go anywhere else now with your car nearly on empty."

I switched off the AC, rolled down the window, and lit up. The red T-shirt had disappeared from sight. So far, so good.

"This week sucked!" Nadia grumbled. "First we got hammered at school over the Class XII boards like they're a matter of life and death. And then yesterday my bratty sister stirred—yes, *stirred*—the wand of my eighty-riyal mascara in a pot of talcum powder. Like it was a prop she'd use playing house! When I told her off, she went crying to Mom, who acted like *I* was at fault for screaming at her seven-year-old angel. And on top of that, there's that English exam next week. God, I'm so gonna fail that . . ."

Sweat beaded the back of my neck. Twenty minutes left before she had to get back home. Enough time, in Bilal's opinion, to hit three bases, maybe even score a home run. "The hotter the girl, the fatter her attitude," Bilal had said. "Don't let her sit on your head and dictate terms. Be a man. Under no circumstance must you let on that you're dying for her."

I blew smoke out of the window. "You're head girl," I told Nadia. "You won't fail a test." Which was a lie. She'd failed the last one, I knew, and the one before.

"But I haven't been studying for ages!"

I smashed the butt into the car ashtray. "Fine, then. I'll take you home."

The edge in my voice made her jump. "So soon?"

"It's getting late." I turned the key in the ignition, hoping she wouldn't take the bait. "I don't want to waste any more of your *study* time."

"Farhan, wait." She put a hand on my knee.

Blood rushed to my face. I released the steering wheel and turned to face her. "Not good enough, Nadia."

The engine hummed in the silence. Nadia bit her plump lower lip. Cherry red stained the edges of her front teeth. Then, after one long minute, she leaned forward and put her hands on my shoulders. Slid them around my neck. Opened her mouth, maybe to say something.

I didn't wait to hear it. I stuck in my tongue and simultaneously pushed aside the *abaya* and *dupatta* covering her chest.

She stiffened. A sound emerged from her throat—yes? no? my name?

Who cared as long as her hands remained where they were?

Cotton bra. Lace trim. There didn't appear to be any padding, but I squeezed several times to make sure. I traced the lace with my thumbs and followed it to the back, where the hooks were located. She squeaked when I withdrew my tongue from her mouth and pushed down the bra. The fine hair on her skin gave it a velvety, apricot-like texture. She smelled like expensive perfume. Moments later, a siren sounded in the distance, followed by the honk of car horns.

"Get down," I snapped. Blood rushed to my face.

"W-wha—?" Her scarf had somehow remarkably stayed in place, covering her hair completely, even though the rest of her clothing was in disarray.

I put a hand on her head and shoved it—as gently as I could—down toward her knees.

Red and blue lights flashed in the rearview mirror. Two police cars shot past the Hanoody warehouse—chasing some dude for speeding in a residential area, I guessed. To be safe, I waited five more minutes, my hand still holding Nadia's head in place.

"You can sit again," I said finally, releasing my grip. "They're gone."

She slid down to the edge of the seat. There, she fumbled with the rest of her clothes till she managed to put them back in place. Her bra, which she hadn't managed to clasp properly, wrinkled at the peaks. Black mascara circled the skin around her watery eyes.

"Sorry," I said.

She smacked my mouth with the palm of her hand. "You maniac! I don't want to see you again. Ever."

"What are you talking about?" My lips were stinging. "I saved you from being lashed by the police!"

"Oh thank God, thank *God* for the police!" She shuddered and wrapped her arms around herself. "I thought a few kisses would appease you, but . . . God, if not for them, you'd have probably raped me!"

The words did not sink in at first.

"What do you mean?"

"Don't you understand English?" Nadia's lower lip curled. "In any case, I've made this disgusting date well worth your gasoline money."

A muffled laugh floated to my ears from behind the broken wall. "Y-you're kidding, r-right?" My face burned. "You were s-so . . . You *wanted* it, Nadia. You asked f-for—"

"Take me home." She ripped a few tissues from the box in the glove compartment and wiped her mouth with slow, measured strokes. "Now."

Abdullah had told me about such girls. NATO, he called them. No action, talk only. The ones who kissed like whores and then cried like virgins.

"I would have told her to get out of the car and driven off," he said later. "Let her walk home by herself. But seriously, Farhan, to say 'Y-yes, N-n-n-nadia,' and drive her back home like she asked you to? Were you wearing bangles?"

Bilal laughed. "You looked like you'd just crapped your pants."

Then, a month later, Abdullah forwarded me a text and a video clip on my phone.

In the text, cricket captain Ashraf Haque claimed to have

set the record as the first Qala Academy boy to hit a home run with the head girl at the Hanoody warehouse a week after their very first coffee-shop date, in his secondhand Honda Civic.

No one seemed to care that the video was of poor quality or that the girl's face was only partially visible or that her breasts weren't as full and firm as the ones I remembered seeing on Nadia. Within a day of the clip being sent out, Haque's reputation changed from being another perverted toilet stall masturbator to the luckiest guy in school.

It was only after Nadia left for India for further studies—still staunchly denying any involvement with "that jerk"—that Bilal revealed the secret to Haque's success. "A single cup of coffee, my man," he told me. "A single freaking cup. You can bet every guy she went out with wished *he'd* thought of the idea first."

"He drugged her?" Abdullah looked, for the first time, disgusted and self-righteous. "That's messed up."

"Who cares?" My mouth still stung from the memory of Nadia's slap. "Everyone knows what a slut Durrani is."

"Yeah, maybe. But I draw the line at drugging a girl. It's a whole other level of creepy."

I paid no attention to Abdullah, who pretended to be religious and God-fearing in front of the adults, and then went on to blow hundreds of riyals on cigarettes and porn videos he bought online from one of those "secure sites" that even the Saudi censors could not censor.

Bilal's words stuck in my head. Some nights, before I fell asleep, I pictured Nadia the way she had been that afternoon. Before the police had interrupted. Before she had intimidated and emasculated me with her violated-virgin act.

AGE 17

The first girl I used the drug on, Aliya Chowdhury, probably did not even need it. She was in love with me and would have done it anyway. But the drug calmed her down. She even cried in the car when I broke up with her a week later outside the warehouse.

"You're such a jerk," Abdullah told me when I called him the evening of our breakup. No hi or hello. Just that. "That girl was only fourteen."

He'd probably heard the news from Bilal. Or they'd probably decided to spy on me again—this time without my permission—and seen everything.

"Hello to you too." I laughed. "What's wrong, Abdullah? Are you so whipped by the girl you're going out with that you've forgotten to have fun? What's her name again? Zarin? Shirin?"

"This has nothing to do with her." Abdullah sounded angry now, almost as angry as he had when I'd gone up to his sister's room two years ago. "You'll be in big trouble someday, you know."

I laughed again, mostly to mask my anger at his words and, under that, a fear I did not want to acknowledge. I thought of Nadia again and then of the Chowdhury girl, the glassy look in her eyes, the relaxed smile on her face.

I thought of Abba, compared my tableau to his.

"Don't worry, *ya* Aboody." I crumpled the paper with the girl's number and e-mail into a ball and tossed it into the basket next to my bed. "I'm not like Haque. I don't need to masturbate to videos of myself having sex with girls."

REENCOUNTER

Zarin

ACCORDING TO THE DOG LADY, IF YOU ever wanted to know what a person was like, all you had to do was peek into their living room through a window or an open door. "A person's home tells you a lot about who they are," I'd overheard her telling Masi once. "Even if you can't see their faces."

In Mumbai, especially in Cama colony, where people often left doors open during the daytime, this was easy enough to do. If you peeped into the Dog Lady's one-room flat, for instance, you'd see *Fussy Old Parsi Widow* written all over it—a large garlanded photo of her husband hanging on a blue wall, a Godrej fridge draped with a pink plastic cover, and flowered white curtains hanging over the windows. In a corner, right next to the kitchen, lay an iron cot with a hard mattress for the Dog

Lady's bad back, and a pair of aluminum bowls, one filled with water and one empty until she filled it with food for her rabid little Pomeranian, Jimmy.

In Jeddah, this sort of scrutiny was nearly impossible. Here, windows were translucent, barred with grilles and draped with curtains or, as with some of the buildings in the old city, with latticed wooden *mashrabiya* screens, shielding a home's privacy from prying eyes. After the morning rush of school buses and vehicles pouring out onto the main roads, the city's inner streets turned quiet. Mothers slipped back into their homes after waving good-bye to their children. Forbidden from driving, the women skulked inside their air-conditioned villas or apartments, waiting until a private car or taxi arrived to pick them up. Heat rose, thickened like soup. Even the shopkeepers didn't move unless it was to shoo stray cats out of their shops. There were days when the silence could be as suffocating as the heat itself.

And it drove Masi mad.

In our first years here, she would sniff at doors and peer at windows, as if hoping to ascertain the kind of person who lived there by the scent of their food or the shadows that hovered behind windowpanes.

"What kind of neighbors are these, Rusi?" I often heard her complain to Masa. "No hi, no hello. Forget about a polite smile; they don't even look at you over here!"

Yet, as the years went on, and we slowly turned from Mumbaikars to Non-Resident Indians who no longer fit in the city, Masi began changing her tune. "People in Mumbai have no sense of privacy! Our Jeddah is our Jeddah. At least over there no one keeps asking me every little detail about myself!"

And she grew quieter and more suspicious around anyone who did. It was a dangerous, simmering sort of quiet that had me tiptoeing around her the way I was now creeping toward our apartment door.

In Jeddah, locked doors and closed windows were the norm. Anything different could mean one of two things:

(a) Your house had been burglarized, or
(b) Your house was in the process of being burglarized.

Which was why, when I found the door to our apartment open a crack one afternoon after coming home from school, I hovered outside the door for a few moments, debating between entering the house and knocking on the door of our nosy neighbor, Halima.

I chose the safe route at first and rapped several times on Halima's door. But no one appeared to be home. I pulled out my cell phone, an old flip Nokia that wasn't supposed to be used for anything except emergencies, and held a finger over the number nine. I could hear Abdullah mocking me in my head. *What?* I imagined him saying. *You think the Saudi policemen are like the American ones? That they'll come running for you the minute you dial 999?*

Calling Abdullah didn't seem like the smart thing to do either. For one, Masi would kill me if she knew I was seeing a boy. And, more important, I was pretty sure that Abdullah wouldn't come running for me if I was in trouble. Swapping spit and the occasional cigarette with a girl for a month and a half did not make her the love of your life.

I did what I could under the circumstances: heart in throat, in silence, eased open the wooden door made heavy by the extra locks and latches Masi had installed the year before after someone broke into an apartment in the building next to ours. A small foyer led right into the living room, which consisted of a navy-blue sofa laminated with plastic (Masi was nearly as phobic of germs as she was of me marrying a gangster like my father), a bamboo armchair pushed up against the wall, a walnut coffee table, a glass showcase with a crystal bust of the prophet Zoroaster, and a nineteen-inch flat-screen TV that Masa had won in a lucky draw at the academy fair a couple of years before.

In the space between the TV and the showcase lay Masi, her arms and legs sprawled over the carpet, breathing hard, her nightgown stuck to her chest. Halima was crouched beside her, sprinkling water over her face from a glass. "It's okay, Khorshed. It's okay. Halima's here now."

My mind registered the absence of danger before my body did, taking in the scene before me. My hand slowly fell back to its side.

What you'd find if you ever peeked into Rustom and Khorshed Wadia's living room: a complete mess.

Which wasn't really as surprising as the embarrassment that unfurled in my belly and flooded my face when Halima finally registered my presence and turned around to greet me, her chubby cheeks sleek with perspiration, her smile strained and extra wide.

Halima was one of the newer tenants of our building, having moved in next door a couple of years ago. From the very beginning, she'd tried to ingratiate herself with Masi, bringing a CorningWare bowl of fava bean stew and fresh lemons one Friday after moving in. She'd stood at our threshold, holding out the bowl wrapped with aluminum foil, and grinned at Masi. "I'm Halima. Your new neighbor."

Then she shoved her way into the apartment, past my speechless aunt, and made herself comfortable on the living room sofa, making stilted conversation with Masi for about fifteen minutes: "What's your name?" "Do you work?" "Your daughter is pretty, *Masha'Allah*." "Oh, she's not your daughter? Then, what a pretty niece." "Where does your husband work?" "How much does he make?"

The final question, which took even me by surprise, had

Masi immediately making an excuse about "guests coming over" and unceremoniously escorting Halima to the door. Not that this seemed to bother our new neighbor.

"I'll be back," Halima had promised. And she was. Time and time again.

Before long, Masi began finding ways and means to avoid Halima, pretending to be sleeping or showering whenever the other woman came knocking at her door.

I wasn't sure if this was the universe's way of giving Masi exactly what she'd asked for a few years before in the way of friendly neighbors. Unlike the other Arab tenants in our building, Halima spoke perfect English and was twice as nosy as Masi herself. I could never look at Halima with a straight face after our first interaction, my lips automatically curving up into a grin when I saw her. Halima seemed oblivious to the mocking nature of my smile, greeting me each time with a smile and a "Hello, little Zarin."

"*As'salamu alaykum*, Halima," I would say in response. The greeting always seemed to make her happy. After the first few times, I even managed to keep the sarcasm out of my voice.

I never knew what Halima saw in Masi or why she always went out of her way to be friendly in spite of my aunt's coldness. But that afternoon I was grateful that it was Halima who was inside our house and not a burglar wielding a crowbar.

"What happened?" I allowed my bag to slide to the floor and closed the door with a click.

"I heard Khorshed screaming. I didn't know if she was in trouble. The door wasn't locked, so I came here with that." Halima pointed at a rolling pin lying on the sofa.

I stared at my aunt's pallid face, which was slowly filling with color, and wondered if she'd forgotten to take her pills again. Our family physician continued to prescribe them at my uncle's insistence, even though they seemed to make little difference in Masi's temperament or mood, only knocking her out cold for a few hours when she took them.

"There is nothing wrong with Khorshed," Masa told Dr. Rensil Thomas when he suggested psychiatric referral. "She's okay when she has enough sleep."

But I knew that what Masa was really afraid of was having people treat Masi the way they treated old Freny Bharucha in Cama colony. Cracked Freny, they used to call her in the years before she was finally diagnosed with Alzheimer's, laughing at how she forgot the simplest of things or lost her way within the compound where she lived. So, to a degree, I saw Masa's point. People in Mumbai—and especially at the colony—weren't exactly sensitive when it came to mental health issues. Masa's colleagues in Jeddah weren't any better. Just a year earlier, I'd heard one of them casually disparage a common friend whose wife had depression, and seen the way Masa's smile had frozen on his face.

Halima pointed at me and then at the phone. "Should I tell your uncle? Call him home?"

I shook my head. Calling Masa would infuriate my aunt, if she wasn't already angry over Halima finding her like this. Masi never liked appearing out of control to anyone. Masa once told me it was because of the life she'd led in Mumbai before I was born, a life that I'd heard her blame my mother for, many times.

"Thank you, Halima," I said. "I'll take care of things from here."

"You sure, little Zarin?" She hesitated, watching Masi, who had not moved from the floor, her eyes still closed.

"Yes. I'm sure."

After checking that the door was locked this time around, I tiptoed back to the living room and stood next to my aunt, watching the rise and fall of her chest, listening to her raspy, shallow breaths.

She whispered something—a name I couldn't quite catch—and then gnashed her teeth.

"Masi?" I called out hesitantly. "Masi?"

"My sister," she muttered in Gujarati. "Get away from my sister."

Always her sister—my mother—haunting a part of her mind I couldn't see. Whenever Masi forgot (or more likely spat out) her meds, my mother always paid her a visit in her head.

Another time, she told me that she'd considered suffocating

me the day I was born. "It was the monsoons. The streets were flooded. The doctor was late and your mother had fallen asleep after the labor. It would have been easy," she had told me. "So easy to get rid of you and, through you, him."

Him meaning my father, of course, the other part of the equation that almost always resulted in a Masi episode.

"She didn't mean it, Zarin," Masa had told me repeatedly when I was ten, in the days after my kitten, Fali, died. "She didn't know Fali would get into trouble if she put it outside. Can't you simply accept that? It was a cat, not a human being!"

It. Like Fali was a thing and not a living creature.

I picked up the glass of water Halima had left on the coffee table and sipped, watching Masi twitch on the floor for a few more moments. Then, slowly and carefully, I poured the rest of it over her face, watching her sputter back to consciousness before taking the glass to the kitchen and placing it in the sink.

In the weeks following Fali's death, I had started slowly. Small pranks like stealing a toothbrush. Muddying the corridor carpet with shoe prints. Dropping a face towel on the wet bathroom floor. Sneaking into the bathroom after Masa went to bed and putting the toilet seat back up, so I could hear them argue about it in the morning.

The small pranks eventually became bigger ones. A newly lit oil lamp blown out the moment Masi left the kitchen after a prayer. Crows flocking to the ledge of the kitchen window, pecking at scattered lumps of golden-brown semolina and whole wheat pudding—the special *malido* Masi had made the night before for my mother's and great-grandfather's annual death-day prayers, littering the orange kitchen tiles with black and gray feathers.

"What did you do?" The long vein at the side of Masi's neck stood out in sharp green relief under her pale skin. The hands at her sides shook. "No beating," I heard her mutter under her breath. *No beating, no beating, no beating*—a mantra she managed to abide by until I started laughing at her and stuck out my tongue.

To my surprise, Masa defended me for once that day, yelling at Masi when he saw the bruise on my cheek. "Why would you do that?" he demanded. "Don't you see how hard she's becoming? How she will become if this continues?"

"So what do you expect me to do, Rusi? Do you want me to beg her to behave? Should I sit around doing nothing—saying 'Please, *dikra*, don't do this!'—while she continues to taunt and disrespect me?"

"She's going through a phase. She will grow out of it. She will find other things to do."

And I did.

Boys entered the picture shortly after I began pranking Masi, the first showing up when I was eleven years old, at the DVD store next to our apartment building in Aziziyah, between the racks of pirated discs, their cases shaded black with Magic Marker, covering every bit of the actresses' exposed skin, and in some instances even their faces.

The boy was around fourteen or fifteen years old, with fair skin and a skullcap over his golden-brown curls. His gaze met mine nearly the instant he entered the store. It wasn't a real surprise. Ever since I'd hit puberty, a lot more boys had begun noticing me. It was in the boobs, I wanted to tell them mockingly. Two fleshy bumps that had sprouted on my chest seemingly overnight, and declared that I was no longer a girl who looked like a boy.

Had this particular fact not annoyed Masi so much, I might have been embarrassed, even made uncomfortable by the attention I was getting. But I had to admit that I was also curious back then about what made her so annoyed. What, I wondered, could happen between a boy and a girl who had hit puberty that could make an already angry aunt angrier?

As if sensing my curiosity, the boy picked up one of the DVDs from the back—an older one released a few years before. A man and woman flanked the sides of the cover, the woman wearing a black dress split up to the thigh, a gun tucked into her garter belt. Someone, probably the DVD store guy, had colored in her legs and arms with green magic marker, giving the effect of an oddly designed *salwar-kameez*.

The boy placed his index finger in his mouth and then, with a glistening tip, traced the arch of the woman's heel, her ankle, her calf, her thigh. The marker probably wasn't permanent because his finger came up green, revealing the bare skin underneath. He curled the finger inward and gestured that I approach. His dark eyes were fixed on my face.

Curious and a little disgusted, I stepped forward. Once, twice. Again. A voice roared in my ears, "ZARIN!" and my feet halted in their tracks.

The DVD slipped from the boy's smudged fingers and clattered onto the floor.

I felt Masa's fingers grip my arm. "Come! We're leaving."

As we were leaving the store, however, I turned around once and caught the boy's eye. He gave me a slight, wobbly smile. It was strange how quickly I went from being disgusted to feeling sorry for him. I smiled back, the barest upward flick of the mouth, a quick nod.

Days later, I saw the boy again outside our apartment building, tossing pebbles at my bedroom window. It was probably the worst thing he could have done because Masi was in my room at the time, placing a load of newly folded laundry on my bed.

A moment later, Masa and I watched, a little shell-shocked, as Masi marched out of the building, her long nightgown whipping outward from her bone-thin body, her hair still covered with the white cotton scarf she wore for prayers, and threw a slipper at the boy, hitting him right in the back as he ran.

When she returned, Masi gripped me by the shoulders and shook me hard, her words buzzing in my ears like bees: "Who was that boy? What was he doing throwing stones at your window? Did you know him? Did you call him here?"

"Stop it!" Masa pulled her off me. "Khorshed, stop! Of course she doesn't know him. He was that boy from the DVD store last week."

"What boy? You didn't tell me anything about a boy!"

"He was . . ." The flush on Masa's face nearly reached the top of his bald head. "He was watching her. I didn't think much of it. Boys and girls at this age. You know what it's like, Khorshed."

"How could you be so foolish?" Masi's head swiveled from window to window, a manic bobble-head doll. "I know you're a man, but don't you even think?"

"I'm sorry! But how could I have known he would follow us?" Masa turned to face me. "Zarin, did you tell him we lived here? Did you ask him to come? You know how wrong that is, don't you?"

"I never even talked to him," I said. "He was the one who was watching me. *He* followed us. I didn't do anything wrong!"

I gritted my teeth. Sure, I wasn't exactly innocent here.

I *had* smiled at the boy at the end. But how could Masa assume I would give our address to anyone anywhere?

"You didn't, did you?" Masi's lips were turning white. "Oh no, you knew nothing!"

"Khorshed, please, it was most likely a mistake." Masa's voice, so sharp and accusing when he'd talked to me, softened, sweetened. "She's only eleven . . . she was probably curious."

———————

It took a few more years for my curiosity to be satisfied. And I had to admit that Abdullah, who started calling me his girlfriend at the end of our third date, did it quite well with his kisses.

In stores, I continued to aggravate Masi, looking boys and men in the eye, forcing them to take second looks with a twist of my hips, a slightly swaying walk.

By the time I was sixteen, I considered myself an expert on boys and the sorts of looks they gave me. It was also during this time that I began questioning my expertise when I discovered another kind of boy, another kind of stare.

———————

A few blocks from our apartment building in Aziziyah stood a Lahm b'Ajin deli shop, one of many meat and cheese franchises owned by the Lahm b'Ajin group of companies headquartered in the capital city of Riyadh. The words *lahm b'ajin* referred to the minced-meat pizzas they initially sold out of a small shop in Riyadh many years before. These days, the same pizzas were sold in the cooked-goods section at each of their deli shops and as frozen goods in big supermarkets like Tamimi and Danube.

Masa worked as plant manager at Lahm b'Ajin's meatpacking factory in Jeddah's fourth industrial city. From what he told us at dinnertime and from the various newspaper articles he pointed out, I understood that the company was expanding rapidly across the Kingdom and the UAE, opening new branches and shutting down old, unprofitable ones.

The deli we visited was one of the few older shops that still turned a profit. Run ever since we came to Jeddah by an old Palestinian named Hamza, it was as familiar to me as the back of my hand, with its gleaming white walls and speckled tiles. Meat hung from hooks at the far end of the store, where the butchery was set up—skinned goat and lamb parts, whole goats in the days leading up to Eid al-Adha. The deli section, at the center, nearly always ran out of the peppercorn-beef salami, but there was usually plenty of smoked turkey on hand. The cases displaying the cheeses at the other end of the butchery always had red plastic roses in them. Masa and Masi knew every man who worked at the deli counter by name, some of whom still called me "Baby," which, though embarrassing, was something I tolerated.

Being treated like I was still seven years old was a small price to pay for a few minutes, sometimes even half an hour, of real freedom if the line at the counter was long—the kind of freedom that Masi had sanctioned, the kind I didn't have to steal. The deli shop was one of the few places Masi sometimes sent me to alone, on errands to pick up a tray of smoked turkey. This had begun happening more and more often over the previous year or so, after Masa got promoted to senior plant manager and began working longer hours and Masi grew more sluggish—probably because of the medication she was taking then.

"Make yourself of use for once," Masi had said one afternoon after I came back from school, and handed me a fifty-riyal note. "And bring back the change."

And so it began. Each time she sent me off, I kept my face neutral, biting the inside of my cheek so I didn't reveal my excitement. I wasn't foolish enough to think Masi would send me on these errands if she ever thought they made me happy.

Seven weeks into dating Abdullah, Masi sent me on another one of these errands. I was in line at the deli counter, which was even slower than usual, and contemplated texting him from my cell phone. It was a risk—my phone was pay-as-you-go and Masa had the habit of going over the bills at the apartment and shouting out discrepancies so that Masi could hear about them: "Zarin, *dikra*, whose number is this?" or "Zarin, *dikra*, are you still getting those spam texts?"

Had I been any other girl, I would have resented this intrusion into my privacy. I had classmates who threw fits if their phones didn't load their texts on time, who smacked their mothers during parent-teacher conferences. I, on the other hand, barely used the Internet except for research—*Yes, even my computer time is monitored*, I wanted to tell those spoiled girls—and knew better than to question the scraps of privilege my guardians threw my way.

A draft of air from the central AC cooled my hot skin. I slipped the phone back into the pocket of my *kameez*. No boy was worth this freedom, I decided. Not even Abdullah.

It was then that I sensed someone watching me, the fine hairs at the back of my neck rising. When I turned around, I wasn't entirely surprised to see that it was a boy standing a few feet away—tall, broad-shouldered, with features that struck me as Persian or, even more specifically, as Parsi, from India: dark, deep-set brown eyes, thick black eyebrows, and a hooked nose.

A new worker, by the looks of his pristine white uniform and cap and unstained Lahm b'Ajin deli apron, a cardboard box of assorted cheeses held closely to his chest. His sturdy hands had multiple cuts on them, probably occupational injuries. But it was the expression on his face that struck me the most.

One of recognition, not lust.

A slight smile hovered over his lips. He stepped forward, opening his mouth to speak.

I never found out what he intended to say to me then because he slipped on a patch of tile, knocking over the yellow wet-floor sign, and fell to the floor with a painful grunt.

Though a part of me wanted to laugh, another part felt a little bad for the boy. I was inching forward to make sure that he was okay when a voice shouted in the background: "Porus! What happened to you, boy?"

Porus.

In India, this wasn't an uncommon name. In India, I wouldn't have thought twice about it. Even here, I might have managed to push it aside had the boy not smiled at the other man: the slight gap between his front teeth sent me reeling back into a past of colony cricket matches and tentative waves.

"S-sorry, sir." His voice had deepened over the years, but he still spoke with the same lilt to his voice, with the same soft Gujarati accent. "I . . . fell down."

I don't know why instead of saying hello, I turned around and fled, ignoring the man at the counter who called for me— "Hey, miss! Don't you want your turkey anymore?"

I barely even registered Masi's reprimand when I reached home—"Why did you stay so long if there was such a long line?"

In my room that night I was the one doing the scolding. Zarin Wadia did not run away from boys, I reminded myself. Zarin Wadia didn't act like a silly, lovestruck Bollywood damsel, hearing cheesy love songs playing in the background when she saw a boy staring at her.

I snorted. Okay, the last bit *definitely* hadn't happened. As for running away—that was silly in itself, but maybe it was from the shock of seeing Porus Dumasia again after so long, I reasoned. The Dumasias had changed residences shortly after we left Mumbai for Jeddah, after Porus's father got a better-paying job. I remembered feeling terribly disappointed upon hearing the news. I had been having a hard time at my new school in Jeddah and was hoping to see a friendly face when I visited Mumbai again, even if I didn't really intend to speak to Porus.

It had been an effective lesson in the ways of the world. People came into our lives, people left. Sometimes for good, like my mother and father. Sometimes they returned, like Masa's old school friend who showed up one night for dinner in Jeddah after nearly fifteen years of no contact, and then was never seen again.

There was no reason to give special meaning to a reencounter, I told myself. Even if it *was* after ten years, and the first boy who had ever called me pretty. I had yet to meet a boy who could flip my world entirely on its head and turn every answer I knew into a question.

Porus

STORIES, MY FATHER USED TO SAY, WOULD always change the course of our lives, the greatest ones being retold over and over again not to simply convey morals or life lessons, but to bring people together. "That is the reason a storyteller tells stories," he declared even during his last days, while lying in the hospital bed. "So he can connect to another human being!"

Pappa was smart in that way even though he didn't go to school for long. He was one of the top salesmen in the life insurance department at the New India Assurance Company until the leukemia began eating away at him, forcing him to quit his job twenty years before retirement, and forcing us to cash in on his own policy the year I turned seventeen.

When it came to storytelling, my mother said that I had Pappa's skills, the same capacity to fabricate truths for survival when needed.

It wasn't a compliment, but it was how I managed to bring her to Jeddah a year after Pappa died. ("Yes, sir. Labor visa, sir. Arabic? Of course I know Arabic. Bad accent? Sorry, sir. What to do? I'm Indian, no? But don't worry, I will learn fast-fast.") It was also how I later got a job at the Lahm b'Ajin deli and cheese shop in Aziziyah. ("Of course I've seen that machine before! And I'm a quick learner.")

It wasn't difficult lying about my age. Twenty-one, I told the labor agents, even though I was eighteen. I was taller than most boys my age, and big-boned like my father. After scraping a thousand rupees together, I managed to get a new birth certificate from the *chawl* near our old Mumbai apartment building where, for the right price, you could buy everything from fake report cards to real Beretta handguns.

Porus Dumasia. S/o Neville and Arnavaz Dumasia. Born June 21, 1993, at the Parsi General Hospital. June 21 was the longest day of the year, Pappa had told me. It was also the first day of summer, a good day for new beginnings, I'd thought when I asked the forger to write it down.

There were times, however, when stories came alive. When someone who you thought you'd never see again stepped back into your world and knocked the wind out of you—the way

Zarin Wadia did to me in the deli in Jeddah a few weeks after I began to work there, her face so familiar that I accidentally tripped over my own feet, my rear slamming hard against the freshly mopped tiles.

For a moment, I sat on the floor, staring at her startled face. The short black hair that curled in waves around her head. The sharp, angled brows over her brown eyes. The tiny birthmark, perfectly placed, right above her soft pink lips.

It was the birthmark that tipped me off, and that look in her eyes—part wildcat, part startled doe. It was the same look she gave me when I first clambered up the sagging wooden stairs of Building Number 4 in Cama colony and stood next to her, waiting, curious about the cute girl with the funny haircut.

Twelve years had passed since then and the haircut was still the same. The girl, however, had morphed, might have stepped out of my favorite story in Pappa's old copy of *Classic Persian Myths*, her heart-shaped face and delicate curves reminding me of the fair, dark-haired Armenian princess Shirin.

"Porus!" my boss yelled. "What happened to you, boy?"

"S-sorry, sir." Heat rushed to my ears and I scrambled to my feet. "I . . . fell down."

By the time I got up, however, she was gone. I shook my head, wondering if my work combined with the Saudi heat was simply making me hallucinate.

But a week later, I saw her at the store again, this time

accompanied by her aunt and uncle, who I recognized from my years at the colony. To my surprise, Rustom Wadia, who might only have patted my head in passing when Pappa was still alive, came up to the counter and started talking to me in Gujarati. "So you're the Parsi old Hamza was telling me about!" He glanced at the new name tag on my apron. "Dumasia, Dumasia . . . You wouldn't happen to know Neville Dumasia, would you? From Cama colony?"

"He was my father," I said. "I don't know if you remember me, Mr. Wadia, but we used to stay in the building across from yours. My mother, Arnavaz, used to give Gujarati tuitions over there."

"Call me Rusi Uncle, my boy. Or just Rusi, if you feel like it. I'm not so old yet."

For the first time in months I felt my mouth curve into a genuine smile. "Okay, Rusi Uncle."

"What a small world we live in! Yes, yes, of course I remember you. In fact, I should have seen it earlier; you look so much like your father, young man. Khorshed? Khorshed, come here. *Arrey*, where has that woman gone to?" he said, waving over his wife, who was standing next to Zarin by the meat-chopping counter in the middle of the store.

"It's a wonder," Rusi Uncle said after he'd made the introductions—or, rather, reintroductions. "Khorshed and I hardly know any Parsis here in Jeddah, you know. So when

Hamza told me that he'd hired you to work here, we decided that we had to meet you."

As we continued talking, I found myself glancing at Zarin from time to time, hoping for a hint of recognition, a sign acknowledging our accidental meeting the week before. Earlier, when her uncle had introduced her to me, she'd simply given me a stiff nod, ignoring the hand I held out to shake hers. She probably didn't even remember who I was. And why would she? Even back then, despite the teasing, I'd known several boys in the colony who had crushes on her. It was partly why they teased her so much. I was one among many.

Now she was staring at the floor, sliding a well-worn sneaker across the speckled tiles. Had it been another girl, I would have taken the hint and given up. But a part of me—a stubborn part that Mamma accused me of inheriting from my father—still remembered the old Zarin. The one who would peek out her window and then slip back into hiding when she caught a glimpse of me. Zarin of the cautious smiles and shy waves. Someone I considered a friend even though we hadn't talked.

Or maybe it was the way her curls looked in the light, black and shiny; the way she exhaled and glanced up at the ceiling, her lips parted in a sigh. Clearly there was something about this girl that short-circuited the rational parts of my brain, that addled me enough to say what I said next.

144

"You know"—I directed the comment to Rusi Uncle again, but kept my eyes on her—"when I saw Zarin at the shop last week I thought I was in a dream. She looks exactly like Shirin from the great love story by Nizami, you know. For a moment I thought I was staring at a painting."

Zarin finally looked up at me and raised an eyebrow. "Interesting. When I first saw you, I thought I was staring at Bakasura. Without the giant mustache and the big teeth."

I felt my face go warm.

"Stop being so rude, dear." Rusi Uncle's voice was pleasant, but there were tight lines around his mouth and his face had turned red. Zarin did not seem to notice. While her uncle studied the blocks of cheeses and meats in the glass display case and asked me a few questions about the products, Zarin looked around at the people in the store, the men in particular, as if she was looking for someone, or maybe even daydreaming.

Zarin's aunt, who was small and insectlike in her movements, did not participate in any of the conversation either. She, too, watched the men, her eyes magnified to giant proportions by her bifocals, ready with a glare for anyone who seemed to reciprocate her niece's interest. Anyone, it seemed, except for me.

Moments later, Zarin let out a sigh and turned back to me,

the only male in the shop her aunt had not deemed worthy of her notice: "Do you have a car?"

———————————

The car was a story in itself. A '98 Nissan station wagon in green, the muffler gone, rust blistering the left back passenger door. "Not very good," the man I bought it from said. "But the price is *superb*, *ya habibi*! You will not get a better car than this!"

A few days after I got it, which was a few days after I'd first met Zarin, I drove up to a small four-story apartment building in Aziziyah with black-and-gold grilles over the windows. I looked at the address Rusi Uncle had scribbled down for me on a piece of paper, making sure it was the right one. "Please do come over, my boy," he had said with a smile. "Both Khorshed and I think that it will be good for Zarin to have a Parsi friend."

As I pulled into an empty parking space, a face peeped out from behind the curtain of a ground-floor window. Moments later Zarin emerged, a scarf carelessly wrapped around her head, her *abaya* unbuttoned at the front, flying open like a cape, revealing a pair of baggy blue jeans and a checkered shirt that could have been a boy's.

Another set of eyes appeared at the window behind Zarin,

the large glasses glinting in the afternoon sunlight. I straightened and waved. "Hello, Aunty, how are you?"

But Zarin's aunt did not reply. It was almost as if she hadn't heard me. Her gaze was trained on us both, but mostly on Zarin, and after a few seconds I lowered my hand, feeling awkward.

Zarin, on the other hand, gave no indication of seeing her aunt or my feeble attempt at common courtesy. "A bloody *khatara*," she called my car. "This car is as old as I am!"

"Good. I was going to name her after you," I said, stroking the bumper lovingly, pleased to see the alarm that flashed across Zarin's face.

Then she laughed. "You were nicer when we were kids."

"So were you." It was the first time she had acknowledged that we knew each other. I couldn't help grinning.

"Why? Because I kept my mouth shut?" She laughed again.

She had a nice laugh, I thought. It brought out the warmth in her face and a sparkle in her eyes.

"Can we go for a drive?" she asked.

I glanced at the window again. The curtain had fallen back in place, but I thought I could see a shadow behind it, waiting.

I hesitated. "But Zarin, your aunt . . . How can I . . . without . . . ?"

"You mean, go in to ask for her permission like a good Parsi boy?" she asked sarcastically. "Don't worry. If she wanted to interrogate you, I wouldn't be standing here next to your car. Even she knows you're not my type."

I was tempted to ask Zarin what exactly her type was. Instead I simply sighed and opened the front passenger door. "Make sure you wear your seat belt."

"Okay," Zarin said the moment she sat down. "I think I was impaled by a spring."

"Im-*what*?"

"Impaled. You know, skewered like a shish kebab?"

I frowned. I was eighteen years old, two years older than this girl, but her English was, I suspected, already at college level, certainly beyond the reach of my Gujarati-medium understanding. "Your English is too high for me. Will you please speak in Gujarati like any normal Parsi girl?"

"I'm not entirely Parsi. I'm half Hindu too. Or that's what my aunt keeps saying. It's a surprise they even let me into the fire temple when I go to Mumbai. I think it's probably because the priest's wife used to like my mother and feels sorry for me."

"Do you always talk like this with everyone?" I asked after a pause, and then realized that she probably did. There was a recklessness about her that reminded me of acrobats in a circus I'd once seen, a trapeze artist leaping high in the air without a net.

She raised an eyebrow. "Why? Are you going to tell your dear Rusi Uncle?"

I felt my ears going red. Saying nothing, I decided to change the subject by turning on the ignition and reversing back onto the road.

Zarin reached out a hand to turn on the AC. I caught hold of her wrist. "No. It will overheat the engine. It will be better if you roll down the window. Also, the radio drains the battery."

She pried my fingers off. "Okay. Got it. No need to get touchy-feely."

For a moment I kept driving. Next to me, she whistled. Some English song, probably. A tune I did not know.

Do you have a boyfriend? I wanted to ask her. Instead, what came out of my mouth was: "You go to school, right?"

"Qala Academy."

"How was your day?"

"Boring."

"Why?"

"What why? School's school. Boring."

"So nothing happened? Nothing at all?"

"Well, I got caught smoking on the terrace. Thank God it was only our English teacher. She loves me because I'm so good at the subject. I sobbed a little bit and she promised not to tell anyone. Just got away with a scolding."

The car jerked to a stop at the signal. "You smoke?"

She smirked. A patch of light slanted across her face, shimmered lightly on her pink lips. "*She* sounded scandalized too. She'd never seen me smoking before this."

149

I glanced at my own reflection in the rearview mirror—my hooked nose, my sweaty forehead, my thick, hairy eyebrows. From this angle I almost looked like a tough guy. Or maybe a demon from Hindu mythology. It was probably the reason Zarin had called me Bakasura in the first place. I wondered if she would be impressed if I told her about the time my friends and I had smoked a *beedi* outside our school in Mumbai, though I would have had to leave out the parts about how disgusting I found the cheap hand-rolled cigarette and how upset Mamma had been when she smelled the smoke on my clothes, making me promise never to do it again.

"When did you start smoking?" I asked instead.

"When I was fourteen," Zarin said. "I used to skip classes sometimes and go up to the academy roof and climb the ladder to sit on the water tank with my bag."

She smiled slightly, a real one, I noticed. "It's quite nice in the afternoons, especially on the breezy days. You can see the whole school from up there, and the grounds. Sometimes in the afternoon, if you time it right, you can even hear the prayers from the mosque. Anyway, there was this girl called Asfiya there too, one of the seniors. She was the one who gave me my first cig. Most of the time, though, I sat with her for the company. It made me think I wasn't quite as alone."

She uncrossed her legs and placed her feet on the floor.

The silence between us stretched and I began to get the feeling that she had grown a little uncomfortable after making that revelation. I wanted to take Zarin to the Al-Hamra Corniche—the fancier part of the city, with giant malls, hotels, and restaurants, where at night you could see the Jeddah Fountain: a white jet of water against the black sky. But being around Zarin made me so nervous that I was sure I would forget where I was going. So instead of turning onto Palestine Street like I'd originally planned, I cut into a familiar inner lane behind Madinah Road, sticking to the comfort of one of the few areas I knew well thanks to having lived there for about a month now. There weren't any malls in this area, but the apartment buildings were clean and well maintained. Instinctively, I took the route back to my house and parked across the street, in my usual spot, under a bent palm tree.

"That's where I live." I pointed out a small brown building. "Right over the barbershop sign."

Zarin leaned forward. She wasn't looking at the building. Her eyes were peering into the distance, as if she was remembering something she had forgotten. "Isn't this the area of the old Hanoody warehouse?"

I frowned, trying to remember. The Arabic signs in Jeddah were still a challenge for me, but I knew most buildings in my area.

"There is some sort of warehouse a few kilometers away

from here," I said. "But I think it's abandoned. No one goes there."

Now, this wasn't exactly true. There were times when I would see a car parked there, a group of guys leaning against the doors and talking. Sometimes there would be a single car with no passengers in sight. I felt strangely uncomfortable thinking about the warehouse, even more so because of the gleam that had come into Zarin's eyes when she heard me talk about it.

"Take me there," she commanded.

"It's abandoned!"

"Fine." She shrugged. "Then I'm going to go to that convenience store and get a pack of cigarettes."

"Wha—wait!" I called out when she began opening the door. "What do you think you're doing? No one's going to sell you cigarettes!"

"Why? Because I'm too young?" She smirked in a way that told me this hadn't stopped her before. "Of course, if you're so worried, we could always go to the warehouse."

A pair of bespectacled eyes floated across my face. Zarin's aunt, furious at finding out Zarin had been smoking. Even more so when she found out that I was the one who'd taken Zarin to the store where she bought the cigarettes. *She might not let you see Zarin again*, I told myself. Though in reality I was more worried about Zarin not wanting to see me if I didn't take her to the warehouse.

I turned on the engine once more. "We aren't stopping there," I said firmly. "I've seen police cars around that area. If they see us together, they will ask questions."

Zarin said nothing. She simply sighed and looked out the window again. Sand feathered the road leading to the warehouse. The buildings in this area were few and far between, their paint yellowing and veined with cracks, the backs of old air conditioners protruding from their walls. Even though the windows were dark, I had the strangest sense of being watched, a feeling I partly attributed to how quiet it was here compared to the bustling center of the city.

I approached the warehouse with caution, keeping an eye out for police cars, pleased to see that there were none around. "There," I said. "Happy now?"

"Rizvi's car," she said softly.

"What?"

"Rizvi. Our head boy."

A black car was parked several feet away from the warehouse, an M3, from the looks of it, dust lightly coating the back wheels and the trunk. In the front sat a guy around my age, maybe a little younger, sunglasses on his handsome face. Next to him sat a girl who appeared to be crying.

"Interesting," Zarin said, but her eyes, I could tell, were on Rizvi and not the girl.

"Is that his girlfriend?"

She shrugged and turned away. "*Was* his girlfriend, probably. He's a bit of a heartthrob around school. Half of the girls in my class have his yearbook picture saved on their phones. Even the teachers drool over him."

I heard the words she wasn't saying and felt the inside of my chest tighten. Instead of making a U-turn and heading back in the direction of my building, I kept going straight, ending up in an area I did not know that well, resulting in a much longer drive than I'd originally intended. I had not wanted to pass the black car again. I had not wanted Rizvi to turn around and see us—see her. But it did not seem to matter. Seeing the boy had sent Zarin back into a daydream. One that made lines appear on her forehead and turned her mouth soft and contemplative. The sun was now setting, and the sky was awash with different shades of red.

"You look beautiful," I said, hoping to distract her from her thoughts.

It worked. She stared at me and for a moment she looked bewildered. Then a car behind me honked. I glanced at the speedometer: I was driving at least ten kilometers below the limit. No wonder my car wasn't rattling.

Zarin covered her mouth with a hand, shoulders shaking. I tore my eyes away from her and sped up again, focusing on the road once more.

It isn't the first time a girl has laughed at you, I told myself. I was fifteen the first time I'd liked a girl at my old school in Mumbai. I still remembered her twinkling brown eyes and neatly plaited hair. The one time I'd tried to approach her in the school corridor, I'd slipped on the freshly mopped floor and fallen flat on my face. Everyone had called me Bozo for weeks afterward because of the way my face looked—pale like a clown's with the exception of my nose, which had a nice big red bruise on it, and my burning cheeks. She and her friends had never been able to look at me again without giggling.

Thankfully, Zarin wasn't like that. After a few seconds she stopped laughing, her face calm and controlled once more, even though her eyes were still bright. I decided to keep my mouth shut and keep driving. We didn't speak until I was parked once more outside her apartment building.

"Thanks." Zarin turned in her seat; her belt, I saw then, had never been buckled. "That was a nice drive."

"Really?" Somewhere inside me, hope bubbled.

She stared at me for a few seconds and then sighed. "Look, Porus. You're a good guy and maybe we can be friends. But don't get any ideas about me, okay? Meaning I'm not going to be your girlfriend. Ever."

"What do you mean?" I blushed. "Maybe I want to be friends with you."

She laughed. "You're joking, right? The whole Shirin story

at the deli, talking up my *masa* and *masi*, calling me *beautiful* . . . yeah, right, you want to be *just* friends."

"You haven't even given me a chance yet," I protested, not knowing where my sudden boldness came from. I took a deep breath. "I may look like Bakasura to you, but you don't know me that well. I may surprise you, you know."

"Okay, you need to stop taking my words so seriously. You don't *really* look like Bakasura. I said that because you annoyed me." She frowned then and stared at my face for a few seconds, almost as if she was seeing it for the first time. She shook her head. "But that isn't even the point. I'm seeing someone, okay? I have a boyfriend."

A boyfriend. It shouldn't have been a surprise to me that someone like her should have one, but I felt the sting anyway. "If you have a boyfriend, why are you here with me?" I challenged.

"You have a car and I needed to get away from Masi and her muttering." She shrugged. "What else?"

"My boss, Hamza, has a car too," I pointed out. "So does that pervert cashier, Ali. I don't see you out with either of them."

She scowled at me in response, but the corners of her mouth twitched. It was that slight movement that gave me hope, that hint of amusement on her lips that propelled me to go on and say: "You know what? I think you will go out with me again.

Maybe as a friend or whatever you call it. But even then, it will have more to do with my charm and conversation skills than this rusty old car."

"Yeah." She rolled her eyes. "Okay."

"Great, so that's settled, then," I said cheerfully. "I'll come see you again next weekend. Maybe one day I can win you over and you will leave that boyfriend of yours for me."

She stared at me for a second and then burst out laughing—a real laugh this time, not a sarcastic one. "You, my friend, have clearly lost your mind."

A week later, an unknown number flashed on my phone.

"Hey," she said. "It's Zarin. Come get me, will you? Text me on this number when you get here."

"What's wrong?" I asked, but she had already hung up by then. A part of me was irritated. Who did this girl think she was? But another, larger part was deeply curious. I knew a little about Zarin's parents from the bits and pieces of information floating around Cama colony when I lived there.

Women had shared stories about Zarin's mother, Dina, the colony beauty who could have married any man she wanted, but instead started working at a cabaret bar once Zarin's great-grandfather died.

"My brother offered to help her, you know," Persis, the Dog Lady, told anyone who would listen. "He said he would marry her, give her a home. But she refused! Said she didn't want to marry someone like him! As if there was something wrong with my brother! Then she went off with that thug and had a baby with him. Mad, I tell you!"

Though Dina eventually moved out of the colony to a fancy apartment in downtown Mumbai, she sometimes showed up to visit her sister—especially after she'd had an argument or a fight with her lover.

The day Zarin's father came over to the colony was one few had ever forgotten. Once, over drinks, a group of men described to my father how the man rode in through the gates on his Harley, calmly marched up the stairs to Building 4, and put a gun to Dina's head.

"You have to give our Dina credit, though," one of the men had said. "She stood her ground, didn't reveal an ounce of fear. Said she wouldn't go home with him if he threatened her like that. Little Zarin is just like her, you know. The way she pummeled her cousin the other day! Would have never imagined such a temper on such a small girl. Maybe she gets that from her father."

Everyone, including Pappa, had laughed at the casual joke. Yet no one ever mentioned or even joked about Dina and Zarin's father in front of the Wadias—not even the gossipy old Dog

Lady. I might have been eight years old back then, but even I could see how the atmosphere shifted when either one of Zarin's guardians walked in on a gossip session, how quickly voices faded and subjects changed.

Zarin was waiting by the door to her apartment building when I pulled up, her face paler than the last time I'd seen her, clutching a small backpack to her chest.

"You came," she said, her voice flat. But she was speaking in Gujarati for once and I could feel my annoyance melting away.

"Yeah, I did. You sounded strange. I got worried."

She sighed and then slipped into the passenger seat. "I didn't mean to call you like that. I didn't mean to call anyone. But my *masa* . . ." Her head snapped up to the window, where I saw two shadows. A man and a woman, holding each other.

"Could we get out of here first?" she asked irritably.

I frowned. I might have had a crush on this girl, but even I had my limits. I opened my mouth, fully intending to tell her that she couldn't order me around like that. But then she raised a hand to tuck a stray lock of hair into her scarf. The loose sleeve of her *abaya* fell to the elbow, revealing a crescent of red and blue circles smudged over her skin.

Seeing the direction of my gaze, she hastily pushed down the sleeve. "What are you looking at?" she snapped.

I gently caught hold of her wrist and pulled the sleeve up

159

again. I would have let her go if she'd struggled, but to my surprise she didn't really resist my grip. Maybe she simply assumed that I was too strong for her. But when I looked up into her eyes, I realized she was tired.

"How did you get these?" I asked, brushing a thumb over an older bruise, which was now turning yellow.

"Masi's fingers."

I looked back up at the window. The shadows were gone. I didn't even bother asking Zarin if they knew I was with her. I released her hand and shifted the gear into Drive. "Where do you want to go?"

Jeddah's Corniche was the only part of the city that sometimes reminded me of Mumbai. One weekend, I had finally taken my mother out to the central Corniche, a lively patch of coastline bustling with families in the evenings. Arab boys of my age and younger rode beach buggies in the sand and sometimes on the boardwalk. A half hour before sunset, the Jeddah Fountain opened to the public, propelling over a thousand feet of water into the air from the middle of the Red Sea.

We bought corn on the cob from a chatty Malayali who stood behind a bright yellow Mazola Cooking Oil stand and steamed full husks in water before brushing them with butter and sprinkling on salt. He often complained of other hawkers at the southern end of the beach, men who wheeled in corns in barrows and roasted them over open fires, the way they did in India.

"My corn is better," the Malayali insisted. "Sweeter. And you do not taste charcoal in your mouth. Right, no?"

"Right," I said. I did not tell him that the charcoal taste was associated with some of my happiest memories of my father and of Mumbai.

On bad days, when the pain of missing Pappa grew too much and Mamma sat praying next to the altar in our kitchen for hours on end, I drove to the north end of the Corniche to be by myself, to stare at the waves until my body was fooled into thinking that it too was floating with the foam, past the little white Island Mosque with the pink domes, across the Red Sea. I walked along the shore and stood by the rocks near the mosque, a few feet away from the families spread out on mats with bags of sandwiches, packs of Pepsi, and aluminum containers of AlBaik chicken. Children splashed nearby, laughing hysterically in the shallows. Their voices didn't matter much after a while; the waves that crashed against the craggy rocks often drowned out most noises, allowing the thoughts in my head to turn liquid, to slosh lazily around in my brain and lap at its sides.

It was here that I took Zarin now, parking next to the

boardwalk, with a clear view of the mosque. I rolled down my window and sucked in a deep breath of the sea air: clean, hot, tinged with salt. In the distance a municipal dredger lay flat and black against the water, leaving behind a stream of white foam.

There were days in Jeddah when the smell of the sea was much stronger, so strong that it stuck to the clothes my mother hung to dry on our small balcony, a stiff, fishy smell that never seemed to go away no matter how much deodorant I used. "It was never like this in Mumbai," Mamma would grumble, pressing the iron hard onto my shirt, as if she expected to burn the smell out of the cloth.

Zarin stared out at the water now, crushed like the fabric of a woman's sari, a dull steel blue that caught glints of red and yellow from the setting sun.

"We used to come here," she said, speaking for the first time after our silent car ride. "Masa, Masi, and I. When I was six. Masa used to take my hand and walk with me along the shore. Masi would walk on his other side. People used to think we were a family."

"You *are* a family."

"You're kidding, right?"

"I would be if I knew what I was joking about."

She finally turned around to face me, but didn't really look me in the eye. "It was ridiculous. The reason for our fight. She was complaining about how much she hated certain things about Jeddah. 'Our India is our India.' " Zarin mimicked her aunt as she spoke the last few words. "And stuff like that. But when she goes to India, she praises Jeddah to the skies and complains about how dirty Mumbai is. She was being a hypocrite. I called her out on it. I should have kept my mouth shut."

I cleared my throat. "Does she hit you a lot?"

She shrugged. "Not as much as she used to."

"But Rusi Uncle—"

"Does nothing. Well, to be fair, he does tell her off sometimes. But he also keeps saying that I shouldn't shoot my mouth off at her. He always takes her side. Even when I'm right." She finally focused her gaze on mine. "I was so angry. I wanted to get out of there."

"And I was the first person you thought of? I didn't know you thought of this as your getaway car," I joked, trying to lighten the mood.

She smirked. "I guess I could have picked better, huh?"

"Like your boyfriend," I said pointedly. "You do have one, don't you? Or did you lie about that as well?"

"Yeah, sure. Call my boyfriend, whose existence neither Masa nor Masi knows about, and get into even more trouble. That would have been classic. Why don't I ask them to ship me off to Mumbai and marry me to some good Parsi boy over there?"

"What's wrong with Parsi boys?" I couldn't help feeling offended. "And you're too young to get married anyway."

She rummaged through her backpack and pulled out a pack of cigarettes. "Hey!" she shouted when I plucked it out of her hands. "Give that back!"

"You're not smoking those things in my car. Besides, do you know how much they can damage your lungs?"

"Come on," Zarin insisted. "No one cares."

"Well, maybe they should," I said.

Something flickered in her eyes. She held out her hand again. "Will you give it back to me if I promise I won't smoke?"

Yeah, right. I pocketed the pack.

"Fine, keep it," she said irritably. "There was only one left anyway."

"A small but important victory."

"It has suddenly become clear to me why you don't have a girlfriend."

"I didn't know furnaces could be girlfriends."

Her eyes widened for a brief moment. The way her mouth twitched should have tipped me off before the laugh bubbled out of her. Belly-deep. Real. "Okay, wise guy," she said, once she'd caught her breath. "You got me. *This* time."

I should have known I was in trouble from that moment. Because, though she didn't know it, she'd gotten me as well.

Just when I'd been about to write her off, she laughed that laugh and I fell for her again.

———————————

That first phone call set the tone for a ritual of sorts. Zarin would call—mostly moments before she wanted to go somewhere—and ask if I wanted to "go out." When we met, she would make it a point to say we were "friends only." I would tease her about this—"Why are you being so specific? Are you afraid of falling for me?"

It wasn't easy reconciling the image of Zarin I had in my head with the girl I found in Jeddah. In Mumbai, I had always thought of Zarin as clever but quiet—a girl who preferred sitting by herself and who observed more than she spoke. Ten years later, while I found some of these things to be true, I also had to account for her quick wit, her biting sense of humor, and her general moodiness on the days when she didn't get a proper nicotine fix.

Though she didn't show it very often, Zarin had a softer side as well. When I talked about Pappa or my old life in Mumbai, she listened, sometimes even contributing an anecdote of her own. On my bad days, she made me laugh. It was odd, I thought, how she seemed to sense the change in my moods almost instantly. The only other person who could see through my poker face was my mother. When I mentioned this to her, Zarin said: "You can never lie to another liar."

Having Zarin in my life broke the monotony of working at the deli and lightened the crushing grief that had come with my father's death, a feeling that could go away for days on end and then suddenly return the moment I saw a man with salt-and-pepper hair or smelled the pages of an old book.

My mother, who had spoken to Khorshed Aunty a few times after I introduced them, didn't approve of my friendship with Zarin.

"Khorshed has told me a few things about this girl," Mamma told me. "About her misbehavior at school and at home. She doesn't think twice about the things she does. She doesn't care about the people around her; she's so rude, even to her own *masi* and *masa*."

"They are not always kind to her," I argued, remembering the bruises I had seen on her arm. "It's not . . . things are not always what they seem."

My mother looked at me for a long moment. Her eyes were sad. "Porus, you are so much like your father. Always giving people the benefit of the doubt. Sometimes it is as much a curse as it is a blessing. Please listen to what I'm saying. Think long and hard before you get too involved with this girl."

Yet, when it came to Zarin, anything that resembled thought always went out the window. There was something about her that instinctively drew me, that I could not explain to myself, let alone to my mother.

The nights I couldn't sleep, I took to sneaking out and driving around aimlessly—something that was easier to do in Jeddah than it was in Mumbai, where many of the roads were narrow and poorly lit. In Jeddah, streetlights burned like fireflies, following me everywhere from the dazzling glamor of Palestine Street to quiet residential lanes. I could pretend I was with Pappa, showing him the city the way Zarin had showed it to me, pointing out landmarks that flashed by between palm trees, joking about how lucky I was that the gas here was cheaper than drinking water.

Once, on a whim, I even drove to Aziziyah and parked across the street near Zarin's small, four-story apartment building, a few feet behind the municipal garbage bin. A gibbous moon hung in the sky and for several moments I sat in silence, mesmerized, until a pair of cats leaped out of the garbage bin, their screeches piercing the air.

I jerked upright, heart pounding. Lights glared down at me, reflecting in the hood of my car. They made me realize suddenly how bright everything was—how easy it would be for anyone to look outside and catch me lurking. If Zarin saw me now, she would probably call me a stalker. Or maybe even a roadside Romeo, the way the boys at the deli did whenever they caught me staring at her. I was about to drive off again when a shadow appeared at the ground-floor window of Zarin's apartment, followed by the brush of a pale hand against the grille. "I get nightmares," Zarin had told me. "Sometimes I think it's better if I don't sleep."

I wondered if it was her now, if she would turn around and catch me watching her. But she never did. Seconds later, the hand disappeared and the shadow went back to bed.

A GIRL LIKE ANY OTHER

Zarin

THERE WERE DIFFERENT KINDS OF LOVE, Porus said. The kind that struck you instantaneously—"Lust at first sight!" I interrupted—and the kind that grew with time—"Desperation!"—which was what he hoped would happen between him and me.

"It doesn't work that way, Zarin," he said irritably. "Falling in love does not mean you're desperate."

"Of course it does!" I countered. "There's no other way I would fall in love with you."

Pain flashed in his eyes, as quick as liquid, and then was gone with a blink. My own smart mouth didn't surprise me. It was the regret that came with using it on Porus that did. I was never known for censoring myself when talking to anyone, especially not the boys I went out with. But saying something intentionally (mostly unintentionally) cruel to Porus always made me feel guilty. Any other boy would have left by now.

To my surprise, apart from the few rare occasions when he revealed his pain, Porus generally laughed at me. *Tohfani*, he called me in Gujarati. *Tempestuous*.

It was an apt description. If I was like a tempest, then Porus was like a rock, solid and unflappable. And, as bad as this sounded, each time he laughed at my cruelty, I couldn't help but test his limits, see how much he could take before snapping back.

"Do you ever get angry?" I asked him one day at the deli, though my tone was more curious than taunting. "I mean, don't you want to bash in someone's head at times?"

"Yours, you mean?" His lips curved up into a small smile—the kind he sometimes flashed at giddy female customers. I was annoyed to feel my heart skip a beat.

"You don't want to see me angry, Zarin," he said. "I have a really bad temper."

"Yeah, right," I said with a snort, even though I sometimes wondered if he was telling the truth, if his biceps were really as rock hard as they had felt when my fingers had accidentally brushed against them that one time in his car.

I could have, perhaps, ignored my irritation over Porus's

Gandhian temperament or unexpected charisma. But somehow he'd also penetrated the barriers Masa and Masi had set up for me as a girl. "Such a decent boy!" Masa called him, and this annoyed me the most. Masi also approved of Porus, though I knew this had less to do with decency and more to do with the fact that Porus was Parsi—a pure Parsi born of two Parsi parents—which automatically made him 99 percent better than any other guy who liked her half-Hindu niece.

"Our people are our people," I would often hear her tell Persis. "If there were some nice Parsi families—some nice Parsi boys—around here, I would not feel so anxious about her."

As hypocritical as I found them both over this idea, I couldn't really complain about it. Being with Porus was one of the few ways I could leave the house without having to sneak out, and sometimes he even acted as a cover for my dates with Abdullah, though he didn't like that.

Porus had penetrated some of my barriers too. Unlike Abdullah, Porus was easy to talk to about Mumbai and being Parsi. I didn't have to think twice before switching from English to Gujarati when I spoke with Porus; didn't have to figure out ways to explain a joke about Masi humming during prayers or the eccentricities of the Dog Lady at Cama colony. I didn't even mind it when Porus texted me a cheesy picture and quote that said *Keep Calm and Love a Parsi.* (Even though, for the sake of appearances, I texted back, "You wish.")

There was wonder in Porus's eyes about everything Jeddah. And, if I was honest, everything me. He asked me questions ranging from what book I'd take with me if I was stranded on a desert island to what I thought about women not being allowed to drive in Saudi Arabia. I'd never talked like this with a boy before. Not even Abdullah.

Though I had initially enjoyed the lack of personal conversation on my dates with Abdullah, nowadays it left me feeling a little bored, as it left us very little to do except eat, smoke, or kiss. There were times when we would drive past the familiar palm tree engraving and WELCOME TO JEDDAH sign near the arch on Madinah Road and I would remember Porus and his comment about how he'd never seen so many date palms in one place. Abdullah would ask why I was smiling and I'd say "No reason," which made me feel incredibly guilty.

But Abdullah never seemed to notice how distracted I was, often brushing aside any attempts at conversation with a hard kiss on my mouth. Slowly but surely, he tried to take things further than kissing, inching his hand up my thigh or my torso, always getting pissed off when I stopped him from unbuttoning the hooks on the back of my *kameez* or pulling down the elastic of my *salwar*.

The Thursday before, we'd had our biggest fight about the subject.

"Since when did you turn into a prude?" he'd asked me. "Boyfriends and girlfriends do these things. There's nothing wrong with it."

"Maybe—if you're in America," I pointed out. "I told you I'm not ready yet, Abdullah. I mean, we've only been dating for a couple of months."

Abdullah snorted. "Give me a break, Zarin. It's that deli boy, isn't it? You have the hots for him now."

"Porus is my *friend*. He knows I'm with you."

"Yeah, well, if that's the case, I really don't know what your problem is."

I didn't know either. As much as I liked kissing Abdullah, the idea of having sex with him made me uneasy, felt *wrong* on some level. It was something I could barely explain to myself, let alone to a boy who worked off his sexual frustration by calling me a tease and then giving me the silent treatment for the entire twenty-minute drive back to my apartment building.

With Porus, everything was different. For one: he was my friend, not my boyfriend. Two: despite his annoying comments about how he was going to win me over, I knew he would never really pressure me into doing anything. There was something about Porus, a kindness in his eyes, maybe, or

175

that goofy smile of his that made me instinctively feel safe around him. His curiosity was endless, his questions moving randomly from one subject to another, making me talk and talk and talk until I blurted out things I had never meant to in the first place.

"Do you want *me* to talk to Rusi Uncle?" Porus had asked one day, and pointed toward a new bruise on my arm. "Maybe if I told him, he would stop it."

I'd vehemently shaken my head. Masi's "anxiety issues," as Masa called them, often took precedence over whatever she did to me, though I didn't tell this to Porus.

"Please, *dikra*," Masa would plead whenever I told him. "Please try to be patient with her."

Masa, who would lose his own patience whenever I said that Masi simply used her illness as a shield for her mean behavior. Who had never seen the calculating look in her eyes when she'd smacked her head the day Fali died.

"It's nothing," I had snapped at Porus. "People beat their kids all the time. Even our teachers beat us at school." The week before, I'd seen our Physics teacher twisting some hapless Class VI girl's ear for wearing the wrong-colored shoes to the school assembly. "It isn't anything new. I'm not a weakling, Porus. I can handle it."

"You're not weak if you talk to someone about your abuse. Beating children is wrong. My father always said so. He never beat me, and neither did my mother."

176

"It's more complicated than that." I'd forced myself to look away from his penetrating stare. "I'm not like you, you know. I'm not a nice person."

Even Porus's mother knew this. I'd overheard Masi talking to her plenty of times about my bad behavior when she visited our apartment. "What to do, Arnavaz? Children these days! They never listen."

Once, I overheard the two of them discussing my mother: "I don't even want to talk about the things they called her," Masi told Arnavaz Aunty. "The things they said behind her back. When our grandfather died, Dina didn't want anyone's help. She got up one day, went off to the cabaret bar near the *chawl*, and got a job there. She said that it was for me. For her little sister.

"But no one cared about that. In this world, no one cares if you are starving to death. No one even looks at you. They only care when you start doing things they don't approve of—like dancing with your clothes off. Zarin doesn't understand this. She thinks I am ungrateful. She calls me a hypocrite. She is so much like Dina in that way that it terrifies me."

There were times when I wondered if Porus would have been better suited to living with Masa and Masi than I was— if he could have been that steady, patient child Masa always longed for.

"Love is the answer," Porus told me, when I asked him once. "Love is always the answer when things go wrong."

A day later Farhan Rizvi's sister, Asma, used a similar phrase during the Class XI English debate at Qala Academy, before she began waxing poetic about an eye for an eye making the whole world blind—and about how women who were victims of domestic abuse should *not* retaliate with deadly violence against their aggressors.

"There are other things that women have to often think of," Asma announced, her cheeks turning pink, the way they always did when she spoke in public. "Their children, for instance. What example does it set for the child if both parents are violent? Who will teach the child right from wrong? Also, who is to say that the husband isn't capable of change?"

I watched the judges sitting at a table in front of the stage, strained expressions on their faces. There were two from the boys' section, and two from the girls'. I recognized our headmistress in her long Pakistani-style *salwar-kameez* and our English teacher, Khan Madam, who was wearing her usual sari and white cardigan, her hennaed hair vivid in the bright lights of the auditorium. Her eyes met mine, the skin around them ringed brown. She gave me a slight smile and looked away.

One afternoon when I'd gone to see her in the staff room for a book, the sleeve of her sweater had slipped a bit and I'd seen a mark on her arm that looked a lot like a bruise. The mark had made something inside me tighten and for a brief moment I wanted to show her my own bruises—the scar on my knee that looked like a crater, the brown patch on my left arm from the time Masi had hit it with a hot spoon. *We are alike, you and I,* I wanted to say. But then Khan Madam had looked up into my eyes and asked, "Is something the matter?" and the moment passed. "No, ma'am," I'd replied. How could she help me, this woman who could not help herself? I'd walked away, pretending I had seen nothing.

Mishal Al-Abdulaziz sat across from me, with the team arguing against the topic. Over the past month or so, I had caught her and Layla watching me from time to time and giving me dirty looks. Earlier in the week, they'd been sneering at me, at one point pausing in midconversation to burst into laughter. While it wasn't uncommon for either Mishal or Layla to do such things, ever since my fight with Abdullah I couldn't help wondering if they somehow knew about it, even though my mind told me I was being paranoid. Abdullah did not discuss me with his sister, I reminded myself. "If I told Mishal anything, it would spread over the whole school," he'd told me once. "Don't worry. I would never tell her anything about us."

At the moment, however, Mishal wasn't watching me. She was calmly making notes in her book, probably for the rebuttal. Or maybe it was an intimidation tactic for the opposition. Already I could see the way it was affecting the others on my team: Alisha Babu, who was calmer than any other girl I knew, was making notes like a maniac, copying down Asma's speech word for word.

But I kept only one ear on Asma's argument. I could already tell it wouldn't be any good from the vague way she had begun. I allowed my mind to wander for a while. To Abdullah, first. The puzzling discomfort that always seemed to accompany any thoughts of having sex with him. The anger he displayed now—more and more frequently. I thought of Porus. How strange that a boy so burly could be hurt with a few chosen words. Then, out of the blue, I thought of Farhan Rizvi. A boy I'd seen only from a distance. A boy whose pictures I sometimes studied in my bedroom after my fights with Abdullah, wondering, imagining what it would have been like if he'd seen me smile at him two years before.

Alisha's elbow nudged mine. "Your turn!" she said.

He vanished into the lights and a hundred faces were staring at me then—girls from classes IX, X, and XI forced out of their classes into the ground-floor auditorium used for indoor sports and exhibitions, girls shutting their eyes, scribbling notes to each other, girls bored out of their minds over a debate they'd probably expected to be more exciting considering the topic: "Is it permissible for victims of domestic abuse to retaliate with deadly violence or other illegal action?"

I hastily got to my feet, leaving the papers behind. I placed my hands on both sides of the podium and looked the audience right in the eye: "Should women who are victims of domestic abuse respond by any means possible? Even if it includes deadly violence? Is violence right or morally permissible? Is the case as simple as saying 'an eye for an eye makes the whole world blind'?" I paused, waiting for the silence to spread around the room, a tactic I'd seen the headmistress use when she gave her speeches.

"Is it as simple as turning the other cheek and hoping the husband will suddenly remember the love he once had for his wife—as Ms. Rizvi suggested? Or will it simply mean another visit to the hospital, as it was for Savitri Sharma in Amritsar, Punjab? A woman who was placed in intensive care for severe burns because she didn't bring her husband's family the car they wanted as part of her dowry? Or will the case be that of Megan Forester in Columbus, Ohio, whose husband held their daughter at gunpoint so Megan would not leave him? What if these women had reacted differently? What if they had fought back? In self-defense?"

I looked at the judges again to gauge their reactions. Instead of looking disinterested and bored, the male judges were listening closely to what I had to say. Our headmistress was smiling and nodding her head. Only Khan Madam looked pale and uneasy.

"Seema Rao in Mumbai did this in 2013. She hit her husband

on the head with a cricket bat before he sliced into her with a knife. It was later discovered that her husband was mentally ill. With her quick actions, she managed to save herself and her husband. The judge assigned to the case found her actions justified even though under normal circumstances they would be illegal."

Little witch, Masi had called me when she first smelled the cigarettes on me when I was in Class X. I could still remember the pinch of her nails, the burn of the hot spoon on my skin, her scream in my ear when I brought my foot down in retaliation, crushing her toes with the heel of my shoe. It was the only time I'd ever fought back physically. She had never tried that on me again.

"When we talk about violence, we do not always talk about death," I said. "Sometimes violence can mean the difference between life and death. The difference between waiting for someone's help and continuing to suffer abuse, and helping yourself when you most need it. Even the law recognizes this idea of self-preservation. In Seema Rao's case, the Mumbai High Court judge defined it as the absolute right of human beings to protect themselves from harm—with violence, if necessary."

I paused and looked around the quiet auditorium. "When I went through these cases for my research, I came across so many instances when the victim of the abuse said 'I wish I'd done something.' Or 'I wish I hadn't been so scared.' And you know what? I wish they had as well. I wish they hadn't been scared and that they had tried to fight back. Because maybe if they had, they would have found that the law was on their side.

"Thank you."

I sat down next to my teammates again, my face flushed, my heart racing, the applause ringing in my ears. Alisha gripped my wrist. "You got the most claps so far! Khan Madam looked like she was about to cry. The opposition doesn't stand a chance!"

But I wasn't too sure. Over the years, I'd learned not to underestimate the tall girl who now stood from her chair and made her way to the podium.

Mishal mimicked my posture at the stand, placing her hands on both sides. "My partner has already discussed the moral issues pertaining to retaliating with violence in a violent situation. So I will not go into that. I will address the legal issues pertaining to the topic. Or self-defense, as Ms. Wadia calls it. Yet is self-defense so easy to prove in a court of law? The first question a lawyer will ask you is: Why not a divorce? The law allows a woman to escape the abuse of a violent spouse. We don't live in the Middle Ages anymore. What is the need to retaliate with violence? Why risk a jail sentence or the loss of one's children in a custody battle? Yes, the law may permit you to defend yourself—but the burden of proving yourself innocent in such scenarios may be much harder than the burden of being a divorced woman."

My teammates scribbled furiously, some arguments about women having little to no choice in countries like Saudi Arabia, etc., etc., but I could already see that Mishal's argument had changed things around, knitting everything that her team members had said earlier into something more structured, cohesive. They would be winning the team trophy, no matter what we said during rebuttals; I was quite sure of that.

Ten minutes later, after Mishal and I faced off again in one-minute comebacks, my prediction proved right.

"The winning team," our headmistress announced, "is the Against team, led by Mishal Al-Abdulaziz!"

Alisha hung her head. "Who cares?" I whispered in her ear. "It's a silly debate."

A lie. I'd worked hard on this debate. Harder than anything I'd ever worked on in school.

"Now, choosing the best speaker was a bit difficult," the headmistress continued when the applause died down. "There were two contenders—one from each team—both so good they could end up pursuing legal careers in the future." She smiled. "But there is a winner. By one mark: Zarin Wadia from the For team! Mishal Al-Abdulaziz was a very close—"

Her voice was drowned by the applause that broke out for me, which was much louder than that for the winning team.

The audience had spoken, and it was clear which side they'd supported. "We should've won," my teammates whispered to one another, their voices full of angry triumph. "See?"

What I saw was the look on Mishal's face. She was smiling, but it was a smile of disappointment and for a moment I felt sorry for her, having felt that same dejection seconds before, when my team lost. She was the only one onstage who didn't congratulate me, but I didn't realize that until much later, when I boarded the school bus to head back home. I looked at my reflection in the window—my eyes were brighter than usual and my face still held the afterglow of victory. I grinned to myself, teeth flashing bright, and for a second I wasn't the Zarin Wadia everyone knew, but a girl, a normal schoolgirl who had won something and was proud of it.

Out of the corner of my eye, I grew aware of someone else watching me. I turned warily. It was a boy wearing sunglasses, leaning against the door of a black car, a BMW. His head was tilted sideways and he had a slight smile on his face. Under normal circumstances, I would have raised an eyebrow or even smiled back. But this was Farhan Rizvi. And he was openly checking me out. Heat rose to my cheeks and again, for the second time in my life, I wasn't quite sure what I was supposed to do.

I didn't have the time to do much anyway. A moment later, Asma came racing out of the gateway, scattering girls left and right, her *abaya* flying, a small gold trophy clutched in her hand. She gave her brother a high five and then brandished the little gold cup.

I won. I could read her lips. *I won, Farhan-bhai.*

I turned away from both of them and focused on the seat in front of me—the maroon leather discolored to a fleshy pink by the sun, the white thread holding it together unraveling, exposing yellow sponge. I plucked at a thread curling up into the air, dug my nails into the soft leather. I took a deep breath and willed myself to calm down. I examined my trophy again— a small silver-and-gold cup with *Best Speaker* engraved on the front.

When I looked up, I saw Mishal standing at her usual place at the front of the bus. She was staring at me with an odd smile on her face, one I couldn't quite understand.

"Congrats!" I called out, raising a hand, not realizing at first that it was the one that held the trophy. Mishal's face hardened and she sat down without saying thanks. Obviously she thought I was making fun of her. I hesitated for a moment, wondering if I should approach and tell her that it had been unintentional.

"Okay, girls, settle down!" the bus driver called from the front. I would apologize afterward, I told myself. But somehow I knew it was too late. The moment was already gone. I turned off the knob of the air conditioner overhead and closed my eyes, giving in fully to the afternoon heat and the head-ache that now seemed to press on me from all sides.

The next morning, Mishal approached me a few minutes into break.

"Hey, Zarin. Can I talk to you for a bit?" She slid into the empty chair next to mine.

I closed my book. "Hi. Sure." I hesitated for a brief moment. "By the way, I didn't mean . . . I wasn't rubbing it in your face yesterday when I said 'congrats,' you know. I meant it. You did a good job in the debate."

Mishal's eyes narrowed for a split second, as if surprised. Then she shook her head. Smiled, even. "That's okay. You win some, you lose some, I guess."

"Right."

There was an awkward silence. "You wanted to—"

"Look." Mishal leaned in to keep our conversation private. "I know you're going out with Abdullah." A small shock went through me, but Mishal kept going, placing a hand over my arm. "I don't really care about that, okay? It doesn't really matter to me who he messes around with in his spare time."

"As it shouldn't," I said calmly. I should have known this was too good to be true.

"You should hear the things he says about you." She laughed, her pretty face glowing even more than usual. "Let's see. He called you a tease, didn't he? Oh yes, I can see from your face that he did. He was telling his friends about it this weekend."

She went on to tell me the other names Abdullah called me. Some so awful that they were unforgivable.

The things they called her, Masi had said about my mother. *The things they said behind her back.*

The smile Mishal gave me was almost gentle. She rose to her feet again. "Anyway, I wanted to say congrats too," she said in a clear voice. "You did a good job at the debate, even if you were a little emotional."

Mishal

IT DIDN'T SURPRISE ME WHEN ZARIN phoned Abdullah that evening to confront him about the things I'd said. What did surprise me was that she did not give him my name—like it didn't even matter that her only source of information against her boyfriend was a girl who hated her in school.

Luck favored me even more when Abdullah did not choose to deny her allegations. I bit my lip to hold back a laugh. Though I was no longer afraid of being the target of my brother's wrath, the less he knew about my involvement in this, the better. As far as Abdullah was concerned, I was clueless about his "secret relationship" with Zarin, even though it was thanks to me that their relationship was still secret from the rest of the school. I rolled my eyes as my brother's voice rose in pitch and volume.

In any case, what I'd done didn't really matter. From the sound of their conversation—if you could call a five-minute insult fest a conversation—it seemed that the relationship had already been a little rocky and a breakup would have been inevitable at some point. Zarin probably thought the same thing, especially when Abdullah lost his temper and said: "Who told you? Was it one of my friends? Are you screwing one of them now?"

I carefully switched the cordless phone I was using to eavesdrop on their conversation from my right ear to the left.

Not now, I thought, mentally answering my brother's question. But if the way she and Rizvi had looked at each other after the debate yesterday was any indication, it would happen fairly soon.

Rizvi had stared at her so hard I thought his eyes would pop right out of his shades. It was also clear that Zarin was not unaffected. I had watched the slow drop of her smile when she realized Rizvi was watching. The nervous way she bit her lip. How quickly she'd turned around after Asma burst through the gates, her cheeks flushed pink. In that moment, she wasn't the Zarin Wadia I knew, but a girl like any other in the face of a crush: insecure, tongue-tied, and shy.

"Don't bother calling me again," Zarin told Abdullah before hanging up.

I waited for Abdullah to slam the receiver on his end before clicking off the phone and placing it back in its cradle. I thought back to the insults Abdullah had thrown my way over the years. Crybaby. Twit. Blabbermouth. Fool. I muffled my laughter in my pillow. *Who is the fool, Abdullah?* I wanted to ask him. *Who is the fool now?*

When I finally ventured out of my room, I found Abdullah stretched out on the living room sofa, his bare feet resting on the coffee table, the television switched on, but muted.

"What happened?" I asked. "I heard you yelling on the phone."

He shrugged. "I broke up with this girl I was seeing."

I sat down next to Abdullah. "Do you want to talk about it?" I asked softly.

"She knew I was talking to my friends about her. That I called her . . . some terrible things." His swallow was audible in the silence. "Don't even know how she found out—she wouldn't tell me."

Heat rose to my cheeks at this statement, but thankfully Abdullah didn't seem to notice.

"It doesn't matter," he was saying. "It's not like I said anything behind her back that I didn't say to her face." Abdullah let out a bitter laugh. "I thought I'd finally found someone who was different from everyone else. A girl who didn't need to yak the whole time, someone I thought I actually liked. But she was like every other girl I know—luring me with her body for free food and cigarettes."

I frowned. Abdullah's words did not surprise me. But the pain in his voice did—a pain I had last seen the day Father married Jawahir, when my brother and I were still children. I studied his glassy eyes, the straight nose, so much like our mother's, the cleft in his chin that I used to poke as a little girl, wondering if it was the indent of someone's finger. My heart swelled uncomfortably and I began to wonder if I had done the right thing.

Then I shook my head. It didn't matter, I reminded myself. It didn't matter how much Abdullah liked Zarin. Father would never have allowed Abdullah to marry a non-Muslim. In fact, it was better that they broke up now, rather than later. Who knew what Abdullah would have done if they'd grown closer, if they'd fallen in *love*? They might have eloped, even run away for good, leaving me alone in Jeddah—with our vacant mother in this big house, at the mercy of Father and Jawahir. My stomach clenched at the thought. As bad as my relationship with Abdullah could be at times, I knew that when it came down to it, he would never let anyone harm me or our mother. He was the only person Father talked to these days, the one who kept Jawahir's visits to our house to a bare minimum, the one who still, somehow, held our dysfunctional family in place.

"You're probably better off without her," I said after a pause. "I mean, sometimes bad things happen for a good reason, right?"

Abdullah stared at me for a moment. There was a strange expression on his face—anger, mingled with sadness.

"I'm going to go take a shower," he said abruptly. "You better check on Mother to see if she'll come downstairs for dinner."

As a child, a bee had once landed on my finger. In those days, I had not known enough to be scared of it. I'd studied its elliptical insect body, the black and yellow stripes on its back, its small translucent wings, and listened to the soft humming noise it made. When I'd reached out to touch it, it reacted predictably, rising into the air with an angry buzz, leaving me with a stinging boil on my hand—and a sense of confusion mingled with inexplicable loss.

That evening, when Abdullah walked away from me, I felt the same way—as if I'd come close to seeing something strange and incredible, only to have it slip away before I could fully grasp it.

Instead of updating BlueNiqab with the news of my brother's epic breakup with Zarin, I went over to Mother's room.

"Ummi?" I gently knocked on the door. "Ummi, it's me. I know you don't like being disturbed, but I . . . I need to talk."

On the other side of the door, I could hear the faint, familiar strains of a sitar. On her good days, Mother played *sarangi* music by Ustad Sultan Khan. Flute compositions by Pandit Hariprasad Chaurasia. Even some old Bollywood semiclassical pieces by singer Lata Mangeshkar. On her bad days, though, it was always maestro Ravi Shankar. Ravi Shankar and his sitar.

My hand curled into a fist. Silence. Withdrawal. Sudden switches from relatively calm to very sad. I knew the symptoms. I'd googled them a year earlier, along with the cures for clinical depression.

I slammed my fist against the door. It rattled in the frame. The music stopped.

"I need to talk to you," I told the door loudly. "I really need to talk to you, but you're not here. You never are. I mean, it was one thing when Abu left us for Jawahir, but did you have to abandon us too? Do you know Abdullah and I barely talk now? That Abu and Jawahir are talking about marrying me off to the first guy they find?

"You . . . you make me so angry, Ummi! It's like you've

completely forgotten you have kids of your own. Neither Abdullah nor I exist for you anymore. And I don't know if I can ever forgive you for it."

That night, my mother played no more music. And it was only as I was falling asleep that I began to wonder why.

Porus

TILL ZARIN, I HAD, FOR THE MOST PART, known enough about what I needed to say to be considered reasonably charming around women. In the business of selling meat and cheese at the deli shop, I had to keep my wits about me. "The woman may be your customer," my boss told me, "but you cannot let that intimidate you. You must always be in charge."

In charge, like some of the men I worked with—men like Hamza himself, who unloaded twenty-kilo bags of meat and cheese off the truck with the green-and-yellow Lahm b'Ajin logo without gritting their teeth or squinting their eyes. Men who could curse at each other and then smile and charm at the counter, selling our customers (mainly women) sliced beef and turkey, blocks of *jibneh*, *akkawi*, and *shanklish* cheese rings covered with *ʒaatar* and pine nuts. "Peppered salami with that, *sayeedati*?" "Smoked turkey? Of course." "You are French, no?"

"You cannot be charming with everyone though," my boss had cautioned. "Some women do not like you smiling at them. Some women want you to be polite and courteous and not look into their faces directly, even if they are covered with a *niqab*."

I practiced that same courtesy on Zarin the week after she won that debate of hers—though not exactly for the same reasons: never looking at her in the face directly, while she smoked four Marlboros in my car within half an hour. I knew that if I did look at her directly, she would simply bat her eyelashes and I would foolishly end up giving her whatever she wanted—in this case, more cigarettes.

"No," I said when she held out her hand for the fifth one. "You've had enough."

"Another!"

"I said no, *na*?"

" 'I said no, *na*?' " she mimicked, her voice high and whiny. "Stop being a *muttawa*, Porus. You know I'm stressed."

Stress that may have been caused by anything, from something her *masi* may have done at home to something that may have happened at her school. I knew she would not tell me about it right away, and by now I knew better than to ask her about it directly. Distraction, I had learned, was one way to get Zarin to start talking about herself—even a little bit—and so that's what I began to do.

I began telling her about the great love story between Khusrow, Shirin, and Farhad—a tale that Pappa had told me so often when he was alive that it stayed in my mind, word for word, long after he died. The story, Pappa had told me, represented love in its many forms. Khusrow's jealousy, Farhad's passion, and Shirin's confusion in choosing between the Sassanian king she was destined to marry, and the poor stonecutter who devoted his life to tunneling an entire passageway for her through an impenetrable mountain.

Zarin, as expected, did not seem that impressed. She called Khusrow a Peeping Tom: "What else do you call a man who stares at a woman from behind the bushes while she's bathing?"

Farhad, on the other hand, was a fool. "So some old lady tells him that Shirin is dead and he kills himself because of it?" Zarin said.

"He loved her," I said, willing her to see Farhad the way I saw him. "He spent years tunneling through the great mountain of Beysitoun so that two rivers joined and became one. He accepted Khusrow's challenge and fulfilled it. He had even begun to win over Shirin's heart with his devotion. Imagine what it must have made him feel like to hear that his love, his very reason for living, was gone?"

"*Psh*. I'm sure there were less tiring women out there. He should have spent his energy on them instead of some princess."

"I don't think it mattered to him that she was a princess. And maybe he wasn't doing it for her. Maybe he was doing it to show Khusrow that even an ordinary man could do great things. That he could win over the heart of an unreachable woman by showing her his love and devotion and expecting nothing in return. Why else would Khusrow grow so jealous that he would send over that old woman to plant false rumors about Shirin's death in Farhad's ears? For Farhad, even an accidental glance from Shirin had been enough—a joy, a miracle. He proved how selfless love could be."

She shook her head and laughed. "You are so cheesy."

"Yeah, yeah, I know it sounds cheesy or whatever, but you are undervaluing the strength of emotions. Farhad's emotions gave him strength; he channeled them into great art."

"What was the point, though? His main goal was to get the girl, right? And he didn't. He believed a howling old lady that Shirin was dead and cracked open his skull with a rock." She waved her hand in the air and her mouth curved down. "What a waste of art."

"Love isn't wasted, Zarin!"

But I didn't think she understood. To her, Romeo and Juliet, Layla and Majnun, Shirin and Farhad were myths—"people who did ridiculous things long ago and then died over it. In the name of love, of course."

I told her the story of my own parents—of how my father first met my mother and impressed her by racing after a pickpocket who had snatched her purse on Balaram Street. How Mamma spent day after day next to Pappa in the hospital when he was diagnosed with leukemia, how they prayed together every Friday to ease their troubles.

"Oh, aren't *you* lucky?" Zarin had responded, and then held out her hand again. "Cigarette, Porus. Please! I can feel the nicotine draining out of me as we speak."

The trouble with girls was that they never told you what they were thinking. In Zarin's case, the truth often came out in roundabout ways, eked out in little statements and opinions, usually after she'd smoked a good number of cigarettes.

Even then, when it came to her childhood, Zarin was pretty closed off. "My parents died and I came to live with my aunt and uncle. What else is there to tell?" she had remarked once. However, over the weeks, I learned to tell how angry Zarin was by the number of cigarettes she smoked. One meant Normal Zarin. Slightly calm, slightly grumpy. Two meant Annoyed. Three or more meant Really Annoyed or Going-to-Kill-You Annoyed and most times I didn't even know which.

"You have enough nicotine in your system." I pulled out a can of Vimto from my bag and popped it open. "Here. Have this instead. And maybe, once you're in a better mood, you will tell me why you're acting crankier than usual."

Zarin sighed, but accepted the soda after a moment. She stared out the window—in the direction of an Arab family spread out on a mat under one of those abstract art sculptures that acted as landmarks at the Corniche and on Jeddah roads. Jeddah, with its giant globe and giant gold fist; with monuments of cars bursting out of a block of concrete and four hanging stained-glass lanterns that lit up at night in glowing colors. A city of sudden and surprising art, mostly abstract. Zarin's favorite was a sculpture of a boat made with Arabic calligraphy.

However, that day, I knew she wasn't thinking about sculptures. "Come and pick me up after school," she'd told me over the phone that morning. And, fool that I was, I didn't even think of asking why, although I had to shuffle shifts at work, irritating Hamza so much that he threatened to cut my next paycheck.

"Look, Zarin, you have to tell me what is wrong now. I am in trouble at work because of you."

"You were in trouble before that anyway."

She was referring to the time when a group of boys at the deli had stuck a note on my back with the Arabic word for *dog* written on it in bold letters.

"Kalb." Zarin had pulled off the note when she'd come to the deli for a pack of sliced turkey. *"Kaaf, laam,* and *ba.* See?"

She had tried to teach me the Lahm b'Ajin logo as well— pillars of Arabic letters in green over a background of sunny yellow stitched onto the left pocket of my apron; letters, if one looked at them from a distance, that took on the shape of a farmhouse and a silo. *"Laam, ha, meem, ba, ain, jeem, ya, noon,"* Zarin had said. "Repeat after me; it's not so hard."

The letters had swirled in my mind: the loops and slashes indecipherable from each other, joining to form meaningless squiggles. "I'm glad you told me what this means, Zarin, but I'm pretty sure it was a harmless prank. I don't see why I have to learn this. What is the point?"

"The point? Are you serious? The point is you have to know this stuff! Knowledge is power, Porus. You can control people if you know their language. You can shut them up. I can teach you some swear words too, you know."

She'd spewed out a series of words and phrases that made my ears heat up.

"Thanks, but I don't think my boss would like that very much."

"Oooooh, look at *you* blushing. Is it because I'm a girl?"

Now, inside my car, she sipped a bit of the soda—so delicate and ladylike that I could almost believe she was one.

"Besides, if you were in trouble at work, you shouldn't have come. I didn't force you. I could've called someone else."

Which was exactly what I was afraid of when it came to her: her absolute carelessness about who she went out with. Even when I told her about her GMC-driving boyfriend, about how I'd seen him hanging around Bilal, a boy with a reputation so bad that my boss had banned him from entering our store. "He's a druggie," I'd told her about Bilal. "He has some *wasta* high up with the authorities, which is why he hasn't been arrested yet."

She looked at me now and somehow sensed what I was thinking. "Abdullah isn't a druggie," she insisted, referring to the GMC boy by name for the first time. "He smokes and he is a jerk, but he doesn't do drugs. In any case, I broke up with him, so you shouldn't really worry about it anymore."

On any other day, the news would have had me doing cartwheels. But there was a look on Zarin's face that was so dejected it did little to lighten my heart. In the distance, the twin chimneys of the Jeddah desalination plant smoked plumes of gray into the orange sky. I stared out at them for a long moment, an odd prickling sensation at the back of my throat. "You broke up with him?" I asked finally. "When? I mean, what happened?"

She shrugged. "We were fighting anyway and then I found out that he was talking smack about me behind my back.

When I confronted him about it over the phone last week, he didn't even try to deny it. Got flustered and started harping about how I was *leading him on* and how much money he'd already spent on me, like I owed him or something. The pig."

I said nothing. I had wondered for a long time if they'd gone further than kissing or touching, she and this Abdullah guy. Such things happened here, in hotel rooms, or in cars. "Fast-fast" the boys at the deli called those encounters. Even faster now with Skype and FaceTime added to the mix. "Boys and girls these days have no shame," my boss lamented.

More than that, though, I wondered if she had liked Abdullah. Loved him, even.

"They don't exist in real life," Zarin said after a pause. "Guys like Shirin's Farhad. Guys who do whatever they can unconditionally for some girl. Well, maybe your dad. But he was an exception. In real life, no guy would ever race after pickpockets, dig tunnels through mountains for a girl he barely knows. Heck, he wouldn't even care if she was getting murdered. No one does anything in this world without some kind of expectation."

She rolled down the window farther and tossed the half-finished Vimto out of it. It hit the tarmac with a clang and then rolled across the concrete until it fell over the edge into the water, leaving behind a puddle of grape-colored liquid.

It reminded me of the puddle in Mumbai two years before, that puddle of blood drying in the sun, turning black where the blood congealed. The mugger lying in it, his body broken and then curled like a question mark. I had been the one to deliver the punch that had burst his nose. It was the one time when I turned from ordinary sixteen-year-old Porus Dumasia to one of many in a full-on Mumbai mob.

I had not known the mugger. Yet the man had been both no one to me and *someone*. A complete stranger. A representation of the man who'd accosted my parents on their way back home from the hospital the month before. Who'd demanded Pappa's wallet from him and then sliced into him with a knife before he ripped my mother's gold chain from her throat and kicked her in the ribs. "*Chor!*" someone had yelled from the crowd. "*Chor!*" I'd shouted with the rest of them.

Thief. Thief. Beat. Beat.

The rhythm gained momentum with every kick, every punch. A constable hovered at the sidelines, stick in hand, unsure about intervening at the risk of getting pummeled by our bare, bloody hands. Behind him, a traffic policeman continued working from his position, his shirt bright white in the sun, his whistle gleaming, cheeks puffed as he blew sharp toots and moved his hands, waving cars and mopeds along; for him it was just another day in Mumbai. They said it took two hours after the mob dispersed to move the body away, and that was because it was impeding the six o'clock office rush from walking along the road to return home.

Now, two years later, I took a deep breath. "Maybe you're right," I told Zarin. "What Farhad felt for Shirin was rare. It does take a lot to get that kind of passion from a guy. It happens once in a lifetime maybe, such love. But . . ." I hesitated here, wondering if she would even believe me. ". . . even an ordinary guy can feel that way, Zarin. He may not dig through a mountain for you, but he will do other things. Little things like remembering your birthday, bringing you gifts for no reason, making sure you get the bigger half of a sandwich. It's the little things that turn into big things, anyway. That can change someone absolutely ordinary into someone who you can one day love back."

She stared at me for a long moment. Later, I didn't remember which one of us moved first. All I remembered was the feel of her lips settling on mine like a butterfly, my own pressing back in response. Her fingers brushed the hollow at the base of my throat and I wondered if she could feel how rapid my pulse was. I'd kissed a couple of girls in Mumbai, before Pappa's cancer diagnosis, but I didn't remember feeling like this.

Unwilling to break the kiss, I shifted my mouth to breathe through my nostrils. Our teeth clicked gently. Zarin cradled my jaw with her hands, readjusting our misaligned mouths so quickly that in hindsight I was pretty sure it had been instinctive. I pulled her lower lip into my mouth and sucked carefully.

Maybe that's what scared her. Or maybe she heard something in the distance. The next thing I knew, she was pulling away from me, breathing hard.

"That was a mistake," she said quietly. "It can't happen again."

"Zarin, please, don't do this."

But instead of laughing at me or rolling her eyes, she gave me a sad smile. "That boy you were telling me about before. What if I can't?"

"Can't what?"

"Love him back."

The kiss and her subsequent rejection had frazzled me so much that it took me a moment to remember what she was referring to.

I said nothing in response. The sun dipped into the ocean, staining the sky red. It would be time to take her home soon. Inside my throat was something that felt like a giant ball. I wondered if it was my heart.

Farhan

THE GIRL'S SCENT WAS THE FIRST THING
that hit me—a mix of flowers and sandalwood that cut
through the milky smells of the dead skinned goats hanging
from hooks in the corner of the Lahm b'Ajin deli shop on
Aziziyah, over the heads of the uniformed men working at the
counters—a smell that was fresh and gardenlike and female.
It brushed past me along with the girl, her *abaya* sleeve accidentally slapping against my arm. She was wearing one of
those *abaya*s that had sequins and corded wire designs on the
sleeves and the bottom, the kind that scraped my skin as
she passed by, leaving behind a thin white scratch.

   She stormed into the store, ignoring the surprised looks she
attracted from the people around her, ignoring everyone

except for the tall boy who stood behind the glass display case in his white deli uniform and cap, and flashed him a small middle finger stained yellow with nicotine. If the perfume and her walk hadn't caught my attention already, *that* definitely would have.

"This is for being a busybody and following me to Durrat Al-Arus." She rolled her finger back into a fist. "Have you heard of the MYOB concept, Porus? It means *Mind Your Own Business*."

"Good afternoon to you too," the deli boy said, his voice as cold as the blocks of feta in the display case.

I recognized him now. It was the new Indian they'd hired a few weeks before, the one with the fuzzy eyebrows and the funny name, the one who had thrown Bilal out of the store on the owner's orders.

"And I will not mind my own business," the boy was telling her. "Not when you go around acting like a—"

"Like a what? A man-izer? A slut?" Her laughter possessed the qualities of a newly cut glass pane: clean, crystalline, and sharp around the edges. "He was a guy, Porus. A guy I smoked with. We didn't do anything!"

Her *abaya*, unbuttoned at the front, was nearly slipping off her shoulders. Underneath, she wore white *salwar* bottoms and a navy-blue *kameez* with a Qala Academy logo embroidered in white on the front hip pocket. The flat, starched white *dupatta* was pinned at her shoulders and draped in a V across her chest in the standard schoolgirl style, stopping short of covering the tips of her small, firm breasts.

The deli boy's pale face reddened. "Now you listen to me . . ."

Pathetic. I didn't even have to listen to the guy to figure out the impression he was making on the girl; in spite of his six-foot height and muscle, you could see that he wasn't the one who wore the pants in this relationship, if there was one.

The girl's fingers were pressed to the glass covering the cheese blocks. A narrow, untanned mark bounded her wrist, the imprint of a watch she hadn't bothered to put on that morning. I stared at the creamy strip of skin, wondering if it was the same shade or even lighter in other areas untouched by sunlight.

"May I help you?" the deli boy asked me, his scowl at odds with his polite salesman tone.

"I'm fine, thanks," I said without taking my eyes off the girl. She flashed a glance at me. Eyes dark and acidic. A face that, when I'd managed to get my eyes off her tight little body, looked strangely familiar.

Then it hit me. It was the girl from the bus. The pretty one I'd locked eyes with before my sister came rushing toward me with her silly debate trophy. A girl who had seemed terribly shy then, but did not seem so shy now.

I smiled.

She raised an eyebrow and turned back to the deli boy. "Hurry up," she said. "You know she'll kill me if I'm late."

The boy gave her a tray of finely sliced turkey wrapped in plastic.

I was supposed to pick up something similar for Ammi— slices of roast beef with peppercorn, I think she'd said—but who cared about that now?

I stepped behind the girl, partly blocking her way as she turned to leave, and pulled out a pack of Marlboros from the pocket of my jeans. "Want a ride back home?"

She frowned slightly.

"You can't ride with him!" the deli boy snapped. "You don't even know him!"

Her gaze moved from the cigarettes in my hand to Abba's silver Rolex on my wrist to the muscles on my upper arm.

"Good-bye, Porus." She finally looked into my eyes. "I do know him."

"Really? Who is he?"

She smiled at Porus and said, "Mr. MYOB."

People called me a smooth talker ever since I was a boy. I could charm a smile out of the grouchiest old bag in the room if I put my mind to it; it was a trait I'd inherited from Abba, my mother said. My mother, who I'd always thought was clueless to my father's screwing ways until the day I found her sitting alone in the living room, watching static on the TV.

"Where's Abba?" I'd asked.

"Out," Ammi said. "As always."

"On business again?" I had hesitated before asking the question. I knew Abba's business trips had been done with the week before. He should've been home now. Unless . . .

She'd let out a laugh. High and sharp. "Oh yes. *Business.*"

Abdullah, the only one who knew about the situation, shrugged. "It is what it is, man. I mean, my dad has two wives and he pretends that one of them doesn't exist. At least your dad still comes to see your mom and spends time with you and your sister."

And maybe Abdullah was right—to a point. While Abdullah's mother had turned into a zombie after her husband's second marriage, my mother carried on with life as always, never showing how it affected her, always sleeping with Abba in the same room, in the same bed where Abba had banged other women in the past.

Asma and I were the ones Ammi focused on, Asma more than me, thankfully, being a girl. I was her show pony, the handsome son she liked to bring out to her friends whenever they came over to our house. Sometimes it would be the aunty with the bulldog face. Sometimes the other aunty, who was shyer and prettier and easier to charm. When Ammi asked me to come out and say hi, I knew my real job was to smile the way Abba did, to say things like: "Hello there, Aunty. How are you? Looking as beautiful as ever."

Then they would tell Ammi: "Oh yes, he looks so much like his father." Or "Such a charming young man."

The aunties' daughters were a different story. Ammi's friends' daughters were untouchable, no matter how hot—as I had learned through experience, when I'd started e-mailing Bulldog Aunty's hot daughter in Class X. The stupid girl told her mother about it and Bulldog Aunty wanted to get us engaged. It ended quickly enough though. Ammi dismissed the proposal by saying I was too young to be committed— "They're children! It's much too soon. Let them be friends and write to each other and—"

"Let them *write* to each other?" the aunty said, and for the first time I found her looking at me with an expression other than her usual *such a good boy* one. "What will people say about my daughter if they find out she's been having friendships with boys? Girls from good families don't do such things!"

"Her good little girl was probably the one who contacted Farhan in the first place!" Ammi said irritably after the aunty left. She patted me on the arm. "Forget about her, *beta*. Girls like that only want to entrap rich and handsome boys like you into marriage."

The girl, as expected, had different plans from the mother: *i luv u n wil run away wid u, farhan,* she texted me one day.

I never wrote back—not that I was really worried about entrapment or anything like that. I simply found someone else to e-mail. I almost always did.

Bilal said that girls had this crappy sense of entitlement when it came to being treated "right" by guys. "You have to see how far you can push them," he said. "How much they will put up with before they tell you to back off. You can be really surprised by the lengths a girl will go to when it comes to pleasing a guy she likes."

The girl from the deli, however, was different from the get-go. The way she walked a little ahead of me, as if she didn't care whether I was following her or not—as if she was *sure* I would follow her—the way she stopped in front of my car— exactly my car, even though there was another black Beamer parked on the street outside. She stared at me again with a slight frown.

"Where do you want me to—"

"Not now." Her voice was low and curt. "There's a man watching us from the store. Be an elder brother, Rizvi. Pretend I'm Asma. Open the car and let's get out of here."

She's playing your game, Farhan miyan, I could hear Bilal say in my head.

But the way she said my name, *Rizvi*, like she knew me the way Abdullah knew me. The way she knew enough not to get breathy and excited the way most girls I went out with did— at least not outside the car where anyone could see us. For a second I wondered if she was that chick Abdullah had been telling me about, the one who broke his heart along with his ego.

A slight smile hovered on her lips. "Scared, Rizvi? Maybe I should walk home."

And in that moment neither Abdullah nor Bilal mattered anymore.

"I don't scare easily," I said.

———

Once inside the car though, I didn't ask her where she wanted to go. I got the sense that she didn't really want to go home anyway. Or maybe it was another game of push—testing her limits, seeing what it would take to freak her out.

A few kilometers down the road, the game began. "Corniche first," she said. "It's usually quiet in the afternoons. Good for a smoke."

I said nothing and fiddled with the controls of the radio until

I found a station playing some Calvin Harris remix. I wanted to see if she was like Nadia, if she would get pissed when I didn't reply.

She didn't. Maybe she simply trusted me. Maybe she could see through the game. Maybe both.

I pulled up to a parking spot parallel to the shore on the North Corniche, next to the mosque I used to visit as a boy.

I offered her a cigarette from my pack.

"Excellent." The lighter sparked and the lower half of her face glowed orange for a brief moment. "So what kind of fridge do you have at home, Rizvi?"

Ignoring the question, I plucked a cigarette from the pack and lit up. "I thought you were gonna tell me more about your boyfriend back there."

"Porus?" She rolled her eyes. "He's not my boyfriend."

I shrugged and exhaled cigarette smoke. "If you say so. I wouldn't want to be the proverbial bone in the meat of someone else's relationship."

There was surprise in her laughter, a suggestion of genuine amusement. "Good one, Rizvi," she said. "But you still haven't answered my question. What kind of fridge do you have at home?"

"Before I answer your weird question, I'd like to know your name. Unless"—I leaned closer—"your question is simply an excuse to see where I live."

"Oh don't be ridiculous." The smoke she blew in my direction stung my eyes. I leaned back again. "If we're stopped by a *muttawa* or some other stick-wielding authority figure, we will obviously need to lie and say that we're brother and sister. In which case, my name will be Asma Rizvi, not Zarin Wadia, which I will tell them before they whisk us off to separate areas for interrogation purposes and ask basic questions for which both of us should be able to give the same answers if—"

"Wait," I interrupted, her words finally registering in my brain. "What's your name again?"

She tilted her head sideways and smirked, almost as if she'd expected me to ask the question. "Zarin Wadia."

"Would you by any chance be the same Zarin my friend Abdullah keeps talking about?"

"Maybe I am. Is there a problem?"

There wasn't. Not really. It didn't bother me that this girl had gone out with Abdullah in the past or that she'd unceremoniously dumped him over the phone a couple of weeks before. When it came to girls, Abdullah and I had a deal: sisters were off-limits, but not exes. Especially hot exes. I studied Zarin's face—her short black curls, the smooth hollow at the base of her neck, the unusual paleness of her skin highlighted even more by the delicate blush on her cheeks. What her motives were for going out with me, I did not know. Then again, I realized, I did not care.

"Whirlpool," I said finally. "The fridge I have at home, that is. It's rather big. White, maybe off-white."

"White or off-white? Be specific."

She went through nearly three cigarettes while I shifted uncomfortably behind the wheel and answered questions about my parents, about Asma, about my aunt who gave Hindi tuitions in a building across from the academy's girls' section, even the name of the convenience store across from my apartment complex.

She flicked the last glowing butt out the window. "That's good enough."

I did a quick three-sixty of our surroundings. In the distance, a black speck that was a lone man watching the waves. The afternoon sun beat down on my car. It was a risk. The man could decide to turn around and walk this way anytime. A car could drive up behind us, could slow down to see what we were up to. But then I looked at Zarin's face again and her lips parted slightly, almost as if she'd turned a little breathless.

I leaned in.

Her mouth was smoky and moist. Her hair smelled like sandalwood incense and shampoo. But when my hand crept up her ribs, she pushed away.

Her breath came out hard and fast, though we hadn't kissed for more than a few seconds. There was a look in her eyes that could have been confusion or nerves. Or maybe it was her heart. Pumping like mine from the adrenaline rush of being in danger.

"It's getting late." She withdrew her nails from my wrist; there were little crescents now, right below the place where her *abaya* had brushed my skin. "That turkey's beginning to stink up your car."

Chem was where Bilal first told me about the "relaxant"—a vial of clear liquid that, in the right proportions, loosened your limbs and tied up your tongue, shutting down parts of the brain that didn't need to be active. "Colorless, odorless, tasteless," he said. "A few drops in water or a nice fruity drink. Drops, remember. And don't go mixing it in alcohol either. You want the girl to experience paradise with you, not go there directly."

Days after my date with Zarin, he brought the vial to me outside the classroom, slipping it into the back pocket of my pants while he passed me in the corridor before our lab session. It was the second time I'd bought it from him. "Don't sit on it," he said. "That's about a thousand riyals in your pocket."

Bilal had taken the money in advance. The price had spiked slightly since the Chowdhury girl. I never knew where he got his stuff from. Friends in high places, he always told me when I asked. Friends in high, high places.

"Thanks, man." I kept my voice as low as he did. "See you at lunch."

The corridor was empty, but we always talked like this as an extra precaution. As the bell for the third period rang, I opened the door to the lab and made my way to the desk at the very back of the room, next to a cabinet full of dusty beakers and old lab manuals. I glanced around quickly; apart from the lab assistant who was busy setting up things at the front of the room, as usual, I was the only one there. Thanks to the head boy prep the principal subjected me to every other week for some school event or another, second periods on those Mondays were always half free—or at least I never went back to them once my fifteen-minute session with Siddiqui ended.

I gently removed the vial from my pocket and transferred it to a secure little pouch in my backpack. About a minute later, the lab began filling up. Abdullah tossed his textbook and lab manual on our shared desk, rattling the empty test tubes in their stand.

"Hey," he said in a cool voice.

"Hey," I said.

Our conversation the weekend before had not gone very well, especially when he found out about me and Zarin. We hadn't spoken since then, which was why I was surprised when he sat down next to me and asked: "Are you seeing her again?"

I looked at him carefully. "Yeah. This Thursday, in fact."

He gave me a tight smile. "Good luck."

I felt a slight twinge of guilt, but then pushed it away. We had an understanding about these things, I reminded myself. Abdullah knew that. I thought back to my kiss with Zarin last week. Her breathlessness. Those small, surprisingly strong fingers gripping my arms. *That turkey's beginning to stink up your car.* The words had stayed in my head, teasing, tantalizing, taunting all night long, showing up when I least expected them to, like right now. My fingers tightened around the textbook for a split second, the knuckles pink and white. The way I wanted her skin to be when I was done with her. I edged my pack under the seat with the tip of my sneaker, careful so it did not touch any of the chair's legs.

"Old Rawoof failed half of XII 2 with the viva questions first period," Abdullah said after a minute. "We can't expect anything less from Dawood Madam, she's in high board-exam-prep mode. I think I'm losing my mind, man! And why does it smell like farts around here?"

The air in the chem lab didn't smell any different from the usual: a combination of ink, sweat, and sulfur. But I knew what Abdullah was up to. Angry though he may have been with me initially, this was his way of giving me the green light, of saying that we were cool again and that he didn't care what I did anymore, ex-girlfriend or not. I did not know what exactly had caused his change of heart. Maybe he was tired of our cold war. Or maybe he simply wanted to remain in the loop about what would happen next with Zarin and find out if I would succeed where he had failed. We were competitive in that way, Abdullah and I. Especially when it came to girls.

I smirked for a split second and then put on another face—the one that looked like I was seconds from throwing up. "Probably the essence of old Rawoof," I said. "Beans and puke."

And then Abdullah and I stuck our hands under our armpits and made farting sounds over and over until some of the other guys joined in, until the whole class forgot we had oral exams and started chanting, "Gas! Gas! Gas! Gas!"—ignoring the pathetic excuse for a lab assistant—until Dawood Madam entered the room and yelled at us to shut up.

BLOOD

Zarin

"ZARIN, I'VE BEEN MEANING TO ASK YOU something," Porus said a couple of days after our fight at the deli. It was the sort of thing he usually did when we had a disagreement or a blowup—asking random questions or making small talk to ease the tension simmering between us.

"Okay," I said warily. "What did you want to know?"

"I am wondering if you are—wait, no," he began, suddenly switching to English. "I am wondering if there was something you've wanted desperately. Something you've waited for your whole life."

I could tell that he was still flustered. For some reason, Porus always started speaking in English around me when he was nervous, a quirk that, if I was being honest with myself, I found quite adorable.

"Growing up and moving out of Masi's house," I said.

"I know that. I am meaning . . . apart from that."

To be happy. The answer that came to my mind was simple. Raw. Too raw to relate to another person, let alone someone as attuned to my emotions as Porus.

"What else is there to look forward to?" I replied.

Which pretty much ended that conversation.

Maybe I should have been kinder. Maybe I should have just told him he had onion breath and changed the entire topic of conversation to Tic Tacs and Juicy Fruit. But I'd just received an e-mail from Farhan Rizvi that morning and hadn't been thinking too clearly.

And it would have been a lie anyway. Porus's breath wasn't bad. I'd never found myself shrinking away from him for that particular reason, even though his uniform (and his car) did occasionally smell of meat and feta cheese. Porus wasn't that bad looking for a guy. He was tall and broad-shouldered, his deep voice often making him sound older than he really was. I'd seen a few female customers staring at him in the deli from time to time, blushing when he smiled at them, though he seemed fairly oblivious to their interest. Even his shaggy eyebrows added to his appeal.

The reality was that Porus was nice. Too nice for the likes

of me. Porus may have claimed to like me more than any other girl he'd known, but if his mother asked him to stop dating me (which, considering the things Masi had told her about me, was extremely likely), he would, like the good Parsi boy that he was. This wouldn't be unusual. I'd seen it happen several times in Mumbai, to other girls in Cama colony, and had sworn I wouldn't be one of them.

As for the kiss? Simple. It was an anomaly. A heat-of-the-moment thing. It didn't matter how soft his lips had felt or how perfectly they had fit against mine, I told myself firmly. It would have been foolish to think otherwise.

Abdullah once told me that Saudi society didn't permit guys and girls to meet up alone because it was impossible for the relationship to remain platonic. "Think about it," he'd said. "Our bodies are engineered for it. It's like putting a key and a lock next to each other and not expecting someone to try and see how they fit."

At times like this I wished I had a girl for a friend instead of boys trying to jump my bones or Porus with his puppy-eyed devotion. Sometimes I even thought about my mother and wished she could be here to give me advice, even though thinking about her cramped up my insides. There were nights when I would see the flash of something silver in my dreams, shadows around me, long and thin like the legs of a stork, the feel of something warm and sticky trickling over my lips.

Without even understanding why, I knew the dreams had to do with my mother. Not a knife, I would tell myself, whenever I woke up from these dreams, my clothes sticking to my back, my body twisted at that angle I'd always associated with nightmares. Maybe it was the flash of a stainless-steel plate from which she may have fed me as a small girl. And maybe the liquid wasn't blood, but warm milk that I'd shut my mouth to. To this day, I could not and would not drink milk, despite Masi's rages and beatings.

The only other person I'd probably have asked any boy-related questions was Asfiya, the girl I used to sit with when I smoked on the water tank, even though we had never really talked much when we were up there. I'd overheard the teachers saying that Asfiya got engaged after graduation. Right at the age of seventeen to a guy she had seen once, over Skype. "Everything happens with technology these days, but that is the way arranged marriages still work," Khan Madam had told our Physics teacher. "Marriage comes first. Love, if any, grows later and increases with time."

I wondered if the opposite was true for love marriages. If the love in those cases simply decreased instead of growing. Or was it marriage that created the problem, that made love lose its luster, the way it seemed to have for my aunt and uncle, who called each other darling or *jaanu* or sweetheart, but always with caution, sometimes even with a trace of venom?

With Farhan Rizvi, however, things were different. For one: I wasn't in love with him, even though he was the first guy I'd ever had a real crush on. A guy whose kiss temporarily sent every other guy I'd known flying out of my head. Except for the very first time in his car, when I unwittingly compared the kiss to the one I'd shared with Porus. It had confused me so much that I pulled away from him after a few seconds. I didn't know what was going on with me. I could have resolved everything by telling Porus: *Yes, it's Rizvi. He's the one I was waiting for.*

But it would have been a lie. And Porus wouldn't have understood anyway. "You don't really know what you're doing," he told me in a rare fit of temper the day after I first went out with Rizvi. "You think you're so smart. That you know everything. But you don't, Zarin. You can't always be in control. I've seen guys like your head boy Rizvi. I know what they're like. They go out with different girls every week. He'll use you and toss you out like everyone else."

"Have you ever considered that those stories may be rumors?" I asked angrily. "That they may have no basis in fact? Look, Porus, if you're still angry about that kiss we had—"

"I'm not talking about that." He gave me a disgusted look. "I'm trying to tell you that there's no smoke without fire. I did not like your ex-boyfriend, but at least *that* guy had some scruples. Farhan Rizvi has none."

"You don't even know him!"

"And *you* don't know how he was watching you at the deli. He's not a good guy. Mark my words on this."

How was he watching me? I would have asked if he hadn't been so angry. Was it the way he had watched me at the fair all those years ago? Moments before head girl Durrani came waltzing in? The thought stirred me more than I would have liked to admit.

"No way," Rizvi said, when I told him about the incident at the fair. "I would have remembered you for sure."

It was a line, I knew. One he probably fed every other girl. I dealt with it by taking a drag of my cigarette and blowing smoke in his face. "That'll teach you to forget me," I said as he coughed.

My anger dissipated when I watched his eyes darken, the pupils dilating ever so slightly. A smile hovered on his face before he launched himself at me, the kisses deep and rough, the way I liked them. It scared me—this sexual pull he seemed to have on me—how it grew harder and harder to deny him from doing things that I would never have allowed Abdullah or any other guy to do.

"Stop!" I gasped out. I tugged at his fingers, removing them from where they'd been rubbing up against my underwear. "This is . . . It's our second date, Farhan."

His eyes hardened for a split second, but it happened so fast that I thought it was my imagination. He shook his head and laughed. "Chill, Zarin. You're like a little cat at times. So skittish and ready to pounce. You need to relax a little more."

Days later, there was a new rumor flying in school about him. About how he had gotten a Class IX girl pregnant several months before and how she'd had to be flown to India to get an abortion. The news had come from Mishal, who claimed to have read it on an online blog and then spread it across the classroom before the girl's cousin, Maha Chowdhury, had any chance to do damage control. "It was a basic gallbladder operation!" she sputtered at Mishal. "You know how bad Jeddah water is! It gives you stones!"

"It g-gives y-you s-s-stones!" Mishal had mimicked back, which made most of her friends burst out laughing. "If it was that *basic*, it would've been cheaper to have the operation done here in Jeddah. Why fly to India for it?" The rest of the girls either watched in silence or went on with eating their lunch. No one interfered. It was the way things worked at Qala Academy, or at least in our classroom, when Mishal decided to sink her claws into someone.

"Stop it, Mishal," I'd said when Maha burst into tears. I also told Mishal in no uncertain terms what she could do with herself and her rumors.

It was perhaps Mishal's good fortune and my bad one that Khan Madam entered the class at that very moment to fetch her missing spectacles and heard my last sentence. I was made to kneel outside the classroom for the rest of the day with my arms in the air for "talking like a foul-mouthed ruffian!"

The trouble with rumors was that they had the tendency to stick. To coat over your logic like tea stains on teeth. What was even more troublesome was that there had been times in the past when they turned out to be accurate. Like the time Mishal told everyone about Chandni Chillarwalla running away from home to avoid getting engaged to a guy her parents wanted her to marry. Chandni herself confirmed the rumor a year later in a truth or dare game during a free period. The one about the head girl's multiple boyfriends also appeared to be true. I had seen it for myself, long before, when I was in Class IX—Nadia slipping away from the line of girls trooping in through the school gates and into a strange car. Even the story Mishal had spread about me going out with that Syrian guy way back when had been true, though I never knew where she'd gotten that info from.

Of course, rumors often had a way of floating into the boys' section. Here, they got screwed up to the point of ridiculousness. For instance, according to Farhan Rizvi, Chandni Chillarwalla did not run away to her friend's house, but tried to elope with a secret boyfriend. Head girl Durrani not only had multiple boyfriends, but had also participated in a sex tape with a creepy guy from Qala Academy. As for me? I had gone out with two Syrian guys at the same time. And my cigarettes contained weed, not tobacco.

I laughed when Rizvi told me about this on our third date—in his e-mail he'd called it *a late picnic lunch*, which had turned out to be a large tray of barbecued chicken and French fries inside his car at the old Hanoody warehouse near Porus's apartment building.

"Who told you this?" I tossed a chicken bone back into the tray. "I mean, weed? Seriously?"

Rizvi simply shrugged in response and laughed. His lips glistened with grease from the chicken. A bit of barbecue sauce clung to the edge of his mouth. If it had been Abdullah, I would have maybe raised a finger, playfully flicked the reddish-brown speck from the spot and put it on my tongue. With Rizvi, however, I didn't. Something in his expression warned me against it, or maybe it was the rumors again, crawling insectlike under my skin.

To distract myself, I looked around the barren, sandy area that made up the warehouse parking lot. Cigarette butts littered the place, along with old soda cans and aluminum foil wadded up in shining wrinkled balls. Masi, who used and reused aluminum foil at home and covered her stove with it, would have cursed at the waste.

Thoughts of my aunt led to thoughts of my uncle, who had, over the past week or so, tried to get me to confide in him.

"He's a nice boy, no, that Porus?" Masa had asked. "A good hard worker."

"Yeah, I guess he works hard."

"A nice, nice boy. Good. Decent. You don't find boys like that these days."

I shrugged, wondering where this was leading. "Maybe."

He cleared his throat. "Do you have something you want to tell me, Zarin, *dikra*?"

The Boyfriend Question. I knew it from the way his Adam's apple moved in his throat, the gentle clicking sound he made with his mouth closed.

"No, Rusi Masa." I had looked right into his eyes as I said it. "I don't."

It had been the truth. Abdullah and I were done, and as tipsy as Rizvi's kisses may have made me, we'd only been on two dates so far. As for Porus . . . I shook my head. I couldn't think of him now. I wouldn't.

I watched Rizvi rip into the last chicken leg in the tray, sucking at the gray bone once the meat was gone until I could see the dark marrow in its center. Something about the image stirred an old memory I had of him, making the words slip out before I could stop them.

"I saw you here with a girl once," I said. "She was crying."

His shoulders—those broad shoulders that I'd admired as a fourteen-year-old—tightened for a brief moment. He tossed the bone back on the tray. "Breakups can be tough at times," he said. "What can you do?"

"Yeah," I said. "What can you do?"

He smiled at me and I smiled back, but there was a slight shift in the air, a tension that had not been there before. I wondered if the girl had been the one Mishal had been telling everyone about: Maha Chowdhury's pregnant cousin.

My skin prickled and for a second I was tempted to ask him to drive me home. I shook my head, irritated by this sudden rush of nerves.

"Thanks for the lunch." I blotted the grease from my lips with a paper napkin. "It was really good, even though the chicken does feel like lead in my stomach," I said, trying to lighten the mood.

He stared at me for a moment, and that's when I saw it again: that quick flash of ice in his eyes, the slightest narrowing of his lips before he smiled.

"You're welcome. Do you want a drink? I'm thirsty after eating this food." He turned around and rummaged inside his backpack. A rustle of tins and paper before I heard the familiar hiss of a soda can being opened.

He handed me the Vimto. "You said you liked this one, right?" He removed another can for himself and popped it open. He grinned at me and a dimple formed deep in his left cheek. "Will be a good palate cleanser. Hopefully we both don't taste too much like chicken."

I glanced at the clock on the dashboard: 3 p.m. I had told Masi that I would be held up by debate practice today; I had to be back home in half an hour. "Fine," I relented. "But *one* drink."

There were a few things I remembered clearly after that. The taste of the grape soda. Fizzy, sickly sweet, warmed by the sun. The feel of his hand, hot with grease, sliding up my *salwar*-clad thigh. "It's okay, Zarin," he whispered. "Relax."

I was dreaming of the man again. Tossing me high into the air. *Majhi mulgi*, he said in Marathi. *My girl.*

"Where did you hear this phrase?" Masa had asked when I'd asked him for the meaning one day.

"Nowhere," I'd said.

As always, the man was a shadow, leaning over me at first, draping me in darkness until he threw me up, high, high, high, so high I could almost touch the glowing bulb overhead and the moths dancing around it. *Touch it*, he coaxed. *Go on, touch the light.*

I reached out with a hand.

In the background, a woman screamed. *Stop it. Stop it.* Was it Masi? I could not tell.

The leather inside the car burned hot from lying too long in the Jeddah sun. My head pounded and I tried to move. But my limbs felt like four bags of wet cement. Something scraped against my knee.

A curse and then the shadowy man turned into a boy with shining golden eyes.

I saw the priest at our fire temple.

Daily prayer, he said, was not the only requirement for crossing the Chinvat Bridge successfully. Zoroastrians also had to live a life that embodied three important precepts: *humata*, *hukta*, and *huvareshta*.

Humata: good thoughts. For Masi: hypocrite. For Masa: spineless. For Porus: nagging.

Hukta: good words. For Masi: "Kindly do me a favor and buzz off." For Masa: "Quit the concerned-parent act." For Porus: "Find someone else to pester, Mr. High-and-Mighty."

Huvareshta: good deeds. I saw Masi searching for the *malido* in the fridge—the *malido* I had intentionally fed the crows by the kitchen window. I mimicked Masi's screechy falsetto in front of Masa, watching him grow scarlet with rage. I

blew cigarette smoke into Porus's face and laughed when he
coughed.

I saw the boy with the golden eyes again. His hand inched up
my bare knee, fiddled with the loop of my underwear.

Then light burst through: a thousand brilliant bits of glass.
Air washed over my face: warm and smoky, with specks of
sand.

Shadows struggled above. When they dispersed, there was
blood on the face of the golden-eyed boy. I wondered if he was
a vampire, and the silly thought made me want to laugh. Laugh,
laugh, and laugh until I could scream, scream, and scream.

Cloth slid over my skin once more, followed by the sound
of metal buttons clicking, up to my throat. A voice whispered
in my ear, as soft as flowers: "He didn't hurt you, did he?"

I don't know, I wanted to say.

But my tongue was tied and I could not whisper back.

Porus

I KNEW SOMETHING WAS WRONG THE moment I felt the phone vibrate in my pocket. Call it gut instinct. Or maybe it was the knot I'd been carrying around in my stomach ever since the day Zarin had kissed me and then started dating Farhan Rizvi. Instead of ignoring the instrument the way I normally would have while working, I put down the cardboard box I was holding and picked up.

"Hello? Porus?" A familiar voice, brusque and anxious. Zarin's aunt. "Is Zarin there with you?"

"No, Khorshed Aunty. I'm at work. I haven't seen her this afternoon." I flattened my back to the wall next to the loading dock outside the deli and pressed the phone to my ear, ignoring Ali, who was glaring at me for leaving my box in the truck. I raised a finger: *one minute*. Ali rolled his eyes and nudged me hard with an elbow on his way back inside.

"She hasn't come home. She said she had debate practice, but that should have been over an hour ago. She isn't even picking up her phone."

I bit my lip. "Debate practice" had been Zarin's excuse for sneaking out on dates with Abdullah in the past. I guessed she was using the same MO with Rizvi.

"She wouldn't notice if I was gone," Zarin had said of her *masi*. "There have been times when I've come home and found her so drugged up from her pills that she barely knew I was there. She'd wake up and start asking me what I thought of the lunch she'd cooked up. Like I could even think of eating after seeing her like that."

"It must be the buses. Sometimes they can b-be late," I stammered now, hoping Khorshed Aunty wouldn't question my lie. The buses were, to my knowledge, never late. And boy or no boy, Zarin had never taken this long to get home before.

At the other end of the line, there was a barely suppressed sob. "Could you . . . could you go and check on her. I'm so sorry to bother you like this, dear, but Rusi is not picking up his phone at the office . . . I . . . I didn't know who else to call."

As badly as this woman had treated Zarin, I couldn't help but feel sorry for her now. I was also worried. In India, as terrible as the red tape could be at times, we could have tried calling the police, tried filing a missing person's report. In Saudi Arabia, things were different. Neither of us knew enough Arabic to communicate with the authorities. And if the religious police got involved, there was no saying what would happen.

Zarin liked to talk about them dismissively, telling me that nothing would go wrong, that Jeddah wasn't as heavily regulated as the capital city, Riyadh, where the Hai'a was headquartered. But I'd heard stories at the deli about surprise raids at homes over here, based on a tip about alcohol or drugs. I'd also read articles online about young Saudi and expat couples getting arrested at coffee shops for "acting suspiciously" and being taken for interrogation to the Hai'a office in Jeddah. In extreme cases, involving adultery, the couple was imprisoned or sentenced to multiple lashings. Zarin knew a little Arabic, but not enough to explain herself in a scenario like this. What if they misunderstood her? Or what if they didn't ask for any explanation and simply assumed the worst? As much as I despised Rizvi, there was no way I wanted to see Zarin get into trouble with the authorities for going out with him.

"Leave everything to me, Aunty." The words settled heavily in my gut. "I'll find her. I promise."

I hung up and instantly dialed Zarin's number. A couple of rings later, it went to voice mail.

I swore out loud, unable to think of how else I could reach her. I closed my eyes and tried to remember everything she'd ever told me about Farhan Rizvi, everything I'd heard from the boys at the deli. My mind switched over to the first time I'd ever seen the guy. Sunglasses. Crying girl. Black car. Warehouse.

I shot a glance at Ali, who was unloading the final box of Swiss cheese from the delivery truck. "I have to go," I told him.

"What?" Ali's face was red with effort. "You can't ditch work like that! The boss will have your hide."

"It's an emergency. My mother." The lie fell easily from my lips, eliminating the need to tell him anything else. "I really need to go. I'll take your next shift, I promise."

Ali frowned and opened his mouth as if to say something.

I didn't wait to find out what it was.

On a normal day, it would have taken me twelve minutes to get to the warehouse. Today, it took nine. If I hadn't been contemplating the various horrific scenarios I could possibly find Zarin in, I would have cheered over the fact that my car hadn't given me an ounce of trouble the entire ride.

Outside the car, the sun burned. If I closed my eyes, I knew it would turn red against my eyelids. I squinted in the light glinting against a shard of glass near the rusted warehouse gates and spotted a black car in the distance, amid the dusty buildings.

I burst out, my sneakers pounding the tarmac, and paused a few feet away, taking in the scene. A shadow moved in the back seat of the black car. Rizvi. He raised his hand and brought it down, as if hitting something. Someone. I didn't try opening the door. I didn't even think before reaching down to pick up a rock from the debris surrounding the building and smashing it through his window.

What had he done to her?

How far had he gone?

I didn't know. Couldn't be sure. After breaking Rizvi's window and then his nose, I didn't even have the time to check Zarin for bruises. To my surprise, Rizvi didn't try to fight back. He held on to his broken septum and whimpered.

If it hadn't been for the green-and-white police car I'd seen a few blocks from the warehouse—a restless *shurta* who seemed keen on issuing multiple parking tickets that afternoon—I knew I would have killed Rizvi.

I pulled Zarin's clothes back into place and buttoned her *abaya* shut before carrying her to my car. She was heavy for someone so small. Or maybe it was the effects of whatever drug he'd given her. I carefully laid her on the back seat of my car. I was close enough to smell barbecued chicken and, under that, a hint of Pond's powder. I tried to hold on to that faint floral fragrance, to the first time I'd smelled it as a boy, and then the other time, the week before, when she'd buried her fingers in my hair and fused her lips with mine.

"Shh," I whispered when she made a noise. "You're safe. You're safe now."

There was no way I could take her home like this. If I'd lived alone, I could have taken her back to my apartment, but I lived with my mother and she would be there and there was no way I could explain anything to her without the news getting back to Zarin's family. The best I could do was drive around and wait for the effects of the drug to wear off.

At the traffic signal a few blocks from the warehouse, I saw the cop again, this time in the car right next to mine. I kept facing forward. The air was sour and rippled with heat, blurring the road and cars ahead of me. My clothes stuck to my back. Every breath felt like I was inhaling sweat. My right eye twitched—a trait Mamma attributed to nerves, Pappa to bad luck or danger. I gritted my teeth. Now wasn't the time to think of cursed lemons or black cats. Casually, I glanced sideways. The *shurta* was staring at something on his cell phone. Then, as if sensing my gaze, he looked up and nodded.

I nodded back and turned to face the traffic lights again. A drop of sweat inched down my temple and slid toward my ear.

It took every bit of my willpower not to gun the engine when the light turned green, to look left and then right and gradually release the brakes, moving forward, merging with the traffic like I was a normal teenage guy headed back home from school or work and not carrying a drowsy girl in the back seat of my car.

A few minutes in, Zarin began stirring in the back. "Porus?" Her voice was hoarse. "Is it you? Am I in your car?"

"Yeah, it's me. Don't . . . don't sit up yet." I drove around a few more blocks before finally pulling into a parking spot at a quiet apartment building. When I opened the back passenger door, she was still lying on the cloth-covered seats, her eyes closed. It was the first time she'd willingly complied with any of my instructions. Or maybe she was too tired to fight.

There was enough room for me to slip in, to carefully raise her head and place it in my lap. I stroked her sweaty forehead. "Are you all right? Did he hurt you?"

"I . . . I don't know," she said after a pause. "I was so out of it. I am so out of it now."

"I need to take you back home." I kept my voice low, gentle. "Your aunt was the one who called me about you missing. She is really worried."

Groaning, Zarin finally began rising up. I helped her into

a sitting position. In my arms she felt birdlike. Breakable. Perhaps she was. Perhaps she always had been and I had foolishly allowed myself to be thrown off by her sharp words and bravado.

"She'll be furious. She'll turn into an evil Hindi-film stepmother and tell me to take my blackened face back to the gutter where it belongs. She'll probably be right. You should have let me die, Porus. Because if we go home, she's going to kill me."

"Hush," I said, even though her words settled uneasily in my belly. "Stop saying such things." I belted her into the front seat. "We're going home."

Khorshed Aunty's reaction, however, ended up being closer to what Zarin had predicted. Seconds after verifying that both of us were still standing, her sharp little eyes narrowed in on other things—Zarin's oddly swaying gait, the rip at the hem of her *abaya*. Her nose wrinkled and I knew she could smell the grease from the chicken as well.

"Where were you?" Her voice was high and thin. "Where were you, worthless girl? Who did you blacken your face with?"

In other circumstances, I might have laughed at how accurately Zarin had predicted her *masi*'s reaction and her words.

Unfortunately, there was nothing funny about the way I had found Rizvi hovering over her semiconscious body, nothing funny about what was happening now, in Zarin's own house, where instead of checking her to see if she was okay, her own aunt looked like she was about to hit her.

Outside the window, the sky was turning a reddish brown, a shade darker than the housecoat Khorshed Aunty was now wearing, a color that I knew would coat the apartment buildings, the trees, and the cars in shades of rust.

It was the shade that colored Rusi Uncle's shiny bald head and narrow cheeks when he entered the apartment several minutes later, filling in the craters left by smallpox, giving the illusion of smoothness. "Khorshed," he said breathlessly. "I was in a meeting. I left as soon as—"

"Finally," she interrupted, and then laughed, high and strange. "Finally the lord of Lahm b'Ajin shows up at his humble abode."

"I'm sorry, but—"

"Now." She turned sideways and, for the first time, Rusi Uncle seemed to notice that he had an audience. He glanced quickly at me and then at Zarin, who was still wearing her *abaya* and scarf and clutching her schoolbag.

"Now maybe you will tell the truth." Khorshed Aunty pointed at her husband, but kept her eyes on me. "Tell him! Tell him where you've been this whole time!"

Rusi Uncle fumbled with the bag in his hands before placing it on the sofa. "Khorshed, what is——"

"Ask him!" Khorshed Aunty shouted. A vein protruded from her temple and the side of her neck. "Ask this foolish boy how long it took him to bring her here after I called! Not that you would care, would you, Rusi? Busy, busy, always busy. So busy that you don't even care that your own niece hasn't come back home by the time she was supposed to."

"Aunty, I was at work," I pleaded. "I couldn't leave for another half hour, forty-five minutes. When I reached the school she was waiting there with two other girls. The bus was late and——"

"Rubbish! The buses are always idling there! If you have to lie, at least do it properly."

A cool draft of air breezed through my sticky shirt before the AC made a soft clicking noise and then shut off.

My hands fisted and for the first time I felt the scrapes on them. Fresh ones, some of them still red. I did not even remember how they had come about. Did not recall the shards of glass slicing my skin open after I threw the rock through Rizvi's window and reached in with my arm to unlock the door. I had never even felt the pain. Zarin drew a curve in the carpet with her toe. Her hands shook the way I'd seen them before when she was craving a cigarette. A lump lodged in my throat.

"What happened to your hands?" Rusi Uncle's gaze had moved from Zarin to me. His voice was full of suspicion.

"Accident at work. Happens sometimes."

Next to me, I could feel Zarin shaking even more, even though she didn't speak and kept her gaze lowered to the floor.

Rusi Uncle took a step toward her. "Zarin, *dikra*, what's wrong? Come on, you can tell Rusi Masa."

Maybe she would have if it had been just him. I'd always gotten the sense that Zarin's relationship with her uncle would have been a lot better had it not been for the man's wife.

Zarin stepped back, stumbled. I wrapped an arm around her out of instinct. The air around us smelled of barbecue sauce and sweat.

"Bathroom," Zarin whispered. It was the first time she had spoken since we'd stepped into the house fifteen minutes before. She slipped out from under my arm and for a few seconds I continued standing there, clutching air.

"Why are you still wearing your *abaya*?" Khorshed Aunty shouted. "Hang it up in the cupboard, at least! And why are you taking your bag with you?"

Zarin looked back once and then dropped her bag in the corridor outside the bathroom with a thud. Seconds later, a strip of light peered from under the door, followed by the whir of the exhaust fan. I frowned, feeling anxiety creep in, the same sort that had congealed in my belly when her aunt first called me, but this time stronger, so strong that it felt like a stone.

Khorshed Aunty's nails dug into my arm. "My niece stumbled out of your car like a drug addict and you tell me that she was at debate practice! Do you think I'm a fool? Do you think I did not notice the tear in her *abaya*?"

I resisted the urge to throw her off. It suddenly began to make perfect sense to me why Zarin hated this woman so much. *Don't you care?* I wanted to shout. *Don't you care that she's in pain?*

"I swear to God, Aunty, she's okay," I said tightly. "She probably snagged it on something sharp and—"

"Lies!" The blood drained from Khorshed Aunty's lips. "Lies you both are telling me!"

But then Rusi Uncle stepped up, carefully placed his hands on his wife's shoulders, and pressed his thumbs into the flesh there. He murmured softly into her ear. Over and over, until her grip on my arm loosened. He pulled her arms back to her sides and gently rubbed. It wasn't an unusual action; I remembered my father doing the same thing for my mother when she was angry, but the resignation on Rusi Uncle's face told me that he had done this more times than he would have liked to.

Finally, he looked up at me. "If anything has happened to

our niece, we have the right to know. You must tell us the truth, Porus. Was Zarin at debate practice?"

His voice was so kind that for a moment I faltered, almost telling him everything that I had seen. But then I remembered Zarin's face and how terrified she had been.

"Yes," I said. "Of course she was."

His eyes hardened at my reply and for a second I thought he would hit me. But he continued stroking his wife's trembling hands. "Don't lie to me. Where was she, really? With a boy? You must tell the truth now, Porus."

"I am telling the truth," I insisted, wishing I was half as strong as my father when it came to convincing people. I wanted to close my eyes and seek out Pappa's presence the way I did some mornings while praying before the altar in our apartment's small kitchen. Pappa would know what to do, would know exactly what to say. I glanced quickly at the bathroom door. If Zarin and I had been alone, I would have knocked, hammered on it until she came out or let me in. But here, in front of her aunt and uncle, things felt different. I was no longer a friend but a stranger, intruding on a family's private embarrassment. I wondered if Zarin too felt this way, like a perpetual intruder between this man, this woman, and their dysfunctional relationship.

I caught Rusi Uncle's face, reflected in the window. When my eyes met his, he looked away.

"You can go now," Rusi Uncle told me in a cold voice. He made sure he didn't look at me again. "Thank you for bringing Zarin home."

I hesitated. "Uncle, I—"

"Go, Porus." The bite in his voice made me step back. "Just go."

Zarin

THERE WAS NO BLOOD. NOT THE WAY there was supposed to be if you were a virgin. I'd heard whispers at school that some girls didn't bleed, didn't even realize something had happened to them until they were a few weeks in, like Maha Chowdhury's cousin.

My period, which came a couple of days later, eventually proved that nothing had happened with Rizvi on that day, nothing at least that would have me withdrawing from school with the excuse of a swollen belly. But something had. Something that made me wake up at night, sweating and sick, vomiting the dinner I'd eaten hours before.

"Stomach flu," Dr. Thomas said, when Masa took me to see him. "A pretty bad one, but nothing serious. It could have been something she ate outside."

But it was more than a bug and both Masa and Masi knew this.

"What happened that day?" Masi kept asking me, over and over again. "Was it a boy? Tell me!"

"Nothing happened!" I kept telling her in response. "I was sick, okay?"

I braced myself for her blows—a favorite tactic of hers to coax the truth out of me—but to my surprise, Masi did not raise her hand. It was almost as if she was afraid to touch me now, as if she could somehow sense the invisible stain that Rizvi had left on my skin.

"I tried," I heard her telling Masa over the phone. "I tried so hard, Rusi, but she won't tell me anything."

When Masa came home that evening, he found me sitting on my bed, my Physics textbook on my lap.

"Zarin." Masa started to reach out for me, but his hand paused when I inched away from his touch. "Zarin, *dikra*, will you please tell me what's going on?"

"N-nothing," I said, hating the way my voice shook in front of him. "I'm s-studying. I have my Physics mock exam on Wednesday."

"Zarin, we are worried about you . . . You aren't acting like yourself."

"I'm fine," I insisted. "It's the flu."

Silence filled the room.

"Maybe you will tell me later," he said after a pause. His voice was so quiet that I wasn't sure if he was speaking to himself or to me. "You will tell me later, won't you?"

"There's nothing to tell." I stared at the words in the book, the letters blurring together, until I finally heard his receding footsteps. My stomach churned and for a second I was afraid I would throw up again. I tossed the book aside and closed my eyes.

What did he want me to say? That I had had a crush on a boy who later tried to rape me? That I'd ignored Porus's warnings, the rumors, and worst, my own instincts?

Where did he touch you? I could imagine the religious police asking. *With what body part?* Rizvi would deny everything, or worse, hire a lawyer who would point out that I was the one who had initiated things that first time at the deli. That everything that had happened afterward was consensual, even though I only wanted to kiss Rizvi (a thought that now made me want to hurl).

Who do you think they will believe? a voice that sounded like Mishal Al-Abdulaziz's taunted in my head. *A good-looking all-rounder who is head boy at his school, or a female who everyone thinks is a few rungs short of juvenile delinquency?*

"You are girls," I remembered the Physics teacher announcing one day when we were especially rowdy in class. "You can't get away with acting like boys."

In the days that followed, Masa and Masi did not approach me again. They watched me from a distance, evading my gaze when I looked at them, whispering furiously whenever I exited a room: *Did she tell you what happened that day?* or *Was she screaming in her sleep again?*

It reminded me of the time I first moved to Cama colony after my mother's death, when I sat for days in one corner of my aunt and uncle's apartment after the funeral. "She doesn't remember?" Masi had sounded furious. "How can she not remember?"—and I knew that they were talking about the way my mother had died and how they found me next to her, covered in blood. They said I spoke to no one afterward and that I hadn't even cried.

At the Tower of Silence in Mumbai, where the funeral had been held, I could not look at my mother's face. The pallbearers brought in a dog on a leash, a skinny beast covered with white fur and with two brown spots over its eyes. The dog sniffed my mother's toes and then her ankles, testing for a sign, any sign that she might still be alive. But she wasn't and that was confirmed in the prayers that the masked priests recited, loud words that were meant to stitch the skin over the wound of her earthly sins.

Post-Rizvi, nightmares—especially those involving my mother—had become more frequent. In my dreams, my mother hummed softly the way she had on my fourth birthday, her fingers brushing the smooth marble wall of our apartment building in Jeddah. My mother, singing, deaf to my cries while I crawled naked in the stairwell after her, trying to evade the voices I could hear behind me—voices that laughed at me and called out my name.

Almost a week after the incident, I saw Rizvi inside the girls' school, lounging against the wall outside the ground-floor auditorium, where he'd come to pick up Asma after our Physics mock exam. His hair was neatly combed and his head boy blazer was buttoned and pressed. His nose, I noticed with some satisfaction, was still in a splint. My heart tightened at the thought of Porus doing this. Going all Farhad over me even though I didn't deserve it.

"Hey," Rizvi called out to me, as if we were old friends or perhaps more. "How was your exam?"

Bile rose to my throat. I had fully intended to duck my head and walk away as quickly as possible, but the audacity with which he addressed me left me stunned for an instant, incapable of movement.

A few feet behind him, I noticed several girls from my class huddled together. They were staring at us and whispering among themselves, their post-exam discussions clearly forgotten. Mishal didn't take part in the conversation. She had grown somewhat silent after Abdullah and I had broken up, completely ignoring me now that I was no longer associated with her brother. Sometimes, however, when I turned around, I would catch her watching me with a strange expression on her face. It was the way she was watching me now. Like I was a train wreck waiting to happen—a thing she couldn't take her eyes off, even though the thought of it sickened her.

Without taking my eyes off Mishal, I unzipped my bag and pulled them out: a pair of knitting needles that glinted silver in the afternoon light, needles that I had carried with me ever since the incident in Rizvi's car.

"Stay away from me," I told him. It was as if another person had taken over me: a girl whose voice was cold and hard, one who could steadily hold something long and sharp inches away from a boy's shocked eyes, even though everything else inside her was shaking. "If you come any closer, I'll poke your eyes out."

Rizvi's mouth hardened. He forced a laugh. He raised his hands and slowly began to back away. "Chill, baby," he said in a voice that would make its way back to the eavesdropping girls. "I wanted to say hello."

"There's no need to," I said equally loudly. "I've already said good-bye."

I stalked off, ignoring the girls who were now gawking at me with a mix of awe and resentment. Voices broke out behind me.

"Wha . . . Did she?"

"Why was she threatening him?"

"Wait a minute . . . Is she crying?"

Someone from the crowd called out my name. I broke into a run, scattering groups of girls, racing until I reached the very end of the long corridor and threw open the door to the girls' bathroom. Ignoring the startled glance of a small Class IX girl brushing her hair in front of the mirror, I locked myself in a stall. Here, in a musty cubicle of four gray walls, surrounded by the sounds of ripping toilet paper, flushes, and running water, I finally allowed myself to convulse. To slide down the door with burning eyes, my cries muffled by the top of my backpack.

Porus

"I DON'T KNOW," I HEARD MY MOTHER whisper over the phone in the living room. "He hasn't told me a thing. Not one thing, Khorshed dear."

Not one thing, despite her constant prodding. "What happened that day?" "You must tell me what happened, Porus. I am your mother!" "I won't tell anyone, I promise."

What they really wanted to know was if something *bad* had happened. Something that would necessitate an abortion or marrying Zarin off as soon as possible.

"It was a debate," I lied over and over again. "I've already told you this."

But in truth, I did not know. Did not know for sure what had happened in the blank space of time between Khorshed

Aunty's panicked phone call to me at the deli and finding Zarin outside that warehouse, lying dazed in the black car, her white *salwar* scrunched around her ankles, Rizvi lying on top of her, his pants unzipped.

I saw him again, a week later, when I went to pick up Zarin from school, white tape holding the bridge of his nose, his lower lip still swollen. I wondered if the police had caught him lurking around the warehouse, if they had found any trace of the drug he used on Zarin. Though maybe he got rid of the evidence and they had to let him go.

It happened sometimes, my boss, Hamza, said. And it wasn't always the police's fault. "I have a friend. He's a policeman, yeah? So many times he wants to keep a boy in jail. Alcohol— even drugs! But the boy's father knows someone high up in the ministry and then *khallas*. Charges dropped! It's about *wasta*, my friend. About who you know."

My gut told me that the bad stuff had already happened, even though a week later Zarin told me she didn't think anything had.

"What do you mean you don't *think* anything happened?"

"Nothing that *matters*, okay?" she snarled. Her eyes were red and there were smudges under them. "I'm not exactly experienced in these matters, but I do believe there is supposed to be *blood* if something did. And there wasn't." Her hands shook in the split second before she fisted them. "No

261

blood, no bruising. So you're not saying a word. Not to anyone!"

"You can't let him get away with this," I said, forcing myself to keep my voice low. "You need to tell someone."

"Tell who? Masi, who will probably kill me? Or the courts over here, who most definitely will? Who do you think they'll believe when an expensive defense lawyer is involved?"

She was right, of course. Reporting the assault here in Saudi Arabia was out of the question. Even in India, society did not look kindly upon girls who made such reports. I had read about the cases in the newspapers, watched them play out on TV. *Your daughter is intact, no?* the police would ask the father. *Then I suggest you don't press charges, sir. It will bring your daughter unnecessary publicity and can even ruin the boy's future.*

A plate of Britannia's hard, rectangular glucose biscuits lay before us along with two steaming cups of tea. I felt Khorshed Aunty pause behind us for a second, then retreat toward the kitchen.

"You wouldn't lie to me, would you?" I said after a pause. It would be trademark Zarin to avoid seeking help and try to handle everything on her own. "You know I wouldn't judge you, right?"

She stared at me, the faintest trace of her old sarcastic smile crossing her lips. "You are usually the one person I find it very difficult to lie to. Strangely enough. Maybe it's because you never tell anything to anyone. You didn't even tell them who I was with, right? You wouldn't even tell your mother. But you don't really believe me."

"I never said that." My voice didn't sound convincing, even to me. I took a bite of the biscuit; it felt like sandpaper in my mouth.

Zarin dunked her own biscuit into a cup of tea, over and over, until the tough crumb weakened, hanging limp, brown and mushy.

"I dream of my mother at night. Sometimes a man. Sometimes there's blood and my mother is lying in a pool of it and I'm lying with her and the man stands over us, laughing. I see faces swimming over me. Faces around the man. Masa. Masi. You. I call your names and reach out for your faces. They disappear. I wake up screaming. Well, not always screaming. But it happened yesterday. Masa said I used to do that when I was a small girl. He says I need to see a doctor." She made a sound that could have been a laugh or a gasp. "I bet he means a gynecologist."

The lump of biscuit fell into the tea and dispersed.

"Don't you think you *should* go see a doctor after what hap—"

"I've told you time and again, nothing happened. *Nothing*, okay?" She was livid, hysterical. "You can tell *everyone else* that too!"

I said nothing. I examined the knuckles on my left hand, fisting it so they grew pale, the skin on a couple peeled off, exposing the flesh, the scars on them barely healed.

It was luck, I wanted to tell her. Dumb luck that I'd thought of the warehouse—that I'd even known about it—when her aunt called me. Luck that I'd seen her with Rizvi a week earlier. Luck that she was here, sitting next to me, instead of lying broken in a ditch somewhere.

Her aunt came rushing out of the kitchen. "What is it? What happened?"

Zarin didn't look at either of us. She took a deep breath and suddenly the anger went out of me. She dipped the rest of her biscuit into the mushy tea and let it fall. "Nothing. Just catching up over tea."

Her aunt's lips trembled and then she opened her mouth as if to say something. Then her mouth closed once more. "Drink it then," she said abruptly. "It will get cold. And Porus, I want you leaving at six sharp. She has studies to do."

"Yes, Khorshed Aunty."

"She treats me like an untouchable." Zarin spoke again once her aunt had retreated, this time careful to keep her voice soft. "Places a tray of food six feet away from where I am. She doesn't force me to sit with them at the dining table anymore either. If I do, they don't talk. It's sickening. I feel like those girls segregated in a separate corner of the house when they're on their period. It's like I'm perpetually bleeding."

I shifted on the sofa. "Maybe I should get going and let you study."

She raised an eyebrow. "If you want to go, go. No one's stopping you. No one even asked you to chauffeur me around either, you know."

"Your uncle did. When he has important stuff at work. You know this, Zarin."

The call had come unexpectedly, in the middle of the night. "I don't have a choice in this," Rusi Uncle had said in a voice that sounded years older. "They are being difficult at the office. You know what they're like, Porus, these Arabs. And I don't trust anyone else. Please, *dikra*. Please help us out."

"You didn't have to say yes, did you?" Zarin asked now, almost as if she had read my mind.

No, I thought. *I didn't have to say yes.* Part of me longed to get up and leave the way I'd said I would. But somehow I couldn't.

"At school, girls call me so many things," Zarin said after a pause, and I didn't know if she was talking to me or to herself. "They think I'm not listening, but I am. All the time."

I placed my half-eaten biscuit back in the saucer. "It doesn't matter what they say."

"Oh no, of course it doesn't. I'm supposed to be used to it by now, isn't that it?" She laughed that strange laugh once more.

"I am not meaning it that way."

"*'I am not meaning it that way,'*" she mimicked, exaggerating my Gujarati accent, her every word a bite.

We both grew silent after that, not speaking for several minutes. The clock in the living room struck six. I sipped my barely touched tea. Cold.

"I need to get going now. I have work." I spoke in Gujarati this time, not trusting myself to speak in English.

"Fine. Go, then."

When I glanced back one last time, she was breaking biscuits into pieces, smaller and smaller, crushing so hard that the crumb finally turned to powder and slid through her fingers like sand.

SHAME

Mishal

THE STORY CAME OUT IN BITS AND PIECES, first over the phone, during a conversation between Abdullah and some guy named Bilal.

"*Really.*" Abdullah sounded fascinated. "He told *me* he did her. Not once, but thrice. Nice and tight, she was, he said."

"Nah. We got drunk last night and the truth came out. He couldn't even get it up. Then his bad luck turned real bad. That girl's Romeo came along and started screaming and beat the crap out of him."

"What? What Romeo?"

"That deli boy. You know, the one with the junkyard of a car?"

"So *that's* how Farhan got his nose broken." Abdullah

laughed as if it was the funniest thing in the world. "He told me he fell in the shower."

"Yeah. A shame really, for Farhan *miyan*. A thousand riyals down the drain."

At school, other rumors were afloat, most of them bearing the headline "Zarin Wadia's Historical Breakup with Farhan Rizvi."

"Did those cigarettes fry her brain cells?" Chandni Chillarwalla shook her head. "Farhan Rizvi. God, if he so much as *looked* at me, I would die of happiness. To have him and then dump him?"

"Good from far, far from good," Alisha Babu retorted. "I thought it was brilliant. I mean, what's the big deal about Rizvi anyway? Sure he's athletic and everything, but there are better-looking guys out there. And his eyes are so creepy, almost yellow like a cat's!"

The dumping rumors didn't really sit well with me, especially since Zarin did nothing to confirm or refute them. After that dramatic confrontation with Rizvi outside the auditorium, she had grown silent. For days, she sat in her corner seat in the back row of the classroom, saying nothing, looking pale. It was only when someone asked her a question that her old arrogance returned—the "Mind your own business" response that made everyone believe that yes, it was quite likely that Zarin Wadia was the only girl in Qala Academy capable of hooking and then breaking the heart of the school heartthrob.

"You should have seen it," Layla said, repeating the story of the confrontation to those who did not know. "He was waiting outside the exam hall for Asma after our mocks. When Zarin came out, he tried talking to her. Said, 'Hey, how are you doing?' She got this disgusted look on her face. Like he was a statue some bird had pooped on in the garden. Then she suddenly dug into her bag and pulled out a pair of knitting needles. I thought she was going to poke his eyes out or something, she looked so furious!"

"Do you think they *did it*?"

Which was really the question most hotly debated among the girls in our batch. The segment who called Zarin a delinquent thought it was quite likely she was no longer a virgin. Another segment, led by Alisha, who had turned into a Zarin Wadia fan girl ever since Zarin had won the Best Speaker award at the debate, called their arguments illogical and antifeminist. "You *do* realize," she told me, "that if Zarin was a boy, no one would be questioning her purity or lack of it. How does one determine virginity anyway? Hymens can break in other ways too."

"Now that sounds gross!"

"This is a sign of *qayamat*. We are going to burn in hell."

"Stop being silly," Alisha said. "I'm sure the Lord has

better things to do than condemn a group of girls discussing their own bodies to hellfire."

"But think about it," someone else argued. "We are young now and most of us have committed sins that may be small, but as the days go on, our sins pile up, don't they? When you face God on judgment day, what are you going to tell Him? How will you account for your misdeeds?"

I glanced at Zarin's empty desk. Marked absent from school for the second time that week for unexplained reasons.

"What do you think?" Layla asked me. "About her and head boy Rizvi?"

"You mean if they did it? Who knows?" I shrugged. "With her reputation, anything is possible."

I didn't tell them that BlueNiqab's Tumblr inbox was inundated with asks and fan mail, different details, sent in by different people:

did u kno abt da warehouse on madinah rd? I bet dats where he tuk her.

A source told me they were doing drugs, Blue! Rizvi was at a house party the night before . . . at a Saudi prince's house. Things got pretty wild, if you get my drift.

A lot of it was nonsense, of course. I was pretty sure Rizvi didn't know anyone in the Saudi royal family, even though his dad did have a good job at the Interior Ministry. Someone (probably a guy) sent in a terribly photoshopped image of Zarin's and Rizvi's faces pasted onto the naked bodies of a man and woman having sex. After examining the disgusting image closely, I deleted it and blocked the sender. I might not have liked Zarin or Rizvi, but even I had my limits.

Traffic on my blog was heavier than it had been during the days of the Nadia Durrani fight, the gossip about Zarin and Rizvi being repeated at school through different sources.

"You know there was this other girl in the twelfth two years ago," Layla said a few days later. "She began complaining of stomach cramps. They hurt her so bad that the teacher had to make her lie down on a row of chairs at the back. Then she was absent for a long, long time. No one knew what happened. Then last year, I found out that she had an abortion in India. She was absent like Zarin. One day, two days a week. No one thought much of it initially."

At some point, the teachers got wind of the tale—at least some version of it. That much was evident from the sudden lectures our Math teacher would launch into in the middle of Algebra, discussing the ills of girls who could not keep their eyes lowered when they passed a group of boys.

"A good girl? A good girl, my children, will look straight ahead and keep walking. A bad girl, on the other hand . . ." He walked the length of the classroom and then turned, though never looking at any girl in particular, not even at Zarin, whose face was studiously bent over her textbook. "She will look back."

Our Physics teacher started out by giving Zarin the cold shoulder at first, completely ignoring her requests to go to the bathroom, and then picking her to answer every possible question she could think of from our textbook.

"Fool!" she would shout when Zarin gave a wrong answer. "This is what happens when you don't pay attention to your studies!"

Beside me, Layla and a few other girls hid smiles behind their hands.

It was only during English and Phys Ed that Zarin found any kind of relief. Khan Madam practiced her usual brand of favoritism by behaving as if nothing was out of the ordinary, even though she had scolded Layla and me many times in the past for inattention in the classroom.

The Phys Ed teacher barely noticed Zarin except to give her permission to sit out the games when Zarin made an excuse about being on her period one week and having stomach flu the next. The teacher went around in her usual *salwar-kameez* and sneakers, blowing her whistle at the rest of us, while Zarin simply sat on the stairs and watched.

Zarin did not take the school bus anymore. Instead, her uncle drove her to school every morning and picked her up every afternoon. Sometimes, a new boy came in his stead; the girls had grown used to seeing his battered green station wagon waiting at the pickup/drop-off point behind some of the better cars there, including Farhan Rizvi's BMW.

"Who's the guy?" Alisha asked Zarin once, about the boy.

"His name is Porus."

"Is he your boyfriend?"

For a second I thought Zarin's eyes appeared watery, but then she blinked and I realized it was a reflection of the fluorescent light overhead. She tilted her head sideways and smiled. "Who do you think he is?"

The rumors, if there had been any hope of them dying out before, continued, evolving again to include this new character in the equation. Zarin and Porus, Porus and Zarin.

Someone sent me a grainy shot of them sitting in Porus's car with the caption *Latest Gossip*, which was a little silly, because neither of them was hiding their relationship. He picked her up from *school*, for God's sake. In front of everyone.

"He's hot, isn't he?" I heard some of my classmates giggling. "Very macho."

Apparently, several others thought the same. I often saw a group of seniors standing by his car, openly appraising him, sometimes even shooting him wide, flirty smiles. Though Porus wasn't traditionally handsome, I could see why he would be appealing to these girls. The stocky build. The scowling eyebrows. The way his face softened when he looked at Zarin, like he had eyes only for her.

"I would love to have someone look at me like that." I could see the hearts forming over Alisha's head. "It makes me feel warm and giddy inside."

"Ugh!" Layla made a face. "Seriously, get a grip on yourself. Did you get a look at his eyebrows?"

I tuned out the argument. It wouldn't be the first one I had heard when it came to the topic of Zarin and her new boyfriend. Every other day different voices rose. Fingers stabbed the air. No one seemed to notice or care about the circles around Zarin's eyes. No one commented on the way Porus watched her when he dropped her off and picked her up; how he sat, straight-backed and stiff; how he always seemed to park as far away from Rizvi's car as he could.

Mother always said that of her two children, I was the one with the instincts, the one who knew when something was off, the one who sensed danger.

Abdullah may have made fun of me wanting to be a psychologist, but he didn't know that I noticed everything: from the tapping of his fingers when he was nervous to the inward movement of his Adam's apple when something shocked him. He did both when I told him the rumors about Zarin and Porus.

"Wow." A muscle in his cheek twitched. He turned up the television again and leaned back against the sofa. "She sure moves *fast*, doesn't she? Then again, why am I not surprised?"

It was the first time he'd even spoken about her since their breakup, the only hint he gave of knowing her in any way. After the rumors about her dumping Rizvi broke out, he mostly stayed confined in his room, huddled in front of the computer typing project reports or e-mails, chatting late into the night with "a friend" on Skype, he told me. To my surprise, he also began to grow a beard. As religious as Abdullah had always pretended to be in front of our father, this was a new step for him. A serious step, I realized, when he occasionally began to invite some of the boys from his Qur'an Studies class to our house.

On the surface, he seemed indifferent—almost bored—with the things that were happening to his ex-girlfriend, except for the time when he'd openly scorned Rizvi's erectile dysfunction in front of Bilal.

But I knew this was not entirely true. While his friends constantly rehashed the incident when they came over to our house, Abdullah remained silent, rarely adding to the conversation, sometimes even growing impatient—"Do you guys have nothing better to talk about?"

I posted tips, answered asks, even made a few jokes about

Zarin and Rizvi and Porus on my blog. But there were times when I wondered why I didn't enjoy the gossip this time around, why, instead of settling inside me with a warm sense of contentment, it simply made me feel uneasy. Though Abdullah never gave any input about Zarin and refused to participate in anything related to Rizvi's attempts to get back at her—"I have better things to do"—I couldn't help wondering if he had known or maybe guessed that something like this would happen if Zarin and Rizvi ever went out. If his lack of involvement in the matter was simply a way of taking revenge on her for breaking up with him.

The only time I heard Abdullah speak up was when Bilal and Rizvi said something about getting even with Zarin's new boyfriend.

"Do you want to go to jail?" My brother's angry voice made me stiffen next to the door behind which I was eavesdropping. "There's only so much your daddy's *wasta* can do to keep you out of it, Farhan."

"Since when did you start wearing your mommy's bangles, Abdullah?" Rizvi sneered back.

Over the next week or so, stories began emerging about fights breaking out near the Hanoody warehouse on the edge of Aziziyah. Cars honking at each other, racing on the narrow street, heedless of the traffic coming in the opposite direction. Though Rizvi's name was never mentioned, I had a strong feeling it had something to do with him—a tactic maybe to intimidate Porus, who supposedly lived nearby.

"I could hear the tires screeching on the road and I live on the fourth floor!" a girl from XI B said. "Horrible noises. They wouldn't even stop for the police!"

A week after she and Porus became an item, Zarin was absent again.

"Another sick day?" Layla asked me during break. She pointed toward Zarin's empty desk.

"Hunt for another boyfriend?" someone guessed.

"Why? Is the deli boy dead?"

In the row ahead of ours, Alisha turned in her seat to glare at Layla, but otherwise said nothing.

"Look!" Layla nudged me. I turned. Zarin had entered the classroom, schoolbag on her shoulders, a pink late slip crumpled in her hand.

"Hi," Alisha said. "We didn't see you yesterday. What happened?"

"I was sick," she said. "Had to see a doctor."

"A gynecologist?" someone behind me muttered. Giggles erupted.

I bit my lip.

Zarin, to her credit, completely ignored us. She dropped her bag on the empty seat by the door and began removing her books and pencil case.

"Should we ask her about her boyfriend?" Layla's voice was quiet with suppressed laughter. "Maybe if we—"

"Maybe if you *what*?"

I turned around to see Zarin standing behind Layla, her hands clenched into fists, her lips white.

"Nothing to do with you." Layla leaned back a little, her voice brusque, nervous.

"Oh really?"

The girls in the row in front of us were watching now, spectators to an unexpected catfight.

"How about I pull your precious hair out of your precious little scarf?" Zarin pushed Layla so hard that she nearly toppled into me, along with her chair.

"Zarin." Alisha rose from her chair. "Zarin, please calm down."

"Why?" Zarin shouted. "So you can continue your gossip fest?"

"It's not like we're saying anything wrong!" Layla's cheeks were two large splotches of red. "You're the one messing around with these guys. What do you expect people to say about you?"

It was then that I noticed the lack of talk and laughter around us, the breath humming in the silent classroom along with the AC. Outside the door, noises buzzed: the chatter of girls and the clatter of their lunch boxes, the squeak of their sneakers across the tiles in the corridor, the thump of balls on tarmac, clanging hard against the backboards of the old basketball hoops on the grounds outside our classroom. My heart strummed.

Zarin stared at us for a few seconds, her eyes finally falling on me. Mixed in with the anger on her face was desperation. It was a look that, for one awful moment, reminded me of Mother, six years before, when she'd begged Father not to take a second wife.

"Forget it," she said quietly.

She stalked out of the room, leaving behind her bag and books, not returning again until the end of the last period, when it was time to go home.

Farhan

THE MEN BILAL HAD RECOMMENDED FOR
the job did not tell me their names. "Safer that way." Bilal
gave me his sly, too-high smile. "What use will you have for
their names anyway? All you should care about is that they're
willing to do this for you and that they know how to keep their
mouths shut."

I stared at them now, one tall and gangly, the other shorter
and stockier, both eyeing the bandage on my nose before examining the hundred-riyal notes I gave them for the advance.
I'd had to filch from Abba's pockets this time around, but as
luck would have it, my father never noticed the missing money.

The Tall One licked his dry lips and pulled out a ski mask.
"Here. Wear this." His tone was clipped, held no room for

excuses. I put it on, wrinkling my nose against the slightly musty smell of the cloth.

"You have to go with them," Bilal had told me soothingly. "To identify the target. You don't have to do anything else."

He must have thought I was as high as he was if he ever expected me to believe that theory. I knew I was there as insurance. In case the police showed up and we got caught. It would be easier for them to hand me in to the cops—"He was involved as well"—instead of taking the entire rap themselves.

But luckily for them, it didn't matter. I wanted to go. I wanted to look at the deli boy when they beat him to a pulp. I brushed a finger over my nose, which would never be straight again. I wanted my revenge.

It had been easier with Zarin. A few rumors, a bunch of anonymous tips to that girlie gossip blog and her whole reputation, not that much to begin with, had been in shreds. From what I'd heard Asma telling her friends—telling anyone who would listen, really—Zarin had turned into a wreck and had once been heard crying in a bathroom.

There were times when I wondered if it was true—if she really was crying—when something that felt a lot like guilt twisted inside me. *Does revenge matter anymore?* The voice in my head sounded a lot like Abdullah's. It wasn't like my reputation was affected. The deli boy hadn't even said anything.

I opened my mouth, ready to call the whole thing off. But then the car jerked to a stop and I realized we were already a block away from the Lahm b'Ajin shop in Aziziyah.

"Are you ready?" the Tall One asked us before slipping brass knuckles onto his left hand.

"These guys, they're good at what they do," I remembered Bilal telling me. "You don't want to make them angry."

I swallowed hard. It was too late to back out now.

A man wearing the white deli hat and uniform and a stained apron emerged from the front with a large package, which he delivered to a waiting car.

"That one?" A hard nudge to my side from the Short One, who was sitting next to me in the back. He nodded toward the employee who was now heading back inside.

I shook my head. No. The boy who had beat me up was taller, broader. I examined the Short One's much smaller frame and wondered if he or the Tall One would really be able to take on Zarin's new boyfriend. But then, as if sensing my doubts, the Short One's eyes squinted as if he was grinning behind his ski mask, and he pulled out something from his bag. The cricket bat looked old, but sturdy. Enough to turn spinners into sixers and bash in hard Parsi-boy heads.

Adrenaline coursed through me and I didn't even care that I was wearing the stuffy ski mask. The cashier looked up at us when we entered—three masked men, the Short One with his cricket bat, the Tall One with a hockey stick. I had been annoyed when Bilal had warned me not to take any weapons for myself. "Safer that way," Bilal had said. "You be their lookout and stay away from the actual fighting. If you get any more bruises, your daddy-*ji* will begin to ask questions, and we don't want that, do we?"

But now, faced with the sole employee at the deli at that time in the afternoon, I was a little relieved that I didn't have a weapon. He didn't even look at me, his eyes trained on the hockey stick the Tall One casually waved in his face. He raised his hands in the air. "I will give you the——"

"Porus," the Tall One interrupted. "Indian boy. We are looking for him."

The man, who was also an Indian, frowned slightly. His mouth tightened before he replied, "No one of that name works here."

The Tall One glanced at me and raised an eyebrow. A mistake? I shook my head.

He turned back to the cashier. "Look here. Tell us where Porus is and no one else gets hurt. You understand me?"

"I don't know who you're talking about." The man refused to budge, refused to tell us where Porus was.

"Ali, huh?" The Tall One traced a finger over the man's name stitched on the apron. His hand arched up, making contact with the man's chin and then his nose. Two quick jabs that had the latter clutching his face, eyes watering. "Or maybe your name is Porus and you are lying to me."

Behind me, the Short One casually picked up the company's funny little figurine near the display case—a grinning cow holding the green-and-yellow Lahm b'Ajin flag—and threw it against the window, cracking the pane.

"No!" the cashier shouted. "Help!"

But there would be no help forthcoming. The deli was housed at the bottom of an old apartment building that had once belonged to the owner's grandfather. There were no other shops in the vicinity, and at this time in the afternoon, the roads were silent.

Bilal had been careful to wait until the deli's owner had a day off. "You never know with that old man," Bilal had said. "He used to be in the military at some point."

But today, apart from the cashier and our target, there were no other employees inside.

It was ridiculous how easily the cashier crumpled under the Tall One's blows, how he began babbling details he'd tried so hard to keep from us before: "Loading dock . . . back entrance . . . next to the toilet."

Maybe it was easier that Porus's back was turned when we crept out and that his arms were loaded with a large crate of salami.

The Tall One did not flinch the way I would have or

hesitate when Porus turned around. The flat of the hockey stick smacked Porus's shoulder first, barely giving the boy any time to express his shock before cracking over his skull. Again and again.

The crate crashed onto the tarmac. When Porus finally managed to grab the stick with his hands, a thin trail of blood was already running down one side of his face. That's when the Short One came in with his cricket bat. But by then, Porus was ready, throwing off the Tall One and leaping to his feet to block the Short One's swings.

It wasn't an easy fight. This much I knew from the sweat beading their foreheads. At one point, I even sensed anxiety, the Tall One glancing quickly at the Short One, before they both launched themselves at Porus.

Porus might have known how to fight. But he hadn't grown up on the streets, fighting in the gutters. United, Bilal's men overpowered him with a slam of the cricket bat over his head and the slap of the hockey stick against his jaw, and he collapsed to the ground in a mess of sweat and blood and spittle.

The Tall One looked at me and nodded. Their job was done. I finally made my way over to the body lying sideways on the ground and leaned over so I could speak in his ear. "An eye for an eye. A nose for a nose," I said before I kicked him in the face.

Zarin

DAYS PASSED LIKE LIQUID TAR SPREADING
over the ground. Thick and glutinous, a blackness clinging
to them as Masa and Masi continued to go about their lives,
pretending as if nothing had happened, until I found one or
the other staring at me, as if expecting me to detonate at any
second.

To fill the silence, Masi left the television on in the living
room while she worked in the kitchen, sometimes pausing to
watch a segment on cooking, or an American talk show where
people came to cry over their past lives and traumas. "Airing
dirty laundry in public," Masi said disgustedly, even though
she was the only one who wanted to watch the show.

Sometimes she used the television as a cover to mask the

phone calls she made to Porus's mother from the telephone next to the kitchen. "I'm sorry to hear that, dear," I heard Masi saying. "I will talk to him if I see him today—make sure he listens to you. Thanks for trying."

So now they were trying to turn Porus against me as well. I stood still for a while, watching her put down the phone and then straighten her spine, as if sensing my presence in the corner. I slipped away before she could see me.

I resisted the urge to pick up my phone and call Porus. I'd taken to calling him these days, late at night, when I jerked awake after nightmares about my mother or Rizvi, a scream choked in my throat. Porus was the one who insisted on me making the phone calls.

"You need to talk to someone. You can't keep things bottled up. Besides, I'm pretty much an insomniac these days," he told me. "When night falls, I think of Pappa and I keep listening for his voice outside my room, talking to a friend on the phone or joking with Mamma. It's like there is this giant hole in my chest that I can't fill up no matter what I do. You do a good job of distracting me."

He did a good job of distracting me, as well, with silly jokes and outlandish Persian myths. Sometimes we didn't even talk, but simply listened to each other breathing over the other end of the phone until we fell asleep.

Once, on a weekday, I surprised him with a phone call when

he was taking a break at work. The happiness in his voice made me glad I had, even though I hung up after a short conversation. I didn't want to get him into any more trouble with his boss, which I knew he had in the past, thanks to his mother telling Masi about it.

It had been a couple of days since we'd last spoken, mostly because the meds I'd taken for the flu had completely knocked me out of commission, earning me a single night of dreamless sleep.

I thought of the argument I had had at school with Layla Sharif that morning and shook my head. I shouldn't have reacted. I should have ignored her. That's what Porus would have done.

Only today, when I called to tell him about this, he didn't pick up.

———

Hours later, when my cell phone rang, a familiar number flashing on the display, my heart skipped a beat, a slight smile grazing my lips. I shut the textbook I was unsuccessfully trying to study from and picked up the phone. "Hey, Porus, I was—"

"Stay away from him!" A woman's voice.

"Arnavaz Aunty?" I asked, shocked. In the time I had

known Porus's mother, she had rarely spoken to me, and never with such venom in her voice. "What happened? Is Porus okay?"

"No thanks to you, he is," his mother spat out. "Ever since he met you he has been ignoring everything around him. His work, his family. Do you know where I spent most of my afternoon? At the hospital where my son was brought in, beaten up and bloody. He won't even tell me what happened or who he fought with. But I'm no fool. I know this has something to do with you."

I tasted metal in my mouth. When I licked my lip, it stung. Somewhere in the background there was a lull in the sound of the television. I sensed another presence in the room, a shadow hovering at the edge of my left eye. Masi.

"Aunty." I struggled to keep my voice steady. "Aunty, please, I didn't know—"

"Of course you didn't know." I could hear from the tone of her voice that she didn't believe me. "Well, remember this, Zarin Wadia, I have only one son. God might have taken my husband, but I won't let the likes of you take away my Porus from me."

From the other end of the line, I heard a groggy male voice. "Mamma? Mamma, who are you talking to?"

I hung up, my stomach swirling the way it did when I'd eaten something bad.

"Who was it?" For the first time, Masi sounded quiet, almost subdued.

I shook my head. Porus hurt—no, seriously injured, because of me. I couldn't bear to say it out loud. I knew that Masi would blame me for it. Though this time she would be fully justified in doing so.

For a moment I wondered if Rizvi was behind the attack. But even if he was, how could anyone prove it?

To my surprise, Masi did not prod me for information the way I expected her to. Instead I felt her watching me the way she had ever since I'd come back home after the incident with Rizvi, examining my flowered pajama pants, my red-and-black flannel shirt. A year before, she'd bought a dozen such shirts for me to wear outside the apartment with my baggy jeans, even though Masa had protested that the clothes made me look like a stick wearing a sack. "You can barely even see her!"

But now I got the sense that Masi was the one who wanted to see, who wanted to peel away my clothes to check for bruises or other signs of damage. Like an over-inquisitive parent, she had begun asking random questions about everything from "Did you brush your teeth?" to "What did you do at school today?" to the most important: "Did you get your period yet?"

My replies, usually monosyllabic, infuriated her. So most days I simply shrugged, saying nothing. There were days when, from the corner of my eye, I would see her hands rise and pause in midair, as if she was remembering something and then slowly backing away. It was easier to stay in my room, pretending to do homework with my textbooks than to sit at the computer in the living room under Masi's beacon-eyed glare. Not that I had anything to look at on the computer these days.

The times I did come out of my room, I sat next to Masa on the sofa in front of the TV while he watched the world news on BBC. Normally, except for a stiff nod, he did nothing to acknowledge my presence, chatting with Masi about dinner and work at the office during commercial breaks.

The only time I saw him show any kind of emotion was during the prank phone calls—anything ranging from *I want to make friendship with you* to *Mine's bigger than the head boy's.*

"Wrong number!" he shouted each time, slamming down the phone.

"Rusi, we need to do something about this," I had overheard Masi tell him once.

"What is there to do?" he asked her sharply. "They are probably bored boys who work at the Saudi PTT." Boys who initially began dialing random numbers with the hopes of hearing female voices, boys who then grew bold enough to speak and attempt to make girlfriends in their own misguided way.

"They do not have Arabic accents," Masi had pointed out.

"They sound like they are Indian or Pakistani." Like they were from my school, I could almost hear her hinting. As usual, Masa ignored her unspoken words.

"Don't reply, then! Do not engage them in conversation! How many times must I tell you this? The more you talk, the more you encourage them."

I, on the other hand, escaped to my bedroom the moment the phone rang, making no move to pick it up even when Masi ordered me to.

The night I talked to Porus's mother, I overheard Masi making a long-distance call to the Dog Lady from the master bedroom. I quietly picked up the extension in the hallway.

". . . sitting in her room every day after school doing God knows what. Rusi keeps telling me to give her space and time. But how much time can I give her?" I heard Masi saying. "Really, Persis, sometimes I think I'm going mad."

On the other end, I heard the Dog Lady let out a sigh. "I don't want to say much, Khorshed, in case I'm wrong. Who knows, with young people these days? But whatever it is, she is still a girl and, more important, *your* girl. If anything bad happens, she can bring shame on your whole family. Remember that your names are attached to her now."

"What do I do, Persis?" Masi pleaded. "What can I do when no one tells me anything?"

"Now, now, don't worry, my dear child. There is a good and reasonable solution to this. She's almost eighteen now, isn't she? No? When—in two years? Well then, it's about time you and Rusi start thinking of getting her married. What about that boy, Porus? You told me that he likes her."

"His mother would never approve of her," Masi said, echoing my thoughts. "Besides, he is only eighteen and can barely support himself and his mother on his salary. How will he take on a wife?"

There was a pause before the Dog Lady spoke again. "I wouldn't normally suggest this, but there are quite a few men in our colony, even divorced men, who are looking for younger girls to marry."

Marriage. I imagined the word swirling around my aunt's mind, sparking in corners and then settling within, warm and soothing, like the smell of butter and cumin in freshly cooked rice. After marriage, I would most likely have to go back to India. No one would mention my mother or my father again. Masa and Masi could continue to stay in Saudi if they wanted to, or even move to a different place, like Dubai.

Neither Persis nor Masi said it, but it was understood: after marriage, I would be my husband's problem, not Masi's. Better if the man in question was fifteen or twenty years older and had a steady job.

A sick feeling spread through me. I wanted it out of my skin.

My cell phone vibrated in the pocket of my pajamas. I opened it to see a series of missed texts from Porus.

i know what mamma did

pls ignore her

zarin r u there pls write when u get this

My hands hovered over the keyboard, a hundred questions resting on my fingertips: *What happened? Are you hurt? Who was it? Did it happen when you were at work?*

And on and on.

But then I thought about what his mother had said to me and couldn't help thinking she was right. No good had—or would—come to Porus from being around or engaging with the likes of me. I swallowed the lump in my throat and turned off the phone.

I woke up that night at around 10:30, stomach cramping, and stumbled into the bathroom to relieve myself. Sweat broke out on my forehead. I was tired. So tired.

Voices buzzed in my brain.

Stay away from him.

. . . divorced men . . . looking for young girls to marry.

He won't even tell me what happened.

I know this has something to do with you.

When I rose to my feet again, white spots appeared before my eyes.

The napkin I had used to wipe my hands was the first thing that fell to the floor. My body followed, head lurching forward, my cheek pressed against the cool bathroom tiles.

———————————

The colors at the Al-Warda Polyclinic in Aziziyah were sterile and functional. White walls, white tiles, white-coated doctors and nurses with white scarves marching the corridors and laughing, chatting in a mix of Malayalam, English, and Arabic.

Their sounds drifted into Dr. Rensil Thomas's office, where I was perched on the examination bench, which was covered with translucent white paper. My head still hurt from the fainting spell and I wondered if it was some delayed aftereffect of the drug Rizvi gave me, even though logic told me this was impossible.

I could feel Masi's gaze on me, so I kept mine lowered and stared at the waxed white floor. Tonight the office smelled like Dettol, cleaned minutes earlier, I guessed, by the clinic's janitor, who now swept past the office, mop in hand.

"Are you mad?" Masi had demanded when Masa suggested

taking me to the clinic half an hour earlier. "What if that fool tells someone? His daughter goes to Zarin's school, remember!"

"*Dr. Thomas* is a professional," Masa had said firmly. "He would never break doctor-patient confidentiality. And we have been going to him for years."

Dr. Thomas entered the room now and shut the door behind him. He had a round face, gray hair, and eyes that crinkled at the corners when he smiled. Masi claimed to never have liked him, but I always got the sense that her dislike stemmed from the way he had suggested counseling for her years earlier. "He thinks I'm mad!" she had raged. "He wants to have me locked up!"

"Good evening, Mr. and Mrs. Wadia. How are you?" Dr. Thomas smiled at us. "Now where's my favorite patient—ah, there you are!" I felt my shoulders relax at the sound of his voice, the South Indian accent I'd been familiar with since I was a child.

"Let's see here." He studied my file. "Your uncle said you fainted in the bathroom? Has this been frequent?"

I shook my head. "It happened tonight."

He went through a list of questions: "Vomiting? Nausea? Blood in the stool?"

Then he put on his stethoscope. "What was the last thing you ate?"

"Um. A bag of chips? At school?" After Porus's mother called me, I'd pretty much lost my appetite. I had locked myself in my room, not bothering to step out. Masi didn't come to fetch me for dinner either. The last thing I remembered was Masa wishing me good night through my closed bedroom door.

"Well, your BP is normal," Dr. Thomas said after taking my blood pressure. "You don't have a temperature either. My guess is that you had a temporary drop in your blood sugar. This can happen when you haven't eaten in a long time. You were probably also dehydrated, which is not uncommon in this country. Do you drink water regularly?"

"Not as regularly as I should."

Dr. Thomas shook his head disapprovingly, but all I could feel was the relief flooding through my veins. It was only dehydration. And lack of food. "So I'm okay, then?"

"You're okay." Dr. Thomas smiled at me, but there was a flicker of something else in his eyes—something that looked like worry. "You need to start eating again, young lady. And stay hydrated."

He turned to Masi. "Now, Mrs. Wadia, would you like to go and have a snack in our cafeteria with Zarin while I write out a prescription for some medication and send Mr. Wadia to the pharmacy? The Cafeteria is downstairs and to the left. Family entrance separate from the one for single men."

"No!" Masi snapped. "Whatever you need to say, you can say in front of me."

Dr. Thomas paused and glanced at Masa. He had been the one who had first observed the anxiety tapping out of Masi's nervous laughs at her appointments, her constant state of alertness when she was around me.

"Mr. Wadia." The doctor hesitated. "My daughter goes to Zarin's school, as you know. And over the past couple of weeks I've been . . . hearing things. You know kids these days, always on their phones, always reading things online."

I felt the blood drain from my cheeks. A face appeared in my head, watchful and quiet, her long black hair pulled back into a ponytail. Dr. Thomas's daughter went to my school, was in my class. But I had never spoken to her. I wondered what had made her tell Dr. Thomas about me. Was it a fluke? Or was Masi right and Dr. Thomas wasn't as professional as my uncle had claimed?

"I would normally not suggest something like this," Dr. Thomas went on, "but your family has been coming to see me for a long time and I was wondering if some of these stresses at school have been having an effect on Zarin's health. If you wanted, I could refer her to someone, maybe a specialist who works with teenagers at Bugshan Hospital."

"Dr. Thomas, I—"

"There is no need for that!" Masi rose to her feet. Her nails dug so hard into Masa's arm, I was sure she would leave marks. "There is no need for anything of that sort. We will be leaving now."

Dr. Thomas stood and raised his hands, as if in supplication. "Please, Mrs. Wadia, I really think this is imp—"

"You think everything is important." Masi's voice was rising now and her lips were slowly turning gray. She slapped away Masa's hands from her shoulders. "No— don't pull at me, Rusi. This man has done enough. Something happens to someone, immediately he says, 'Oh, she is mad! Give her medicine.' More medicine to make her more mad!"

I felt myself freeze, hearing the faint plea of Masa's voice through the rush of blood in my ears.

A knock on the door and a nurse peeked in. "Doctor, is everything all right?"

"No!" Masi shouted. "Nothing is!"

The doctor dabbed his forehead with a handkerchief and stepped toward Masi. "It's okay, sister, you may go. Everything is under control. Mrs. Wadia, I won't call anyone; don't worry. Please sit down. Please."

After several long moments, Masi finally sat down, her eyes darting here and there, as if looking for an escape from the eight-by-ten-foot examination room that suddenly felt ten times smaller than it was.

Dr. Thomas sat down again and scribbled something on his prescription pad.

"Here are some electrolytes. Mix them in water and have Zarin drink it. And please let me know if you need anything else." He stared into my eyes as Masi finally allowed Masa to grip her hand again. "Anything."

In the parking lot, the air was cool. Above us, the stars had been blotted out by clouds and city lights. The air was rich with the smell of earth, and a part of me wondered if it would rain the way it did during the winter. Hard and relentless, the water pooling on balconies, seeping into apartments, cars swimming through the streets like boats. Masa said that the reason Jeddah got flooded every time it rained was because of the poor drainage system. You could drown, I thought now, and no one would even notice.

Outside the emergency entrance, behind the ambulance, two policemen sat in a green-and-white van, watching the paramedics load someone onto a rolling bed. A man was shouting at the medics: *"Yallah! Yallah! Yallah!"*

Beside me, Masi was still breathing hard, her breath emerging in hisses. On her other side, I heard Masa, knew him by the quiet shuffle of his leather shoes on the tarmac.

"Bloody pill pusher!" Masi let out a sudden laugh. "Look how he did *soo-soo* in his pants when I shouted at him. It's like in India. You have to throw a few tantrums sometimes. Why are you looking at me like that, Rusi? I'm fine! And so is this one."

She glared at me. "Specialist, my foot. I am not mad and neither are you. Do you understand, Dina?"

I heard ambulance sirens, the *thocks* of car doors opening and closing. One of the policemen had stepped out of the van and was watching us closely.

"Khorshed dear, this is Zarin," Masa whispered anxiously. I could tell that he had noticed the *shurta*, too. "Dina's daughter. Dina died a long time ago, remember?"

"She's such a bad girl," Masi sobbed, and I was no longer sure if she was talking about my mother or me. "I was so worried."

"Yes, she was very bad this week, weren't you, Zarin?" Masa didn't look at me. "Coming home late with Porus. Not eating her food properly. Worrying Masa-Masi for no reason."

When I was seven, I'd slipped on a patch of wet floor in Qala Academy, my body temporarily suspended in the air, my heart in my throat, pulsing, until I hit the hard tiles, the pain grounding me once more. That evening, I felt much the same as I stared at Masa, only this time there was nowhere to fall, not even the ground.

"Yes." Masa continued to speak, his voice nearly as soothing as Dr. Thomas's as he gently ushered his wife into the car. His body was partly shadowed in the dim lighting, his face a half moon. "She was a bad girl. A bad, bad girl."

It was Alisha Babu who first asked me about my absence. Her fancy blue-and-red class monitor badge was polished to a glistening sheen. "Are you okay?" she asked, approaching me in the corridor outside our classroom. "We missed you in class."

"Fine," I said, unwilling to give any more information. I stared at the candle engraved in the badge's center, the words *Qala Academy* circling it. "Was sick for a while." And I would have remained sick had it not been for the oral part of my English exam, which had to take place today, an exam Masa had insisted I take.

"I do not know what is wrong with you because you won't tell me." Masa's voice had been curt, cold. "But I am not going to have you sitting around the house like this. You must go back to school. Get back into the routine of doing normal things."

I'd agreed because of how stressed Masa had looked. After she'd finally agreed to take the medicine Masa had given her, Masi had slept for nearly a whole day, her guttural snores breaking the silence inside the apartment. Masa, who had taken the day off work, had spent most of it in front of the television, staring at the blank screen. He did not speak to me, except to announce lunch and dinner and later in the evening to tell me that I was going back to school the next day.

Alisha's smile slipped off her face. "Luckily you didn't miss much. They were revising old stuff for the last two days."

My fingers tightened into fists. "Good."

"Yeah." There was a pause. "Zarin, I've been meaning to ask you." She bit her lip and I knew then that this had been planned, that my classmates had probably recruited her to do the dirty work and ask the question no one else had bothered, or perhaps dared, to ask. "Those rumors." Her voice was so soft that it was nearly breathless. "Are they really true?"

Rumors scribbled on bathroom walls and social media feeds and forwarded repeatedly over e-mails. Rumors that had random boys calling me at home and sending me messages, filling up my inbox with lewd pictures and propositions. I was surprised they hadn't discovered my cell number yet, but then I had never given the number to Rizvi and, for some reason, Abdullah had not leaked the information to his friends.

"I don't want to talk about this." I tried to move around Alisha, but she held out an arm to stop me.

"Please, Zarin. Some of us have been talking about this and we want to help you. We are really concerned about what is happening and—"

"If you really were trying to help me, you would mind your business instead of discussing this nonsense over and over again," I said sharply. "Don't think I haven't seen you gossiping with the rest of them and then going silent when I enter the classroom. You say you are *concerned* about me, but what you really want is fodder for your silly little debates with Layla and Mishal."

Alisha went pale. A shadow fell between us.

"Leave it." Layla put a hand on the other girl's arm. She gave me a disgusted glance. "Leave her alone."

I watched them turn around and walk back into the classroom in silence. I did not feel guilty about speaking the way I had to Alisha, for piercing through her fake sympathy. At the end of the day, she was like the rest of them, digging around for a fresh piece of gossip.

I could feel the other girls staring at me as I walked to my desk in the back.

The legs of my chair scraped the floor. I was about to sit down when I heard a giggle. Instinctively I looked at the chair. Someone had made a crude drawing of a penis inches away from a girl's mouth and taped it to the wooden seat. Hisses, muffled laughs when I ripped the picture off the chair and crumpled it into a ball, stuffing it into the deepest recesses of my bag.

"What's the joke?" the Math teacher roared from the front. "Behave yourself, Layla Sharif, or I will throw you out of this classroom!"

I did not look at them. Instead, I opened my school planner and studied the words I'd scribbled last week—the topic Khan Madam had assigned us for our oral exams. It was a formal introduction that would have us speaking about ourselves for a minute or less—without the aid of a paper or cue cards—an exercise that Khan Madam said would be useful when we were older and giving job interviews. *Be truthful about yourself and your accomplishments; do not make up stories,* the instructions said. *However, you may talk about something you wish to accomplish in your life and how you plan to go about the same.*

A simple assignment that on any other day I would have breezed through without any preparation. Now I struggled with it, writing out sentences, scratching them out, ignoring the Math teacher, who was going through the problems that had come up during the mock exams last week. By the time the bell rang for English period, I had a page full of black marks and the following words: *Zarin Wadia. Age sixteen. Student.* The truth, without any embellishments. The truth that I could bear to relay on paper.

Khan Madam smiled when my turn came. "Okay, Zarin," she said. "Time to tell the class a little bit about yourself."

I left the paper on the desk and slowly made my way to the front of the room. A trick to making speeches, Khan Madam had told us once, was to find your focal point. That one member in the audience who seemed to be listening— "sympathetically," Khan Madam called it. A listener whose opinions were malleable, whose judgment could be persuaded to match yours. Today, however, the faces were blank and hostile, none of them standing out to me. Sympathy was out of the question.

"My name is Zarin Wadia," I said. "Who am I? Well, that's an interesting question."

My eyes fell on Mishal. She was leaning forward, her elbows on her desk, staring at me with her sharp eyes, almost as if she was curious about what I had to say.

"When I was seven years old, I pretended that I was a different person," I said, remembering our fight on the playground. "Someone who had a different sort of life. It was a silly thing to do, I know this now, but the trouble then was that I did not know where I came from. Our roots are often a source of pride for us; mine were a constant source of shame. Shame was an emotion I didn't quite understand back then. Oh, I felt it, the way every child feels it. Some people hide, some people fight to cover up their shame. I was always the kind of person who fought. But recent events in my life have made me go into hiding and it hasn't been easy."

I paused for a moment. There was silence in the room. Not a dead one, but a living one, the collective breath of the audience filling the space.

"When people say you're wrong so many times over so many years, when they call you a bad person, you begin to believe them. You begin to hide out of the fear that if you show your face again—to anyone—you will be judged. Sometimes, it gets so bad that you begin to wonder if life is worth living."

I forced myself to smile, hoping no one could see the tremor that had passed through me. "But then you realize—who are these people anyway, who make you feel ashamed of yourself? Do they even matter? Do you even care what they think or say about you behind your back? You didn't before. My name is Zarin Wadia and I am sixteen years old. I am a student at Qala Academy and my favorite subject is English. I do not know what the future holds for me. But today, I'm going to start living in the present again. As of today, I will come out of hiding and go back to being the person you know so well and hate."

The silence continued for a long moment. Long after Khan Madam thanked me in a flustered voice, long after I walked back to my seat. I could feel Mishal staring at me, but I did not look at her. After the period ended and Khan Madam exited the room, a flurry of voices broke out, loud and clear, no longer concerned about whether I could hear them or not.

"No remorse in that girl," someone cried out. "No remorse whatsoever. Any other girl would have been reduced to tears. But she? She has no conscience."

"What does she think?" someone else said. "That she'll scare us into silence with some vague mumbo jumbo? Come on. Everyone knows about her sneaking off with Rizvi earlier last month!"

"Layla, didn't you . . ."

I did not know when I actually stood up, or how I managed to leave the classroom without running into any teacher. Moments later, I found myself locked in a stall at the very end of the girls' bathroom, my head sinking into my hands.

What had I been thinking? That my speech would actually *change* something? That being defiant and angry would win me respect when, in actuality, everyone wanted me to cower and burst into tears?

To live in this world, you needed to follow a certain set of rules and behave in ways society deemed appropriate. My mother did not, of course. Neither did my father. I had spent most of my life seeing Masi trying to compensate for their actions by controlling her own and Masa's, by controlling me. And now, in this stall, I finally began to understand why.

I folded my knees to my chest, my heels resting against the

edge of the closed toilet seat. It would be easy enough to stay here, I decided. To remain locked up for the rest of the day. No one would come looking for me anyway. No one cared. Except maybe Porus.

Moments later, though, the bathroom door slammed open, followed by the harsh voice of a girl bursting into the space outside my stall: ". . . that awful Verghese Madam! Who does she think she is?"

"Shhh," another voice said. "Do you want someone to hear you?"

"Who cares?" the first girl said. "Everyone knows how mean she is. But forget that, did you hear about Zarin Wadia? My cousin Layla told me she had another tantrum today. A couple of days ago I heard her crying in the bathroom down the—oh my God, what's that *smell*?"

My heart hammered. Her words jarred my senses, and for the first time, I registered the dank odor of the bathroom, the stench of urine rising from the stall next to mine, the sweat drenching the front of my uniform.

I remembered the look Masa had given me outside the clinic, right after Masi had had her episode. It was the sort of look he had once reserved solely for my aunt on her bad days—a mix of fear and anger, mingled with disgust.

I could no longer blame him for it. I was disgusted with my-self. Disgusted by how quickly I'd come undone, how easily

I'd let their words affect me. I was doing exactly what I'd said I *wouldn't* do in my speech that morning. Going into hiding. Cowering like an animal in a stinking public lavatory because of some dumb Facebook posts and e-mails, because a bunch of girls were saying crappy things about me.

Five minutes later, when I stepped out of the stall, the bathroom was empty. My hands were shaking so badly that I was tempted to race back and lock myself in the cubicle again.

No, I told myself firmly. *No.* I would not go back into hiding.

I opened the door and forced myself to step outside.

Porus

"WHAT ARE YOU DOING HERE?" MY BOSS, Hamza, eyed the bruise on my jaw, my broken nose held in place with a white splint and bandage. "I thought I told you to go home and relax after the break-in."

His hard gaze told me otherwise. It told me that he knew the break-in at the deli was not a break-in, but a targeted attack on me. *An eye for an eye. A nose for a nose.* There was no point in proving that Rizvi had been the one behind the attack, even though I'd recognized his voice, even though he'd uncovered his face after kicking mine in.

I was well aware of how precarious my position was in this country. A non-Muslim Indian boy who'd made a false birth certificate for a legal work permit. If the authorities discovered that I'd falsified my documents, I would be deported before I could say *ma'salaama*.

Two new security guards now stood by the door of the deli, one with a gun in his belt. I half expected Hamza to call them over and march me to the nearest police station.

Behind me, the other workers whispered among themselves. *It was because of him*, I imagined them saying. *Thanks to his involvement with that girl.*

My mother had blamed Zarin as well. After calling up Zarin to yell at her, she ordered me to stay away from her. "If you go see her again, I will never talk to you," she had said.

If only it was that easy, I thought now. It might have been if Zarin and Rizvi truly cared for each other and if Rizvi wasn't the biggest jerk to grace the face of the planet. If Zarin wasn't being bullied at school.

"I will not have you before my customers in this state." Hamza's face was pink under his gray beard. He motioned me closer to keep our conversation private. "Also, since you are here, we might as well have a talk. You've not been coming to work on time. I've heard you have also been skipping out early, making other people take your shift."

"I don't want the money—"

"Money?" Hamza spat out. "You talk to me about money when whatever personal feud you've been having outside nearly cost me my cashier? I should fire you, you know. You are lucky that you are a good worker and that Hamza Arafat does not let a few thugs stop him from keeping the people he hires."

The AC overhead made a clicking sound, a stray icicle rattling inside. "Shut it off!" Hamza shouted at the boy who was pretending to cut a block of salami. "How many times have I asked you to keep it shut off until the technician comes to inspect it?"

The boy, a sixteen-year-old with a shadow of a mustache, dropped a knife in his haste to switch it off. The machine grunted a couple more times before falling silent.

"Fine then." Hamza's voice sounded louder than usual in the silence. "Since you *are* here, you will make yourself useful. You will stay here today until the technician comes after hours. You will stay out of trouble and not go running off to see someone the minute a phone call comes. If you do feel the need to go out again, please do not come back to-morrow. I cannot have my boys coming and going as they wish. This is your third and final warning. Are you listening to me?"

I did not reply. I thought of Zarin, the shadows around her eyes, the things the other girls had called her when I picked her up from school. *Slut. Whore.*

As if sensing the direction of my thoughts, Hamza sighed and placed a hand on my shoulder. "She is not your sister. Not

315

your wife. Why are you making a fool of yourself over her? Why are you risking your job? Your life?"

My lips stuck together. I moistened them with my tongue. "You are right, sir. Of course you are. But I cannot do what you ask me to."

Hamza's grip on my shoulder tightened. "What do you mean, 'I cannot do what you ask me to'? Have you not been listening to me?"

"I made a promise. To her uncle. I promised I would take care of her. She is my . . . she is my family now."

My mother was going to kill me. The thought flitted through my head and was replaced by images of Zarin's face—smiling at me from between the pillars of an old balcony, lying in the back seat of a car, leached of color.

"Family? She is your family now?" Hamza laughed and clapped his hands. "Look at this one! Look at him!"

He didn't have to tell them; they were looking anyway: Ali the cashier, who'd taken a punch on my behalf, the other boys behind the counters, a few straggling customers.

"This is the classic case of a fool," Hamza said. "Not only that, he thinks I am a fool too! That old Hamza, with his experience and wisdom, is giving him wrong advice. All because of some girl. In the meantime, he brings shame on us."

I focused on the logo on Hamza's apron and remembered the Arabic lesson Zarin had once tried to give me. "*Laam*," I could hear her saying. *"Ha, meem, ba, ain, jeem, ya, noon.* Repeat after me; it's not so hard." It was one of the few times she had been patient and steady around me, the steadiest I had seen her in all the time we'd known each other.

Did I tell her how much she had reminded me of my father then? Pappa, with his endless confidence in me, his endless optimism. Pappa, who told me the story of the Persian poet when he was first diagnosed with leukemia four years ago.

"Once upon a time there was a poet," he had said. "A man who had traveled across a desert somewhere in ancient Persia with a troupe of artists, on his way to Yazd."

At first Pappa told me about the poet's adventures, his rendezvous with other nomads and women with kohl-rimmed eyes. But the story quickly turned grisly. On the way, the troupe was robbed by a gang of bandits. The bandits killed everyone in the troupe except for the poet, whom they decided to torture for fun by cutting off his arms and legs and leaving him there in the scorching sand, at the mercy of the scavengers. The scavengers, great big vultures and birds of prey, attacked his dismembered arms and legs, but not the living whole of him. But the poet knew that this was not out of mercy. The scavengers were simply watching and waiting, their wings beating hot air over his face. Waiting because they knew he would die.

Broken beyond belief, the poet spoke to the One True God,

Pappa had told me. "Ahura Mazda," the poet shouted, invoking the name a priest in his village had taught him. "Ahura Mazda, you have been unfair to me. You have taken away my arms and my legs and now you are taking away my life as well. Well, I am young. Too young to die. I will stay alive for as long as possible. I will fight the odds that I have against me. I will learn to breathe both air and dust. I will learn to crawl through the oceans of sand this desert is peaked with, its cracked salt plains. I will make my way to Yazd, where you reside in the house of fire."

The days and nights, however, ate away at the poet's flesh. When he came face-to-face with the One True God after death, he looked upon his face. "Why?" the poet asked.

And God replied: "Because a bird only learns to fly when its wings are broken."

Those who believed in reincarnation said that the poet was later reborn as a great Persian poet whose name was lost to history.

"They borrowed that nameless poet's ideas, you know," Pappa had said, eyes widening in the way they always did when one of his stories got out of control. "Rumi, Hafiz, those great Sufis."

On a normal day, I would simply have laughed and called him out for making up the whole thing. That morning, though, I had accused him of treating me like a kid. "How can being diagnosed with cancer set you free?" I had demanded. "Will you stop *lying* to me, Pappa?"

But now, as I remembered the story, I felt his presence again. Felt him slide into the room, past the machines, around the counter, and stand next to me, whispering his favorite Rumi quote in my ear.

Hamza caught hold of me by the shoulders. "I hired you because I saw potential." His voice was softer now. "Potential, *ya walad*. You work so hard! Leave the girl. Stop this nonsense. A few more years and you can become supervisor, even manager if you want. I promise. Three more years and I can promote you. I beg you, my boy, don't do this. Don't ruin your future."

I stared at my boss, a man who had trusted me enough to give me a job in this country, perhaps the only man who had, in his own way, tried to fill some of the void Pappa had left behind.

"I—I'm sorry, Hamza. I can't do what you ask of me." It was as much as I could understand, the closest I could come to describing the band that had tightened around my heart at the thought of leaving her alone, at the mercy of her family, those wolves at her school.

Beads of sweat stood out on Hamza's pale skin. "Don't be a fool, boy! You are not thinking clearly."

Maybe I wasn't. But Pappa had always told me that love

didn't think. It was, I understood, the choice between the cage of a safe, unbroken life and one of freedom. If I quit, I could be forced to leave the Kingdom within a week—unless Hamza agreed to transfer my iqama to a new employer and issue a No Objection Certificate. With the savings in my bank account and the certificate, I would be able to scrape by for a couple more months and find another job. But chances of that appeared slim now.

Maybe I was a fool like Hamza said. But at least I would be a fool by choice. I took off my apron and placed it in Hamza's hands. The last thing I heard him yelling through the rush of blood in my ears was my name.

LOVE

Zarin

"YOUR MOTHER WOULD KILL YOU IF SHE knew you were here with me," I told Porus quietly.

"Maybe I'm a glutton for punishment," he replied.

It had been over a week since his mother had called, since Masi's episode in the clinic's parking lot. After those first few texts, Porus hadn't tried to contact me again, and I had been pretty sure he wouldn't.

The trouble with low expectations is that when they're exceeded, your heart begins to tango, and mine acted no differently when Porus showed up at our apartment this afternoon in his work uniform, a bandage on his nose, a bruise on his chin.

"What happened? Have I suddenly grown so handsome that you can't take your eyes off me?"

My fingers reached up to touch the bruise but curled inches short of their goal. "Who did this to you? Was it—?"

"I don't want to talk about that."

I wanted to yell at him. He couldn't do that. He couldn't go around flirting with me, acting like everything was okay when it wasn't. As if sensing my anger or maybe anticipating it, he reached out and squeezed my hand reassuringly. *Please don't be mad,* he seemed to be saying.

Masa, on the other hand, acted like the whole of last week and the week before had not happened. Upon seeing Porus again it was like a switch went off in him and he changed from a sullen, haggard man who blamed me for his problems into the one Porus was used to seeing in the days before Rizvi.

"Hello, Porus, my boy," he boomed, and I wondered if he even knew how fake he sounded. When Porus asked him for permission to take me out for a spin in his car, Masa nodded so hard I thought his head would loosen at the joints that held it to his neck and fall off.

"It will be good for her, getting out of the house," Masa told Porus. "With exams, she's so busy studying these days. Bring her back in time for dinner, will you, Porus?"

Neither Porus nor I looked at each other during this speech, but I knew he was probably wondering why Masa was even bothering to lie. *Everyone knows,* I wanted to tell my uncle. *Everyone knows what a mess of a family we are.*

When I slipped into the passenger seat, I expected Porus to ask me about Masa's strange behavior. He didn't. He simply dug into his bag and produced two sandwiches—greasy chicken shawarmas with pickled cucumbers, soggy fries, and garlic sauce. "Hungry?" he asked me.

I nodded. It wasn't like Masa was starving me over the past week, but with everything that had been going on, my appetite had taken a nosedive. Now though, nestled once more into the slightly worn seat of Porus's car, my mouth watered at the smell of the garlicky chicken. I tore off the wrapper and took a huge bite.

As I ate, Porus drove us to a part of the Corniche that I'd seen once before, on a school field trip when I was younger—a strip of Jeddah coastline that extended for several kilometers in a series of sandy pillars instead of the rock and metal sculptures that dominated the Al-Hamra part of the beach. I wouldn't have minded the longer drive, probably wouldn't even have noticed anything, had Porus not taken us there in his sixteen-year-old green clunker—a vehicle that seemed determined to test out every bump and pothole on the road.

The inside of the Nissan always smelled funky—like feta cheese and mutton, to be specific. And every time Porus drove the car over the speed of sixty kilometers per hour, it rattled until I got a migraine. I had already given Porus a few subtle hints about getting a new set of wheels: "What did you think of the secondhand Honda we saw at the used car lot the other day? It looked decent—only four thousand riyals!" When subtlety proved unsuccessful, I'd progressed to the not-so-subtle hints: "Get rid of it, Porus!" But the whole exercise was pointless. "It's only the high beams and the brake lights that aren't working, Zarin," Porus had said, ignoring my complaints about the rattling noises. "I can get the rewiring done for less than four thousand. Give me some time; I'm waiting for my next paycheck."

I rolled down the car window now and inhaled the salty breeze. The best part about going to the Corniche was the Jeddah Fountain, which could be seen from mostly anywhere, as long as you stuck to the coast. The fountain was closed that morning for maintenance, which on any other day (and with any other boy) would have made the date a flop, shawarma notwithstanding. But I was with Porus. And somehow, despite the awkward silence that had crept up between us during the drive to the beach, I almost felt okay again.

"Do . . ." I hesitated. My hands shook. "Do you have a Marlboro, by chance?"

Porus sighed, but instead of scolding me the way he normally would have, he simply dug around in his bag and pulled out the pack and lighter he kept in there for me. I had known Porus long enough by now to know how he felt about my smoking, could feel it in the hesitant brush of his fingers against my palm. But he said nothing to me that day, and for that I was grateful.

Porus opened his own window a crack. I sucked at the filter and tried to blow smoke rings like *Alice in Wonderland*'s hookah-happy caterpillar, but the smoke dissipated without forming any particular shape. My second attempt was little better, though this time the smoke blew out in a straight line, a mocking imitation of the Jeddah Fountain itself.

I still remembered the first time Masa had pointed the fountain out to me: the base shaped like an incense burner; the water shooting out with such force that it looked like white smoke against the sky. He later told me a tale about little white horses galloping far into the sea, their manes the only things visible over the water. "Where are they?" I asked, looking for the horses, and he'd pointed out their manes—the streaming white froth that we now called sea foam. I never tired of hearing the story back then, and he never tired of repeating it to me.

I reflected on the silent treatment my uncle gave me now, except for that one day when he'd ordered me to start going back to school, his eyes colder than I'd ever seen them, nearly as cold as Masi's had been the day I first entered their apartment in Mumbai.

A monarch butterfly landed on the windshield of Porus's car, its wings fiery orange and black in the sunlight. Seeing it increased the hollow feeling in my chest. *It is strange*, I thought, *how we always recognize our best memories in hind-sight.*

I stubbed out the cigarette in the ashtray.

"Do you want to get out of the car?" I asked, and Porus nodded.

Families were already gathering in groups on various parts of the beach, unrolling picnic mats and laying out containers of food. This particular patch of beach, I remembered now, was a good place for large groups to gather, and also for men to fish in silence. My shoulders relaxed when I realized that there were no teenagers in either of the groups—only adults and small children. I would not run into anyone from school over here.

Tan, hip-high pillars formed a railing in front of us, mark-ing the perimeter of the coastline, with several feet of sand beyond—a guard of sorts between the cars in the parking lot and the sea. They weren't tall enough to really discour-age people from climbing over, though, so that's what I did, my *abaya* hiked up over my hips, and then jumped, landing softly in the wet sand. A second later, I felt Porus touch down beside me. To my surprise, his feet were bare, grains of sand coating them like brown sugar. The soft, white rubber-soled shoes he wore at the deli hung loosely from one hand.

"That sand may not be exactly clean, you know," I pointed

out. Food wrappers, cigarette butts, broken glass shards—you never knew what was lying in there. "I was here a few years ago and accidentally stepped on a dead jellyfish." It was the one thing I'd always remembered about this place and that field trip: the sensation of my bare foot against a slippery, squishy blob. I suppressed a shudder and then scowled when Porus started laughing at me.

"It's not funny," I said. "Some of them sting, you know!"

"Don't care." He wiggled his toes in the sand and stretched out his arms. "It comes with the territory. A little bit like being with you, actually."

My face reddened. "Is that a compliment or an insult?"

Porus grinned in reply. It was so reminiscent of the way he used to be before the Rizvi stuff happened that I felt the ends of my mouth turn up.

"How was your day?" he asked, changing the subject.

"Surprisingly normal." I began walking closer to the sea, making sure to pick a path that *looked* clean—or at least garbage-, glass-, and jellyfish-free. Porus followed.

"A few of the others still had to do speeches in English, so I slept through most of that lesson. Our Physics teacher failed half the class in the mock exams—as expected. What else . . . ? Oh yeah, our Math teacher called us brainless fools and said we would end up giving him a coronary. The rest of the classes were boring as usual."

I had sensed some of the girls watching me from time to time—especially Mishal and Layla—but apart from that, nothing else. No one had tried to bother me that day, or mentioned the rumors in my presence. Maybe it was due to the pressure of final exams, but it seemed that for now they'd gone back to their old default of ignoring my existence. Not that I was complaining.

The sea was quiet that afternoon. Small waves rolled toward the shore, bubbled frothily over sand pockmarked with footprints and left it smooth once more. When I was younger, I was much too nervous about walking into the sea alone, clinging to Masa's hand for dear life, feeling certain that the water would wrap itself around my ankles and pull me in if I wasn't careful. Now, however, I stepped in, farther and farther, even though I had never learned to swim, my feet steadier than they had ever been before, feeling the water slide into my sneakers, seep through the shining black polyester of my *abaya*, up to my knees.

"What are you doing?" Porus's voice was high, nervous.

I looked back at him and frowned. Did he think I was going to . . . ? I felt the blood drain from my face as I realized that drowning was something I might have considered, might have maybe given serious thought to, a few days ago. I shook my head.

"I like being in the water," I said. "Is there a problem?"

Porus bit his lip. "I . . . I almost drowned in the sea when I was seven."

"Oh."

I instantly felt like a heel.

I debated whether or not I ought to offer him my hand and encourage him to come in, but then decided against it. Porus had done enough for me as it was. I stared at his bandaged nose and his bruised chin. My heart twisted. I knew I would never be able to forgive myself if something else happened to Porus because of me.

I forced my legs back up the slippery bank, the bottom half of my *abaya* weighed down slightly by the water. But it didn't matter. My clothes would dry soon enough in this heat. So would my sneakers, when I finally removed them in Porus's car.

Porus held out his hand to help me climb back onto drier ground. But when I tried to pull away, he tightened his grip.

"I will marry you, you know." His deep brown eyes were serious. "I don't care about what happened."

I tugged hard until my hand was free, ignoring the sudden warmth pooling in my cheeks. I wrapped my arms around myself, not knowing why my heart was beating so hard. "Porus. I am not marrying you."

He was silent. The sea rushed forward, bringing with it white foam and debris.

"Why do you love me, Porus? Why are you so desperate to marry me?" I asked when the silence began to grate on my nerves.

There was a long pause before Porus answered again. "When Pappa died, I thought a part of me had been ripped out. I functioned, I joked, I survived, but I didn't really live. Being with you distracted me at first. I mean, you are a pain, you know."

I couldn't help but smile at that. It was true. I *was* a pain.

"But," Porus continued, "in some strange way, being with you reminded me of him again, of the things we did together, the stories he'd told me—the *good* times, you know. The day I first saw you here, I thought of him and that story he told me about Shirin, Khusrow, and Farhad. It was the first time I had thought of him without grief pressing down on my ribs. When I told you those stories from my book, it was like he was sitting right next to me. When I'm with you, I can almost hear him giving me advice again—like, 'Say this to her!' or, 'No, you fool, not that!' Like right now, I can feel him shaking his head at me for making you cry."

I tried to laugh, but all that came out of me was this strange, strangled sound.

He exhaled quietly. "Zarin, you aren't a bad person. Sometimes life does not go the way we want it to and we can't really change that. But it doesn't matter as long as we have someone to love us. Love is more important than anything else in this world. And you deserve love as much as anyone else."

I felt his fingers brush my hand again, his pinkie gently linking with mine. This time, I did not pull away.

It was Masi who shot the missile. Masi who stepped into my room, minutes after my alarm went off on Monday, and stood before the door, glaring at Masa, who hesitantly stepped in as well.

I threw my covers to one side. "What is it? What do you want?"

"We are thinking of getting you married, Zarin, *dikra*." Her smile could have given nightmares to a diabetic. "Do you remember Ratamai's son, Kersi?"

Masa looked down at his hands; they were shaking.

"I am not eighteen, Masi! Besides, Kersi is his mamma's boy, with no spine whatsoever. He probably still asks his mamma for permission before going to the bathroom."

Masi's eyes were hard. "We are your guardians and what we say is final."

I stood up and faced my uncle, who was now shifting his eyes between the both of us, the way he had been shifting, tiptoeing around the house ever since Masi threw a fit at the doctor's office. "Aren't you going to say something about this?" I asked. "Or are you going to keep wearing the bangles she put on you when you got married?"

The clap of a hand, flat against my cheek. The kind that would leave a bruise. But for now I felt nothing except the cool metal of Masa's ring, the tingling warmth it left behind. Slapping. A new first from my uncle.

There was silence.

Masa and I stared at each other. His ears and neck were red.

"Your aunt is right," he said, lowering his arm. "You are not improving one bit. You are going out of control."

Masi's breath came out in a soft, satisfied hush. She wound her hand around Masa's arm. "Come, Rusi," she said in a brisk voice. "We will deal with this later. My dental appointment is at 8:15."

———————

I called Porus without thinking.

"They want to marry me off," I blurted out the minute he picked up. "I was planning to skip school anyway and I have a plan, we can run away and—"

"Calm down. I'm coming."

———————

Traffic on the Al-Harameen Expressway was always heavy: vehicles raced on its lanes at speeds of over 120 kilometers per hour.

Porus refused to run away with me.

"Run away to where?" he asked. "And what will you do without a diploma or degree? Do you want to work in a deli like me?"

I didn't, of course, even though I didn't tell him that. "I could learn," I said, before I could think too much about it. "How hard could it be?"

Porus turned the wheel and the car sped up to join the high-way traffic. "Yeah. You could learn to slaughter baby lambs and goats. Really, Zarin, who are you trying to fool? Besides that, I'm no longer working at the deli."

"What?" The news came as a shock. "Why?"

"I quit a couple of days ago. Doesn't matter why. And don't worry. Old Hamza phoned me last night. He said he would transfer my iqama for me if I wanted to continue working in Jeddah. He even offered to issue a No Objection Certificate! I have enough money to stay here for a couple of months and find another job. In the worst-case scenario—if I have to leave for a while—I can come back on a new employer's visa with-out waiting two whole years, thanks to the NOC."

"I wasn't worried," I lied.

I stared out at the traffic, which was now starting to slow

down. When I told Porus to join the road leading to the expressway this morning instead of taking me to school, I had wanted to get as far away from Aziziyah and my aunt and uncle as humanly possible. Now I felt sick from being cooped up in this car and from realizing how much of Porus's life I'd already messed up. Even though Porus would not admit it, I knew deep down that his decision to quit had had something to do with me.

I rolled down the window to get some fresh air. The smell of exhaust fumes and fresh tarmac filled my nostrils. Coughing, I rolled the window back up. Masa had mentioned something the week before about construction taking place over here; orange arrows marked the detours around the construction site. A flatbed trailer in front of us was carrying stacks of iron rods, probably to one of Jeddah's industrial cities. The rods stuck out beyond the trailer bed, and from time to time Porus would mutter, "One thousand one, one thousand two" under his breath to keep a safe distance between the Nissan and the trailer. The sun glared down at us, making my head pound more than usual. There were no clouds.

"You will be okay, you know," he said. "I will talk to them later if you want. They cannot be thinking of marrying you off. You're much too young."

I said nothing. I stared out the window, watched cars and palm trees blur by.

"Zarin, will you talk to me, please?"

"Talk about what?" I snapped. "About you making a proposal and then backing out when I accept it? Or should we debate the fact that you're a liar like the rest of them? Why don't you take the next exit and drive me home?"

Porus sighed. "That was not acceptance, Zarin. That was you looking for an escape route from whomever your aunt and uncle want you to marry. And I will keep missing every exit until you start talking to me about what's going on in your head."

I closed my eyes. "Isn't it . . . isn't it possible to fall in love with someone with time? You know how they say—marry someone who loves you instead of marrying the one you love?"

His jaw tightened. "What are you saying now? That you think you can learn to love me? With time?"

If I had wanted to be snappy, I could have pointed out that it wouldn't be too much of a chore physically, at least. We had chemistry. He was a good—no, the best—kisser I'd come across. I could admit this much to myself now, after everything that had happened. But I knew I owed him more than that.

Love. I rolled the word in my head, felt it twist in my stomach. I had loved Fali, of course. That much was clear. As clear as the sun in the sky, the bright yellow of his eyes. Porus had been right about that: I *was* a sucker for tiny animals; butchering them would be out of the question. And my mother? I guess I loved my mother. Or the memories of her anyway. The memories that still existed outside the nightmares.

"I don't know if I'm capable of loving anyone," I said honestly. "I like you, Porus. I like you a lot. But love . . . I've never done it before. I don't even know if I have it in me." I was scooped out.

Porus's grip tightened on the steering wheel. "I really want to marry you, you know. In fact, you made me a very tempting offer. But I can't take you up on it. I want you to fall in love with me first."

"Ha." I rolled my eyes, but my lips curved into a smile. "You're going to have to wait a long, long time. Maybe until I'm very old and walking with a cane. Maybe for eternity."

"Eternity." He laughed and my foolish heart skipped a beat. "I like the sound of that."

There was a pause before he spoke again. "Look, why don't you come live with me for a few days? We can talk to your aunt and uncle together."

"Porus." I turned to stare at him. "I can't. Your mother won't—"

"I'll handle my mother," he said firmly.

"But I don't want to be a burden."

"Now you're being melodramatic."

"I'm not!" (Okay, I was.)

Porus smirked at me. Then his face grew serious again.

"Jokes aside, it's okay to rely on other people, Zarin. You don't always have to fight alone."

Had another boy said the same thing, I might have dismissed this. But with Porus I knew it wasn't pretty words and empty promises. He always meant what he said. He'd proven it to me, time and again. I studied his face for a moment longer: eyes squinting against the sun's glare, the curved bridge of his nose, his soft lips parted in a curse for the driver ahead of him, the stubble peppering his strong chin.

I thought about what he had suggested. Not only was the idea of staying with Porus for a few days somewhat soothing, it also allowed me to imagine things that I wouldn't have dared to days earlier. Porus wasn't as hot-tempered as I was. Masa and Masi liked him. With his support, maybe Masa would listen to me about what had happened with Rizvi. And about everything else that was happening at school as well. Maybe they both would.

"Zarin?" Porus asked quietly.

"Okay," I told him, feeling a little relieved even as I spoke. "Yeah, okay, I'll stay with you. But no funny business. You're sleeping on the couch."

I ignored the warmth that flooded my cheeks when he smiled at me.

Then, suddenly: "What the— Why is he stopping?"

The trailer had jerked to a stop. Hazard lights blinked like a pair of yellow eyes. Porus braked—"One thousand one, one thousand two"—and came to a stop; the Nissan's hood was a good foot away from the jutting rods.

"Phew," Porus said, and turned to grin at me for a split second. In that moment, the driver of the car behind us lost control and slammed the Nissan's rear end, sending us flying toward the flatbed. Iron rods broke the windshield. I screamed. There was deep pain. And then there was nothing.

THE COLLECTORS

Mishal

FOUR DAYS AFTER THE ACCIDENT, A classmate who lived two blocks away from Zarin said she saw a mover's truck outside the building Zarin once lived in.

"I saw her uncle there, watching them put a heavy bed in the truck. They're selling mostly books and clothes and some furniture. We went to have a look. The clothes were really ugly; you'd think a boy was wearing them, not her! But there was this pretty little lamp with green leaves. It was a good price too, only ten riyals. But Ammi said no. She said she didn't want anything that once belonged to a dead girl."

Death. An event that had made Zarin more popular than life ever could have.

"Do you think she . . . you know . . . killed herself?" Alisha Babu looked pale. "Because of what was happening?"

Because of what we did, you mean, I thought.

"And killed that boy with her?" Layla snorted. "Don't be ridiculous. It was an accident. An accident, okay? Her aunt and uncle will probably get a lot of money out of the insurance."

Now Layla was the one being ridiculous. But I didn't say anything about that.

In the week after the accident, Alisha, Layla, and I met at my house after school every day under the guise of doing homework and talked about the things we knew about Zarin and the things we didn't. "The Collectors," Layla called us with a laugh. Which was essentially what we had become. Collectors of the news, rumors, and mysteries surrounding Zarin Wadia's death, of the bits and pieces of information about her that seemed to be floating in from time to time like debris from an interesting shipwreck.

It was on one of these days, after one of these meetings, that I found Abdullah up in his room tossing some old magazines and newspapers into a box.

"You can come in," he said, when he saw me lurking outside. "I don't have anything X-rated in here, little sister."

I stepped in. A few issues of *National Geographic*, *Time*, and *Sports Illustrated*, an old copy of the *Saudi Gazette* in which Abdullah's letter to the editor had once appeared.

"Giving them to Father's new charity," he informed me. He scratched at his beard, growing darker now, fuller. The skin on his cheek came up red. "If you have some books or magazines, you can give them too."

He walked to the revolving chair next to the computer and took the books and magazines lying there. I twirled it on its casters. Round and round. "Since when did you become the savior of the poor, illiterate children of the world?"

"Stop that," he said about the chair. After a few more turns, I held it steady once more. He crouched on the floor and rested his wrists against the edges of the box. "I'm getting engaged next month." He looked up at me. "I've been skyping with this girl for a couple of months. Even met her in person last week. Father was the one who showed me her photo."

I moistened my lips, but they were still dry. "Who is she?"

Abdullah's lashes—as long as our mother's—lowered. "One of Jawahir's younger cousins."

"Nice," I said. "Does she look like the witch too?"

Abdullah let out an impatient sigh. "I should have known you would behave like this. Grow up, Mishal. You are not a child anymore. Soon it will be your turn too, you know."

I began turning the chair once more. Round and round.

"I am going to be a psychologist." I did not even know where the words came from; before now, I had barely given

my life after high school any thought. Or maybe I was revealing a long-forgotten dream.

"Who says you can't do that after marriage?"

"I don't want to get married."

"Stop being ridiculous. You're not a boy, Mishal. The older
you get, the lower your chances will be. Father was lucky
enough to get this proposal for you as is."

I held the chair still. Blood rushed to the tips of my fingers.
"What do you mean? What proposal?"

Abdullah tossed the last magazine in the box and slapped
down the cardboard lid. I stared at my nails, at the tiny white
spots that marred their shell-pink smoothness. Abdullah had
the same spots on his nails in exactly the same places. On his
right thumbnail and the index finger of his left hand.

"His mother saw you at one of Jawahir's parties last year
and asked Father for your picture. As far as proposals go, he's
a good one. Real estate in Jeddah and Madinah, investments
in Goldman Sachs. He's fairly young too, only thirty. He
has a son from a previous marriage, of course, but it will be
all right. His first wife died in childbirth." Abdullah stood
up again. He moved closer and brushed his fingers against
my cheek. "It will not be like what we had to face with Mother
and Jawahir. You will have no other woman to contend with,
little Mishal. I've made sure."

His breath smelled of mint gum. Underneath that, cigarettes.

I inched away, step by step, my pink sequined slippers sliding over the floor. I wondered if my feet had fallen asleep or if it simply was the shock of hearing my father's words from Abdullah's mouth. My father who had assured my mother that she would not be abandoned in the days after he'd married Jawahir—*You will keep getting your monthly allowance. I've made sure.*

"You are right," I told Abdullah before I left the room. "I am no longer a child."

"Hello." This time it was a man.

"Hello." My voice came out rusty, the way Mother's did when she hadn't spoken to us for many days. "I'm calling regarding your sale. My friend was there earlier this week and she said there was a lamp. A little one with a lampshade made of green leaves. Do you still have it?"

There was a long moment of silence, a sigh before he replied again. "Yes. Yes, we do."

The smell of dal—thick, meaty, and fragrant—emerged from the kitchen when I entered the apartment, Layla by my side.

Zarin's uncle, tall, thin, and bald, gestured toward the sofa. "Have a seat, girls. Would you like anything? Water, orange juice, Coke?"

"No, Mr. Wadia," I said. "Thank you for offering though."

He nodded. "I will go and get that lamp. It may take some time to find it . . . The house is . . . It hasn't been easy." His shoulders sagged and for a brief, terrible moment I froze, wondering if I was supposed to offer my condolences again.

Utensils clattered in the kitchen. The sound brought him out of his stupor and he straightened once more. "I'll be right back."

"This is so creepy," Layla muttered once he was out of the room. "I don't know why I came here with you."

I took in the pale rectangles left behind on the cream-colored wall—outlines of old photo frames—and the empty space in front of us where a television must have been mounted, grooves in the carpet where there must have been a coffee table next to the navy-blue sofa, which might have been comfortable if it wasn't covered with clear plastic. I brushed a hand over the smooth surface, finding a tiny tear in the cover.

You came because you're a gossip, I wanted to tell Layla. *You came because you wanted to know more about Zarin, like me. Like everyone else.*

I slid my pinkie under the tear to feel the fabric underneath, contemplating if I ought to speak my mind. It wouldn't be the first time that I'd done it to shut Layla up.

But today I bit my tongue. Zarin's apartment building was at least ten kilometers away from our house, and there was no way I could have asked Abdullah to bring me here. In Abdullah's absence Layla's brother, or more realistically Layla, who I'd asked for the favor, was my ride to and from Zarin's house. Layla's brother had offered to wait outside the building while we went in to get the lamp. "Don't think it would be a good idea if so many of us went in," he'd said. "We're strangers, not family."

And, on seeing Zarin's uncle, I'd known he was right. Shadows lurked in each corner of the dimly lit room, trapezoids on the floor from cardboard boxes in various stages of packing. A hard nudge to my side had me turning to face Layla and someone else—a woman wearing red and gold bangles and a flowered nightgown. From the dazed look in her eyes, I guessed that she might have wandered into the room by accident.

There was no doubt in my mind that this was Zarin's aunt. The woman's face was longer and bonier, but they shared the same nose and mouth, the same petite frame. It was like seeing Zarin again through a slightly distorted lens. She squinted at the both of us from behind gold round-framed glasses and tilted her head to the side.

"Zarin's friends?" she asked, and for a second I thought

Zarin herself was speaking to us, with that cool, mocking lilt to her voice.

"No," Layla replied, her voice strained with politeness. "We're her classmates. Here for the sale."

Mrs. Wadia muttered something under her breath that sounded a lot like "Scavengers," and looked up at the ceiling. "That would be a first," she said, addressing the ceiling. "For her to have had girls for friends. Right, Dina?"

Dina? Layla mouthed, but I shook my head. The silence that filled our responses was nearly as thick as the scent of the food from the kitchen.

As if sensing our presence in her living room again, she turned back to us. "Where are my manners? You must be hungry."

"No, Mrs. Wadia, we're—"

"Stay right there."

When she disappeared into the kitchen again, Layla stood up. "I've had enough, Mishal. Let's go. It's taking too long and this is too weird. You can get a lamp from anywhere else."

Years later, I wished that I'd moved faster. That I'd stood up then and there and left the apartment without a backward glance. As it was, I remained indecisive, creeped-out the way Layla was, but perversely, undeniably fascinated the way most people were while watching another person unravel. I was thinking of a way to convince Layla to stay when Zarin's aunt returned, holding two plates filled with rice and the orange-yellow dal we'd been smelling ever since we'd entered the apartment.

She eyed Layla, who sat back down, her face flushing, and then handed one plate to each of us. There were no spoons or forks, but neither Layla nor I asked for any.

Mrs. Wadia's hands rose and quavered in the air. "On the fourth day after death, tradition requires that I cook *dhan-sak*. With three different types of lentils, mutton, pumpkin puree, and brown rice. Why are you looking at me like that, girls? Eat. Eat."

Layla did not touch her plate. But when Mrs. Wadia focused her gaze on me, I hastily dipped three fingers into the mound of rice and took a small bite. The soft, gravy-laden morsel, delicious as it was, stuck to the inside of my throat like phlegm.

" 'Chew, child,' they told me when my grandfather died," Mrs. Wadia said, her voice growing soft, reminiscent. " 'It will not do if you forget to eat.' But tell me, girls. Can you eat when the only person you loved had passed away and left you to live this life with the older sister you hated?"

Layla shifted next to me, her discomfort palpable even though we weren't touching.

"Girls, you are in luck, I . . ." Zarin's uncle appeared in the living room, his voice trailing off when he saw his wife perched on the sofa arm, the barely touched plates of *dhansak* on our laps.

"Khorshed." His fingers tightened around the base of the small lamp he was holding. "What are you doing, dear?"

"They must eat." Her laughter crept up my back, made the fine hairs on my neck rise. "There is too much of it. Who else will eat this food?"

Layla and I put aside the plates and rose as one. "I think we should go. We're very sorry," I said. I could feel Layla glaring at me, and I knew she was angry with me for bringing her here, for making her stay. I didn't blame her. I was angry with myself.

Mr. Wadia thrust the lamp he was holding in my direction. It wasn't even in a box. "Here. For you. Have it as a gift."

For free. I swallowed hard even though there was nothing in my mouth and for a moment, I didn't even want to take it, as pretty as it was with the crystal glass shade and thin gold base.

But my hands made the decision for me, reaching out, curving around the cool fixture. "Thank you," I managed to say.

"Good day, girls," Zarin's uncle told us, but I barely heard him.

"*Dhansak* was her favorite!" Mrs. Wadia cried out. "Her favorite! So why is she not here, Rusi? Why does she not come back?"

"I can't believe you didn't take me with you!" Alisha whined when she found out about the lamp. "I wanted to come as well!"

"I'm sorry," I said, trying to sound sorry about it even though I wasn't. "I . . . forgot."

The old Mishal would have made up a lie and then added more to get the other girl off her back. She would have talked about the apartment and pretended that she'd actually stepped into Zarin's old room. She would have made fun of Zarin's unhinged aunt, her helpless uncle. She would have inserted a punch line about the *dhansak*. A good funeral dinner, she would have called it.

My gaze fell on the lamp again. I said nothing.

Time passed and eventually dissolved the little friendship we'd struck up over the memory of a girl none of us had really known. I lost touch with mostly everyone, except Layla, when I left to study psychology in Riyadh (after successively and *accidentally* pouring cups of scalding-hot tea down the *thob*s of three "eligible Saudi bachelors" and one across the skirt of Abdullah's fiancée when she came to see him, pleased to see Abdullah's pretty white skin turn an angry red).

"How dare you?" Father had said, raising his hand to hit me when he found out about what I'd done to the suitors.

353

"How dare you?" Mother had said, emerging suddenly from her room and slapping his hand away. "Even a *qadi* asks a bride if she wishes to marry a man, and you dare force my daughter into a marriage she does not want?"

Father was so shocked to see Mother after so many years that he backed away at once. Mother turned to me. "I heard you that day. At the door. I'm sorry. I'm so sorry, Mishal. I've been a bad mother. Haven't I?"

"Yes. You have," I told her, before promptly bursting into tears.

This time, however, I wasn't in my room alone. This time, Mother's arms wound around me, frailer than before, but there. Surprisingly, miraculously *there*.

It was strange to see Mother rise from her stupor and begin playing the role of parent again, asking to check my homework like I was seven, even scolding Abdullah once for coming home late. It was strange to tell her of my decision to study psychology and show her the university brochures Layla had given me. I would be alone, I knew. In a different city, perhaps a different country. But at least I would be alone on my own terms.

"It will be fine," Mother said softly, and for a moment I saw her again—the woman who had played with Abdullah and me, who had scolded me for my misbehavior, whose eyes now held a shimmer of pride. "You will be fine."

Mother helped me pack the lamp, which I took with me to Riyadh, first, and later to London, on scholarship. While I was away, she divorced Father and moved back to Lucknow. Abdullah's first fiancée left him and he got married to another girl. Time happened as well. Time smoothed out some of the cracks in our relationship, brought us back on talking, texting, and skyping terms.

"Hey. Do you remember Rizvi? From school?" Abdullah said one morning over Skype.

"Your friend?" I asked, pretending ignorance, even though inwardly I felt myself wince.

"Yeah. Remember how the girls loved him?" Abdullah's smile was weak under his beard. "Well, his mom e-mailed me last week. He's dead."

"What?" My carefully feigned indifference crumbled under the shock of the news. "What do you mean? I mean, how?"

"They found him next to a Dumpster in a back alley in Hyderabad. Drugs. Crack cocaine to be specific."

Both of us were silent for a minute.

"I saw him, you know," Abdullah said. "A couple of years ago. He was living at a friend's place. His dad threw him out of the house after Farhan tried to knife him for not giving him drug money."

The news shouldn't have surprised me, but I still felt stunned by it. So the rumors had been true. Those stories about him and Bilal and . . . I shook my head. What was the point? He was dead now.

"When I met him, he was so high he barely knew who I was." Abdullah's voice grew quiet, thoughtful. "But then he looked up. Just once. And he said, '*Ya* Aboody, I messed up, didn't I? With Nadia. Aliya. Zarin. With all those girls. I see them in my dreams. The drugs, the drugs bring those memories back. But I can't live without those either. I guess this is my punishment, huh?' "

"Wow," I said, unable to come up with anything better.

"Yeah." Abdullah's frown deepened. "Later, he started begging me for money. I was so repulsed. And yet, I pitied him. So I gave him whatever was in my wallet. It was the last time I saw him."

I said nothing. Eventually Abdullah changed the subject and we began discussing other things. But Rizvi's death and his confession stayed on my mind.

So much so that hours later, when I looked up at the night sky, I wondered if she knew. Did dead people know these things?

The lamp, in general, was finicky, as temperamental as its owner had been. There were nights when it stung me if I got too close (the crystal could heat up rather quickly), or times when the bulb refused to light up, no matter how hard I pressed on the switch. Yet the night I found out about Rizvi's death, it worked without any problems. I fell asleep on my back, my hands cupping the back of my head, my gaze raised to the ceiling, where the crystals showered green and yellow bursts of color against the darkness.

EPILOGUE

Zarin

"DO YOU REMEMBER THE FIRST TIME YOU ever felt rain on your face?" Porus asked me. "I remember being a boy then. In a boat with Pappa. There was a light drizzle. I asked Pappa the most foolish question then—is there a sea in the sky?"

The air around me buzzed with electric warmth; I could hear the smile in his voice even though I could no longer see him.

"When I was born, it was raining," I said lightly. "Masi said my mother delivered me at home. Masi said she didn't know if she was going to put me in a crib or choke me to death."

"Now you're being facetious."

"Of course I am."

It was not what I'd imagined, this afterlife. Of all the things I could be doing after death—burning in hell, perhaps, or maybe doing hard labor in purgatory—I was here, hovering in some strange zone between life and death, over the scene of my own accident, talking to Porus the way I would have been at the mall or inside his car on a normal day. Since when had he become my constant—my anchor between life and death? But then, when had he not been my constant?

I thought back to the time in the colony, his big, infectious smile, the blue Tendulkar jersey he always wore. I never knew, never imagined that I would strike up any kind of friendship with him, or that I would see him again in Jeddah. I was never a believer in destiny, but this felt a lot like it.

"So I'm your destiny, huh?"

I scowled. He was reading my thoughts again. "Stop that," I said.

But I didn't mean it. And from the way he squeezed my hand, I could tell that he knew.

"Have you ever been happy?" Porus asked. "I mean, really, Zarin. The way you talk, anyone would think you had the world's worst childhood."

I sighed. "Fine, then. It was at school. The first time I played in the rain. I was seven. The playground had filled up with water. My feet were ankle deep in it and everyone around me was sailing paper boats. When I came back home, Masi was pouring out a bucket from the window. She was so busy doing that, she didn't even yell at me for jumping around on the carpet and making those horrible squishing sounds."

He laughed and everything around me was suddenly more buoyant. My heart swelled with warmth. I felt his fingers loosen ever so slightly.

"Pappa told me that he would be there when I died," he told me. "Of course, when he said that he meant that I would be really old. He expected Mamma to be there with him too."

His pappa, who had always been there at his school functions, until the leukemia confined him to the hospital. His pappa, who had shown him that heaven was a ball of light rising from the sea. I wondered what kinds of creatures lived in those waters, if they truly were as colorful and winged as Porus's father had said.

Of course he would be here, Porus was thinking now. And the minute those thoughts came, panic set in. I tightened my grip on his arm.

"Ouch!"

"Sorry!" My fingers slid down his arm and linked with his hand once more. "I didn't mean to grip so hard. But you were growing heavy again."

I could feel it around me, the weight of unspoken words and memories, anchoring us to the ground, to the wreck on the highway, which was now being cleared away by tow trucks.

Then: "Zarin, I am going to try something, okay? Don't be afraid."

His hand slid from my fingers.

My heart dropped and so did I: a rock in the middle of a pond.

"Porus!" I shouted, panicking. "Porus, what are you doing?" He caught hold of my wrist again and there I remained, bobbing on air, buoyed by his lightness, until he pulled me up again.

"Good one." I forced a laugh. "You had me there."

"It isn't me, Zarin," he said. "It's you. You're the one weighing us down."

"What do you mean, it's me?" My heart felt as thin as a wire; any second now and I would be gasping for air. "It can't be me. It's you who's doing all the thinking! Remembering those moments with your father."

He pulled me closer now, a gentle tug that drew me toward the warmth I'd felt when he first started talking about his father. "Which is what you must do too. You need to remember, Zarin. You need to remember everything and then let go of it. You must allow yourself to feel."

"What's with the 'letting go' stuff? Did you turn into a Buddhist now?" My throat closed. "Besides, I don't have many happy memories."

Porus closed his eyes. Even though we weren't touching

364

each other except with our hands, I could feel the brush of his lashes against my cheek, a moist warmth coating my eyeballs, like a pair of lids shutting over them. I closed my eyes as well. I saw his mother, sitting in her room in Jeddah, watching the cars go by on the road below, laughing when Porus clapped his hands over her eyes and said, "Guess who?" I felt the memory flow through my veins: cool and liquid, like saline through an IV.

When I opened my eyes again, the scene beneath us seemed more distant, separated by a thin filament of cloud. The road was flowing with traffic once more, everyone we knew long gone.

"Do you know what I'm talking about?" he asked me. "Do you understand?"

A shudder went through me. I closed my eyes. In the darkness, a shape slowly emerged. A woman sitting in the corner of a room, her bangles tinkling, singing softly: a moon-filled lullaby. A toddler brushed a tiny hand over her lips. She caught hold of it and kissed the palm.

"Mother?" I found myself saying, and then grew embarrassed by the confusion and longing I heard in my own voice. "Was that my mother?"

Was that me?

Porus's breath washed over my cheek. "Try," he whispered. "Try again."

A man with a mustache and a golden wristwatch tossed me high in the air. "*Majhi mulgi*," my father called me in Marathi. *My girl*. Later, he raised his hand and brought it down on a dark-haired woman, cutting open her lip with the edge of his shiny gold watch. "You will not tell me to leave my job again, Dina!"

A high priest in white robes tended to the holy fire in a fire temple, chanting verses of an old prayer, his face masked in white. The same priest, later during the day, telling Masi he could not officially induct me into the Zoroastrian faith. "Letting her come into the temple with you is one thing, Mrs. Wadia, but doing her *navjote*? I can't. Not without a Parsi father."

A man with red lips and an orange shirt, stroking my hair. "Such pretty lips," he told me. "Such pretty legs." The dark-haired woman again—my mother, I realized—screaming at the man. "You may have been my husband's best friend when he was alive, but if you touch my daughter again, I will kill you."

A woman dressed in a white sari, talking to an old lady with a dog in her arms. "Blood is blood, Khorshed, my dear. What is inside the blood does not change." When I looked up from the book I was reading, they had turned away from me, their faces in shadow.

The man with the red lips pulling out a revolver on a crowded street and pointing it at me. My mother pushing me aside. "Go, Zarin. Run." Her gold bangle felt cool against my cheek. A gun slashed silver through the muggy air. A crack of sound. Blood burst out of her, warm and sticky on my lips.

"What happened?" The woman who asked the question had a mole on her lip, exactly like the one on my mother's. She stared at my blood-covered face and then looked back at the police officer. "What happened to my sister?"

When my mother died, our neighbor Mrs. D'Souza told me that she'd turned into a star—shining at night, I thought to myself years later, the way she always had in a Mumbai dance bar.

I wondered now, as I hovered with Porus over the highway, if my mother too had floated over her own corpse, if she'd ever come by for a final glimpse of me.

"Blood alone does not make someone your family," I'd heard the Dog Lady saying to Masi once. "There are so many families out there—even in our Parsi community—looking for a child to adopt. No one would blame you, you know. No one would blame you for wanting to forget."

I imagined my aunt's face. Her small, dark eyes under the

large bifocals she always wore. Her face, bone thin and weary. Always so afraid.

Maybe it would have been better for her to forget. Better to have let go of me and started over the way the Dog Lady had suggested. To have made new memories and let the old, poisonous ones fade away.

"I cannot," Masi had explained to the Dog Lady. "Rusi is too fond of her. He will never let her go."

But there were times, even then, when I wondered if that was the complete truth. If there had been a little more than just anger in Masi's tight grip on my wrist, in her constant watchfulness, her furious, sometimes venomous diatribes against my mother. *Was it love?* I wondered now. I did not know.

I tried to peer overhead at the stars that I imagined were somewhere over the stratosphere, and felt something within me go out in a soft hush: the rustle of a hundred butterflies, the release of a long-held breath.

A moment later, I felt the air beside me shift. "Do you remember the first time we saw each other?" Porus asked. "Not the very first time, but here. In Jeddah."

"You mean the second time," I corrected him. The odd question, or perhaps the memory itself, made me smile. "You flashed your pearly whites at me and held out your hand to shake mine. I cringed and acted like you had bubonic plague."

"Now you're gripping my hand so tight, it feels like you'll never let go."

I said nothing. Maybe because somehow I sensed that I would eventually have to let go of him. The wistfulness in his voice told me that Porus knew this as well.

"Do you think we'll be reborn?" Porus asked me after a moment. "That we'll see each other in some other lifetime?"

The priest at our fire temple in Mumbai would have said no. Rebirth was a Hindu or Buddhist concept, not Zoroastrian. But who knew the truth? And I wasn't fully Zoroastrian anyway.

"Maybe we will." The words lightened something within me, made me feel hopeful in spite of myself. I laughed. "Maybe I'll even go out with you."

Actually, nix the maybes. We *would* come back, I decided. I *would* go out with him. If he still wanted me.

I felt his warm laughter before I felt his lips. As soft as a breath. As deep as a promise. I had the oddest sensation of being in and out of my body at once, of hearing his thoughts, feeling his joy along with mine. I did not know what would happen after I let go of Porus or he of me. But for now I would not think of that. For now, I would hold on, cling to the flesh of his biceps, to the rounded curve of a kneecap, to the bits and pieces of the earthly bodies we had left behind.

Glossary of Words and Phrases

abaya (Arabic): black cloaklike garment worn by women in
    Saudi Arabia

Ahura Mazda (Avestan): the creator of the world; God,
    according to Zoroastrian scriptures

akhi (Arabic): my brother

arrey (Gujarati/Hindi): oh dear

as'salamu alaykum (Arabic, formal): peace be unto you

Ashem Vohu (Avestan): Zoroastrian prayer

attar (Arabic): perfume

beedi (Hindi): cheap hand-rolled cigarette sold in India

beta (Hindi): son

bhai (Hindi): brother

chor (Hindi): thief

dhansak (Gujarati): Zoroastrian lentil stew

dikra (Gujarati): child

dupatta (Hindi): cloth used as a body or head covering;
    worn with the *salwar-kameez*

Ey su che? (Gujarati): What is this?

habibi (Arabic): literally translated as *love* or *my love*; used
    by friends or lovers or to casually address strangers
    of the same gender

halala (Arabic): unit of the official currency of Saudi Arabia;
    one hundred halalas make up one Saudi riyal

humata, hukta, huvareshta (Avestan): good thoughts, good words, good deeds

inna lillahi wa inna ilaihi raji'un (Arabic): we surely belong to God, and to Him we shall return

iqama (Arabic): Saudi Arabian residence permit or identity card

isha (Arabic): the fifth of five daily prayers in Islam; prayed at night

jaanu (Gujarati): an endearment meaning *life*

Jummah (Arabic): Friday

kabaadi (Hindi): person who buys used goods, usually clothes, in India

kaka (Gujarati): paternal uncle

kameez (Hindi): tunic

Khallas! (Arabic): Enough!

khatara (Hindi): broken-down vehicle

khodai (Gujarati): God

kusti (Gujarati): sacred woolen cord used in Zoroastrian prayers and worn around the waist, over a *sudreh*

loban (Gujarati/Urdu/Arabic): frankincense rock, used in Zoroastrian prayers

ma'salaama (Arabic): good-bye

maghrib (Arabic): the fourth of five daily prayers in Islam; prayed at sunset

Malayali: a person from the south Indian state of Kerala who speaks the Malayalam language

malido (Gujarati): sweet pudding made of semolina, whole
    wheat flour, and nuts, used as an offering in
    Zoroastrian prayers

masa (Gujarati): maternal uncle

Masha'Allah (Arabic): an expression of joy or praise,
    literally translated as *God has willed it*

mashrabiya (Arabic): bay window enclosed with carved
    wooden latticework, found in buildings in Old
    Jeddah and parts of the Arab world

masi (Gujarati): maternal aunt

masjid (Arabic): mosque

miswak (Arabic): a teeth-cleaning twig, a traditional
    alternative to the modern toothbrush

miyan (Urdu): a term of respect; could stand for *sir* or *mister*

muezzin (Arabic): one who calls for prayers from a
    mosque

Mumbaikar (Marathi): a resident of Mumbai

muttawa (Arabic): religious policeman; *plural:* muttawe'en

navjote (Gujarati): ceremony that initiates a child into the
    Zoroastrian faith

niqab (Arabic): veil worn by women in the Arab world

Parsi: a member of the Zoroastrian community in India

qadi (Arabic): Islamic judge

quayamat (Urdu): judgment day

rava (Gujarati): semolina pudding

riyal (Arabic): unit of the official currency of Saudi Arabia

salah (Arabic): Muslim act of prayer, to be observed five
      times every day at prescribed times

salwar (Hindi): pantaloons

sayeedati (Arabic): lady

shurta (Arabic): traffic police

soo-soo (Hindi, slang): urine

sudreh (Gujarati): sacred undershirt worn by Zoroastrians

thob (Arabic): long garment worn by Saudi men and
      women

walad (Arabic): boy

wasta (Arabic): connections or influence (usually with the
      government)

ya (Arabic): vocative particle, used to address a specific
      person; translated as "*O!*"

Author's Note

THE WORD *QALA* IN QALA ACADEMY COMES from *qala't*, which is Arabic for fortress or citadel. When I started writing this book, I intended to explore each room and corridor of this fictional world, and the Saudi Arabia I knew and grew up in. I did not realize how massive this undertaking would be, nor how often I would have to revisit my own past to make sense of my characters' present.

While all the major landmarks and districts in Jeddah are real and still exist, many of the locations mentioned in this novel are fictitious: (Jeddah: Qala Academy, Lahm b'Ajin deli, Al Hanoody Warehouse, Al-Warda Polyclinic; Mumbai: Cama Parsi Colony, Char Chaali). Any inaccuracies are entirely mine.

My own story is different from Zarin's and Mishal's. Yet it does not make their stories any less true, nor does it diminish the reality of living in a world that still defines girls in various ways without letting them define themselves.

This book is a love letter to them all.

Acknowledgments

MY HEARTFELT GRATITUDE TO THE ONTARIO
Arts Council for funding this project.

Thank you:

Mom, for inspiring my love for reading and Dad for being
the first to read everything I wrote.

Bruce Geddes and Sayeeda Jaigirdar, for reading this book
in its many forms over the years and being the best critique
partners anyone could ask for.

MG Vassanji, for being the first to look at Zarin Wadia with
a critical eye.

Joe Ponepinto, for publishing Zarin's story in *The Third
Reader* in 2008, when it was only 5,000 words long.

Barbara Berson, for her valuable advice on a very early draft
of this book.

Eleanor Jackson, for always championing this book
and me.

Susan Dobinick, for seeing this book's potential.

Janine O'Malley, for patiently answering all my questions
and coming up with the best final title.

Elizabeth Clark, for designing this book's beautiful cover.

Melissa Warten, Chandra Wohleber, Mandy Veloso,

Kelsey Marrujo, and everyone else at FSGBYR, for their support in making *A Girl Like That* the best book possible.

Brian Henry, Lauren B. Davis, Sherry Isaac, Mayank Bhatt, and Heather Brissenden, for their encouragement as I was writing this book over the years.

And last, but not least: Jeddah, for the memories.